# Sleepless in Dubai

# Sleepless in Dubai

### SAJNI PATEL

AMULET BOOKS • NEW YORK

Cataloging-in-Publication Data has been applied for and may be obtained from the Library of Congress.

ISBN 978-1-4197-6696-1

Text © 2023 Sajni Patel
Book design by Chelsea Hunter

Printed and bound in U.S.A.
10 9 8 7 6 5 4 3 2 1

Amulet Books are available at special discounts when purchased in quantity for premiums and promotions as well as fundraising or educational use. Special editions can also be created to specification. For details, contact specialsales@abramsbooks.com or the address below.

Amulet Books® is a registered trademark of Harry N. Abrams, Inc.

**ABRAMS** The Art of Books
195 Broadway, New York, NY 10007
abramsbooks.com

*To Prapti—*
*dream big, baby girl*

# CHAPTER ONE

O h, don't mind me!" I crowed into the twilight from the middle of the street, waving at one of our neighborhood Vietnamese uncles to go on by.

He rolled through in his Corolla, glancing at me, perplexed, as I dropped down into peak "Asian squat" and adjusted my camera on the asphalt. My dad would disown me if he saw me like this, but sacrifices had to be made for the one shot that would rule them all! One didn't just pop into the world as an amazing photographer, ya know? One had to scrape up cameras and touch dirty ground and ignore the screaming ache searing up their legs from squatting.

*This* was golden hour.

There was this magical, ethereal, and *itty-bitty* time frame during the late weeks of October in Austin when the setting sun blessed us mere mortals with golden skies like halos. Towering red maple trees in full, autumnal fashion lined my street. Way back in the day, the subdivision had been required to include certain trees in everyone's yards for this very effect. Those early homeowners may not have seen the spectacular end result, but bless the HOA's aggressive insistence for once.

I squinted toward the setting sun as the sky blossomed into shades of enigmatic reds, creamsicle oranges, and lush pinks, then positioned the camera to face the shimmering tunnel of fall maples. They boasted their own array of colors in thick clusters of crimson-and-gold painted strokes, standing tall, branches wide as if saying, "Put aside your pumpkin spice and behold the most majestic element of this glorious season."

A breeze sent the leaves shuddering right as I clicked. *Ugh!* A blur. I had only a few shots—if a strong enough breeze swept through, the entire canopy would fall.

*All right. Let's try again.*

I repositioned the camera, checked, stood, and stepped back. *Way* back so that there wasn't a single pixel of my shadow in the photo.

I used the remote-control feature on my app to take a few shots from afar. I'd checked this angle for weeks and knew this was the best spot, but my brain sent my legs walking farther and farther away just to make sure no unwanted shadows warped the shot.

I was so busy triple-guessing the angle that I hadn't registered the sound of distant, squealing tires from the main road. A car swerved onto our street with a screech; the driver clearly hadn't known the turn was coming.

I lurched forward to grab the camera.

A crunch echoed on the heels of the car's screeching stop.

"No!" I screamed.

I skidded to a halt, taking in the massacre of my most beloved possession. I clamped a hand over my mouth to keep from screaming, my body racked with tremors.

I yelled, "Back up! Back your car up!"

I fixed my gaze on the black, boxy camera under the car. The tire had only partially crushed the camera, so maybe it wasn't totally obliterated.

But as the car eased back, the tire fully rose off the camera, and the camera jerked. The sound it made resembled the final grunt of an actor hamming up their death scene. But it was still a death. The camera was a goner.

Tears welled up in my eyes as panic surged through me.

*No, no, no!*

The driver opened the door and jumped out, stopping to my right, their shadow falling over my form hunched in mourning. I glanced at the scuffs on their kicks and the too-long jeans hems that curled over the lips of their shoes.

"Oh my god. Nikki, are you all right?" a familiar, semi-deep voice asked.

Of course it had to be *him*. My neighbor and former best friend. But better Yash than my parents.

"Where's the other half of my lens?" I asked instead of responding, searching the street and under his car on my hands and knees. The missing piece had vanished.

Yash searched, too, but reappeared with nothing to show for it. "I'm sorry, I don't see it."

Had it been catapulted into a tree? Had it knocked out a bird on its way into someone's yard? We searched for twenty minutes, as far away as three houses down in each direction and on both sides of the street. "There's no way that giant part of a lens could just disappear."

I mean, what in the world! Had it disintegrated? I hadn't even seen it go anywhere. One minute it was attached to my camera, beautiful and whole; and the next minute, half of it had totally vanished into thin air!

I fell on my haunches in front of the demolished camera, muttering, "Dude, you Thanosed my lens."

I gathered everything I could find, picking up shards from the lens and eyeing the cracked screen and its noticeable missing wedge. The main component of the camera was warped.

I rose to my feet, exclaiming, "What have you done?"

Yash startled, his mouth ajar and his eyes huge as they fell to the disaster in my hands. "It's OK! It's OK!"

"No. Dude, it is *not* OK. My parents are going to end me."

"It's just—"

My words came out rushed and hot as I interjected, "Don't even say it's *just* a camera. You know it's not! You know it's my everything, and that it costs a lot of money. You know my dad worked overtime to buy it for me because all I've ever asked for was a camera so I can get better at photography and get an internship. You know I begged my parents for two years for this camera, and I promised on my life to take care of it."

"I wasn't going to say any of that!" He reached out as if he were about to hug me but stopped because he remembered we weren't *exactly* on the best speaking terms. "Of course I know how important this camera is to you. I was going to say it's just going to end badly for me, not you. Look, I'll explain to your parents that it's my fault. I'll pay for it."

"With what money? Yard work doesn't pay *that* well. And don't ask your parents, because sure, they'll pay for it if it makes me feel better, but then it's going to be this weird thing between our parents. It's already weird enough between them after . . ." I stopped myself, my chest heaving as I tried my hardest to keep my anxiety under control.

Yash watched me. His flushed cheeks drained into pallor. Stoicism had replaced his panic.

"Who told you it was OK to speed down the street?" I spat, blinking away this stupid, blurry vision.

"I wasn't speeding," he contested, his voice shaky.

"Didn't you see me running or the camera?"

"I saw you in the corner of my eye as someone far enough from the path of my car. I didn't see the camera."

I grunted.

"Let me help," he pleaded. "Our parents won't find out. I have money."

My eyebrows shot up. "You have eight hundred dollars just lying around?"

He sucked in a breath, as if he didn't know the camera was expensive AF. He knew because I'd lain beside him on his bedroom floor while scrolling through various cameras on multiple sites looking for deals and grunted over how many hours my dad would have to work to afford one.

"Yeah. That's what I thought." Groaning, I spun on my heels and marched toward the house, cradling the distorted remains of the camera against me as I would a beloved, injured pet. The jagged edges scratched my arms and caught on my shirt, but I didn't care.

I refused to look over my shoulder at the boy I'd left standing in the middle of the street and bit into my lower lip. Once, a long time ago, I would've run to him first for anything. He'd been my best friend, the person who snuck out of the house at midnight so we could ride bikes to Taco Bell in the days before either of us had a car. The guy who carried my backpack on his chest, his own backpack on his back, when I was struggling to hold my science project while walking to school. He was the one I'd cried to when some jerk messed with me. Not because I felt bad because of said jerk, but because I'd gotten detention for calling him out in front of the entire student body.

Had this been pre–best friend breakup, Yash and I would've hovered over the broken evidence and come up with a plan not only to hide this from my parents but also to replace the camera. Somehow. Even if it meant Yash moonlighting as a grocery stocker with me.

Unfortunately, there was no "us" and therefore, no plan.

I snuck into the house and trotted up the steps to my room so my parents wouldn't turn the hallway corner and catch me. I dumped the broken pieces onto my bed and flicked a few of the smaller ones, contemplating whether they could possibly fit back together. Could I find someone who knew how to repair cameras when parts of it had been crushed like a bug?

Probably not.

I was irrevocably screwed. I'd not only broken a camera, but I'd broken a promise to my parents to take care of that camera.

They'd always said they could trust me because I kept my word and never (OK, hardly ever) got into trouble. If they didn't view me as responsible enough to care for an item, how were they ever going to let me go off to the internship of my dreams? Out of state. In Washington, DC, of all places!

National Geographic was, ironically and devastatingly, a *photography* internship. My dreams shattered as I tried to piece the sordid mess on my bed back together like a warped jigsaw puzzle. I needed a camera to get that one, spectacular, better-than-the-rest shot that would land the internship; not to mention, I was pretty sure they'd want me to, ya know, have my own camera at said photography internship.

I bit my nail. How fast could I make eight hundred dollars? Also, how fast could I get a job? And again, how to do it all without my parents knowing?

It wasn't until my fingers were cramping from trying to fit the broken pieces back together that the tears, skillfully held at bay, began streaming down my face. I struggled to contain my sobs as my entire postgraduation summer plans were swept away, the same way those maple leaves would be once the first big wind came through.

"Are you OK?" a quiet voice asked from behind me as my shoulders convulsed.

I startled and turned, trying my best to hide the camera wreckage beneath a throw. I quickly wiped my tears and explained, "Just some jerk outside. Never let a guy make you cry, OK?"

Lilly, my eleven-year-old sister, nodded solemnly as she pushed back her curls. Then she tilted her chin and asked, "Want me to beat him up?"

I cracked a smile. "No. That's OK. Also, you shouldn't be fighting."

"Yeah, and boys shouldn't make you cry," she affirmed. "Remember how I got detention? That kid in my class who kept pulling my hair and my teacher only scolded him? He kept doing it. So, one day I just yanked his hair back and asked how he liked it. He cried. I got detention, but I dunno why. *He* didn't get detention. And anyway, I only pulled as hard as he did, and I only did it once. He says stupid stuff like girls are weak, but he's the one who cried. Anyway. I can pull his hair if you want. Whoever made you cry just now. *Extra. Hard.*"

I laughed. "Ruthless girl."

She smiled. "Was it Yash? I don't really want to make him cry."

"Even if he made me cry?"

She rubbed her arm and leaned against the doorframe. "I like Yash. He brings me extra Taco Bell sauce packets."

"Oh my lord. If that's all it takes for a boy to get on your good side, then Yash will always be there. His entire car is filled with sauce packets," I said, recalling all those late nights when we upgraded from bikes to a car for Taco Bell runs. There wasn't a single place in his car that wasn't stashing sauce packets. Open his glove compartment, the console, the pockets behind the front seats, the change thingie. Packets. Everywhere.

"You know?" I'd said to him once. "You can actually buy bottles of Taco Bell sauce at the grocery store."

"But then what sort of Indian would I be?" he'd joked.

"I'm OK," I told Lilly. "Thanks for checking."

"Well, Mummie wanted me to get you. She's all excited," she said, her voice pitching higher, but then she rolled her eyes. It was probably something along the lines of them volunteering us for a festival play or offering us to work kitchen duty during said festival. There was nothing worse than having to work during something fun.

"Ah, OK. Be right down," I told her. I waited for her to leave before I hurried to put every last bit of the camera into a shoebox.

I pushed the shoebox to the back of my closet, dried my face, and took a few breaths. As I walked past my bed, my phone screen lit up with a text. It was probably from my other BFF—or *only* BFF now—Tamara.

But it wasn't a message from her. It was from Yash.

He hadn't texted me in months, not since our falling out. See, I'd made some new friends—which was short-lived in hindsight— who'd talked me into sneaking into clubs. I knew my parents weren't going to let me go.

Yash had seen me sneaking out one time and had gotten on my case when I kept doing it. I'd gotten pissed, because who was he to tell me what to do? But he'd argued to the end of the world that he wasn't telling me what to do, but that maybe I should reconsider it if it was going to jeopardize my freedom and maybe even my internship. And that real friends would tell friends if they were concerned. I'd raised my voice and he'd raised his, per usual, and we got into our typical loudness that turned worse and worse. We'd never fought like that.

Well, one day when Lilly was at her friend's house and my parents had gone out to eat, Yash and I had a big fight. My parents had come home early, and because my mom hadn't been feeling well, they'd been quiet. They'd heard me, loud and clear, tell Yash off about my right to go clubbing if I wanted.

I'd never been more terrified in my life than when I saw my parents come around the corner of the hallway. They'd asked me to repeat what I'd just said. When I'd frozen up from shock, they asked Yash. And Yash, with that sorrowful look in his eyes, *told* them. Granted, I'd ratted myself out first, but in the moment and out of panic, I told them that Yash was the one who'd dinged their car. A secret I promised to keep. And boy, had his sorrowful look turned so fast. He'd gotten upset with me for that.

So, yeah. Our fight had me seeing red because maybe I just wanted to do what I wanted to do. I'd been so pissed at him all summer that it had become natural. And awkward. Especially when my parents sided with Yash. Everything felt like a betrayal, and it still hurt.

Against my better judgement, I swiped to read his text.

**Yash:** I'm sorry about earlier. Can we talk?

Left. On. Read.

# CHAPTER TWO

L illy was sitting on the couch playing on her tablet, her knees pulled to her chest as she slumped against the cushions. Man, how did she get so much stuff? Our parents didn't get me a tablet for the longest time, and when they did it was because school required it. The fact that I had a cell phone was a miracle and a half. And that was only so my parents could get a hold of me whenever they wanted to.

"Did you get the shot?" Papa asked with so much hope it made my insides churn.

"No," I said, feeling defeated and somewhat terrified. He always asked about my photography, so it wasn't as if he wouldn't find out soon. But "chicken" wasn't a strong enough word to describe how scared I was to let him down, to possibly have him decide I wasn't ready for a two-month internship away from home.

"Ah, that's OK. There's always tomorrow!" I added, and helped put away the leftovers from dinner, which I'd devoured earlier so I could rush out the door for the golden hour shot.

Thirty minutes ago, I'd planned to come back for these leftovers. Now? Not so much. My stomach couldn't handle the guilt. As much as I loved cheese enchiladas, looking at the leftovers was making me queasy.

"Come. Come!" Mummie exclaimed, taking my wrist and gently tugging me toward the living room.

Both parents beamed with joy, but their unparalleled bliss could literally be over getting us new school clothes.

I plopped down next to Lilly and spotted the box that read "Diwali" behind the couch. *Oh! Of course!* No wonder they were excited. It was time to put up Diwali decorations.

"Are we still doing decorations and cooking?" I asked. "Since we're going to Dubai this year for celebrations?"

"Of course, beta!" Papa replied as he ripped opened the box, sending the masking tape flying. Out of the four of us, he was the most into decorating for festivals. He was already pulling out string lights and silk marigold garlands. "Let's start tonight!"

Mummie giggled as Lilly tossed aside her tablet and squealed, "Yay! Papa, I want to decide where the lights go!"

"OK!" He beamed up at me even while Lilly fell to the floor in front of the box.

Papa had me smiling in no time. "Oh, Sveta, can you make some cha?" he implored Mummie with big ole puppy dog eyes.

She waved him off, laughing. "Cha! At this hour!"

"What this hour? You know I can sleep after coffee, even. It's festive! The weather is getting chilly, Diwali will be upon us, and we're doing something as a family. Please, love of my life?"

It didn't take long for me to get caught up in his excitement. While Mummie made cha with fresh mint, I pulled a container of homemade, nutty sweets out of the fridge because of course Mummie and I had started making mithai for the season.

In the glow of the lamplight, set low so we could get all cozy, everyone drank a cup of cha, snacked on sweets (call it dessert!), and giddily unraveled a million garlands intertwined with other decor. Not to outdo Christmas, but we had a box for tinsel and sparkly orbs; a box for rangoli essentials; a box for garlands and another for lights; and a box of red and gold Diwali cards, diya holders, and candles. Mummie had snagged them in India, where they were super cheap and available in a variety of styles and colors. The sheer amount would last us forever.

I took lots of pics on my phone to capture the memories.

As color filled up the room, Papa sat back to sip cha and commented, "You're going to be off to college next year."

"Yeah," I replied. "Don't miss me too much."

His eyes misted a little and I pouted. "Don't cry, Papa!"

Mummie playfully hit his arm. "Hah. If you cry, I'm going to cry. Then Nikki will start crying and the neighbors will think something horrible has happened."

"Yeah, Papa," Lilly chimed. "You said this was good. Why are you crying? We'll have more space."

"Hey!" I teased.

"She's just joking," Papa said. "We're not going to touch your room. But this is our last Diwali together for a long time, perhaps."

"I can come home, you know."

"Not during college. You need to make all your classes and exams," he contested. "High school granted some days away, but college is not that simple."

I sighed, not wanting to accept the truth even as I said, "We'll have to wait until Thanksgiving and then winter break, I guess."

Which truly sucked. We didn't celebrate Thanksgiving or Christmas, although we took advantage of the holidays to spend time with family. I would be missing Diwali with my family for the first time. I knew from others in the community and cousins and the college websites that a lot of universities had student groups that put on public events like Diwali and Holi, but it wasn't the same as being with family.

Even this year wasn't going to be like most years.

"We're going to do Diwali big this year. Diwali in Dubai." He clapped his hands once.

"I'm so excited!" Mummie said. "Family, fireworks, friends, and food!"

"But we get that here," I reminded them. I wasn't as thrilled as my parents were. I kinda just wanted to stay in our cozy little nostalgic place.

Mummie added, "Not like how they do in Dubai, second best only to India. It's also closer to some family I haven't seen in years, who you haven't met yet. It'll be a big, fat, Indian Diwali!"

I shook my head but found myself smiling. "It's that way here!"

"No, no, no," Mummie refuted as she placed her cup of cha down and separated decorations for Lilly to sift through. "You don't remember Diwali in India. It's spectacular. And my cousins in Abu Dhabi said Dubai is magical. They have laser and light shows, fireworks, stalls of street food, concerts . . . oh! I can't wait. And it's such a nice, clean, safe city, you know?"

"You can bring your camera," Papa said, making me wince. "It would be wonderful to capture all the moments and to show off your talent to relatives."

"It's not a competition," Mummie warned.

"Why shouldn't I show off, huh? My girls, so smart and talented and responsible."

Eek. Hearing him declare that I was responsible, once a proud sentiment, had warped into something that made me flinch. I'd done two *majorly* irresponsible things, had lost my friendship with Yash over it, and been declared grounded all summer. But I knew he didn't mean it to be upsetting or mocking. So, there was still hope that he saw me as responsible enough to go off for an internship. Of course, he knew I was applying for it. But after what had gone down, there was always a chance that my parents might not let me attend. I had a lot to prove to them.

Papa had that gleam in his eye, like he couldn't wait to brag about us. And if we knew anything about Papa, it was that getting together with uncles brought out the weirdest competitiveness. It had started with Lilly being a super-pooper as a baby. And well, things just escalated from there.

"We're going to decorate at home, still," Papa said as he successfully unraveled a long string of silk marigolds from the nightmarish twine ball of fake flowers.

I rescued a string of lights from the death grip of the mother ball. Sheesh, we really needed to take the time to put away decorations better. Future us will appreciate it.

"No backing out this late," Mummie scolded.

We'd known about the plan to go to Dubai for the holidays for a year now. In fact, my biggest obsession was what to wear. Dubai was a modest country, but I didn't want to suffocate in the heat.

"This will be our last Diwali before you're off to college and our lives change," Mummie said, a hint of solemnness in her voice.

As soon as enough flowers and lights had been laid out, Lilly snatched them and ran to the fireplace, arranging them across the mantel. We had windows to frame, the stairwell banister to decorate, and the section against the stairs to fill with paper flowers and balloons because Lilly loved balloons, so sure, why not?

My parents glanced at each other, and I was certain they felt the impending storm sparking around us. The one everyone had been talking about in hushed conversations. A child was leaving to embark on college and a life of their own, yadda, yadda. My parents were going to cry, weren't they?

Just when I expected tears to roll down Mummie's face, she exhaled and said, "We've invited some friends."

Lilly and I paused and stared at her. "Who?" we asked in unison, but I was bracing for the worst, because it was easy to guess.

Mummie tilted her head to the side. She had a generous hint of mischief in her eyes. "Pranav Uncle and Hetal Auntie."

My jaw dropped. "So . . . wait . . . does that mean . . . ?"

"Hah," she confirmed. "Yash and his parents will be joining us for Diwali."

I almost jumped out of my skin with irrational rage. "What! When did this happen?"

"We've been discussing it over the past year," she replied calmly.

"Bu-but without even asking me?" I sputtered.

Mummie sighed and said, "Before your big fight, you two were inseparable. They were our best friends before Yash was yours.

It was a no-brainer to ask them to join us. This is also Yash's last year at home before he leaves for college. We've always done Diwali with them. This just felt like the right way to send you both off to college."

I harrumphed. There went any fun and relaxation I might've had.

As if reading my thoughts, Papa added, "We hate to see you two fighting."

"That's his fault," I mumbled, looking off into the corner.

Lilly side-eyed me, but she was probably ecstatic about having Yash join us. In her eyes, he had respectable big-brother status.

Papa added firmly, "It's time to put it behind you. Diwali is the season for forgiveness, a chance to let our light shine bright." There was nothing untrue about what he was saying.

Mummie added, "Diwali is about light prevailing over darkness, about good defeating evil. We must forgive in order to fully partake in the festivities. You can't go into Diwali with a dark heart."

I scowled. Since when was putting a friendship behind me considered having a dark heart? That seemed like a bit of an extreme jump! People with dark hearts: Darth Vader, The Joker, Thanos, Nikki.

"Can you do this?" Mummie asked.

"I don't have a choice, do I?" I replied, keeping my eyes downcast. I wasn't about to get smart with her *and* maintain eye contact.

"No," she replied matter-of-factly. Dang, talk about no-nonsense mom-talk. "It's time to forgive and move on."

"But—"

"But what?" she asked curtly and looked me dead in the eye.

But nothing. We all knew I was the one holding the grudge, and I didn't really have much of a reason to. It was just so hard to let it go and I wasn't even sure why.

I didn't respond to my mom but nodded when she said, "Let's get through this and enjoy our last Diwali together before college. No drama, no bickering. Let's make this the best one yet and enjoy every bit of it with the light of the world and not the darkness. There is light in forgiveness, and only darkness by holding grudges. We mustn't hold negativity against others. Especially good people like Yash. Poor boy."

I huffed at that. Poor boy my butt.

I blew out a breath. We had only nine months left before I was off to college and wouldn't have to deal with Yash on a daily basis.

For now, I'd do what my parents asked. Not because they were right but because I wasn't going to let anyone ruin my favorite holiday of the year. I was going to decorate the crap out of our house and enjoy the gum-achingly sugary mithai we'd made and eat all the food and work on rangoli designs and enjoy fireworks.

"Found the tape!" Lilly said, holding up clear packing tape so strong we could use it to hang heavy ornaments from the ceiling. I felt the tension dissipate as Mummie immediately commenced planning what would go where.

Every year, thanks to Mummie's love of YouTube, we thought we could get a little more creative by trying new things. And every year, we ended up doing almost the exact same thing. In fairness, social media people were dedicated and patient, and we were not.

Before we knew it, the plain old mantel had been transformed into a colorful display of flowers and lights and small rangoli-inspired diya holders. Papa moved on to drape garlands over the window frames while Lilly intertwined fairy lights throughout the flowers so it looked like one glowing thread instead of multiple strings pulled together.

Normally we'd be making tons more food. The kitchen would be bursting with clanking pots and pans while my sister and I helped our parents meticulously mix nut flours and spices and saffron. We'd stir slowly while it cooked, laying out thick, sweet concoctions into round, shallow steel dishes to cool. Then we'd cut them into diamond shapes and sprinkle dried rose petals and crushed pista on top.

We'd giggle over how squishy laddoo felt in our hands as we molded them into balls and get frustrated over how we could never fill gughra right—not even with the metal mold for that perfect semioval shape with pinched edges, like tiny half pies filled with pulverized nuts.

The entire house would smell like cardamom and sugar and melted butter. We'd cook way too much and eat nonstop, even as we packed our treats into little plastic bags with bright orange and pink net ribbons to hand out to family and friends.

Yash's grinning face flashed across my thoughts. There was no reminiscing about Diwali without thinking about him. He'd always been there, for as long as I could remember. Nudging my shoulder with his because I was hunching over the counter, flicking my hair because I'd somehow get glitter in it, butting me out of the way when he was trying to sneak food, and trapping my words with laughter by way of tickles.

Yash was tall, like basketball player tall, and was always picked on to hang the high stuff with our dads, to bring down platters and boxes for our moms, to play keep-away with Lilly whenever she cheated at board games. Which was every other time.

I shook my head, shoving his memories out like a bad cold, which wasn't effective at all.

Lilly crawled onto the back of the couch, against the wall, to reach high up to the empty space between two windows in order to slap sticky rangoli patterns onto the wall at crooked angles. She positioned the set of emerald-green paisleys outlined in gold rhinestones for the outer layer at an angle, so it looked like the peacock shapes were spinning. In the center was a ruby red circle outlined in gold rhinestones.

"Wish Yash was here," she muttered, as she struggled to attach shimmering pink pearls above the pattern. "He can reach the high spaces."

I harrumphed, crawled onto the back of the couch against the wall, took the pearls from her, and attached them where she directed.

Climbing back down, I proudly dusted off my hands as if we'd done some hard labor and said, "We don't need boys."

She shrugged with a half-smile and quietly moved on to another box.

The boy wasn't even on our property, and still he haunted us. I just . . . kinda wanted to get Diwali over with. Was that bad? My fave holiday wasn't the same and never would be again. I didn't even know why my parents had insisted on going to Dubai. I just wanted to cook and bake and try new ways to infuse traditional flavors into cakes.

*Actually*, Yash was the one who liked to bake traditional sweets in modern ways. He failed half the time, but the fun had been in trying and in me snapping photos at each step like we were shooting for a famous food magazine.

I grunted, eyeing my parents, who were busy working out decoration details, and slipped out the front door armed with my phone and flashlight. It was getting darker and I had a finite number of minutes to look for the other half of my lens before having to call it a night.

With hurried steps, I went to the road where the macabre accident had happened as the temperature dropped to a nice chill.

With the neighborhood near dead, no cars on the streets, sleepy houses with lights on here and there, streetlamps lighting the way, and a soft breeze cutting through the chill, I turned the corner to the scene of the accident.

There, hunched over bushes across the sidewalk with a flashlight, was Yash. He was in his usual basketball shorts and faded T-shirt, his hair fluffy and wild and falling over his brows. He kept brushing it away from his face every few seconds, and every few seconds it plopped right back down. He stood.

I shielded my eyes from the sudden glare of his beam before he lowered the flashlight and fully turned to me.

"What are you doing?" I asked.

"Looking for your lens," he replied, as if he wanted to add his typical, "Duh," with an exaggerated roll of the eye.

Part of me wanted to thank him and get to looking while we still had some natural light, but the stubborn part of me wanted to pivot on my heels and walk away.

His shoulders deflated. "I can go. I was just trying to help."

I opened my mouth to thank him, to tell him it was OK if he stayed, that two sets of eyes were better than one, but words gurgled at the back of my throat. By the time a breath escaped my lips, Yash was walking back home.

As he passed, a whiff of shampoo hit me and his arm grazed mine, sending a shiver down my spine. I wanted us to be normal again, to laugh with him, to have him help me cover this up the way we'd helped each other so many times before.

I opened my mouth to say something, anything. But in the end, I just stood there, watching him as he disappeared around the corner.

# CHAPTER THREE

fter an hour of snooping in my neighbors' yards, splitting apart their bushes, and kicking through dead leaves while somehow evading merciless fire ant hills, I had *not* found the demolished lens. Yash had truly Thanosed it, and it was forever gone.

I grunted and dragged my feet upstairs and into my room, closing the door behind me as panic clawed at the base of my skull. My parents were going to end me. How were they ever going to trust me again? Between getting busted for the whole clubbing thing and destroying the most expensive thing they'd ever bought for me, why in the world would my parents ever allow me to pursue a photography internship in DC for almost an entire summer? It meant living on my own with absolutely no supervision. *Trust?* What was that?

I changed into pajamas. My parents' voices carried through the hall as they headed to bed. It was all Diwali this and Dubai that and Auntie and Uncle everything. Did we have to do everything with them?

My parents and Yash's parents were best friends, had been since college. Yash and I had been thrown together since birth. We'd been born at the same hospital and went everywhere together. The same schools and parks. The same mandir and festivities.

Our parents had gone to each other's engagement ceremonies and weddings, even had a joint baby shower. They'd bought homes next to each other and installed a gate between the backyards so we could just go on over to each other's houses.

Yash and I used to always use that gate, but now I hadn't touched it all summer. I'd assumed I wouldn't have to spend more than an awkward dinner here and there with him and his family, which was fine because I'd just pop in earbuds and ignore him.

But this? This whole vacationing together was going to be the worst.

I pulled my long ponytail out from underneath my pink-and-gray pajama top and walked over to my desk to look up camera repair shops and, an even bigger stretch, warranty stuff. Seemed like warranty windows never lasted long and almost never included damage caused by close encounters with a car tire.

I sat on the swivel desk chair, turned on my laptop, then happened to glance up. There was a big ole window right in front of my desk, which faced the window of the house next door. Yash's bedroom window, to be exact. He also had his desk and chair set up in front of it, so we could sort of hang out, even when we weren't together.

Through his window, I could see Yash on his phone pacing his room. Who was he talking to, looking all delighted and smiling? Eh, it wasn't my business. Also, why was I even watching him?

After a few minutes, he hung up, sat down at his desk, and ran his hands down his face. Then he leaned back and stared at the ceiling before dropping his head back down to find me watching him.

Oh, shoot! Caught being a creeper, yet I couldn't stop creeping.

We both froze, staring, locked into place like we couldn't move. The only thing I could do was blink and breathe.

After what seemed like forever, Yash gave a small smile and a slight wave.

I didn't respond, didn't move.

He lifted his phone to indicate chatting, but I shook my head. He frowned. He hunched over his desk.

In another minute, he lifted a whiteboard with large, sprawling black letters that read, "I'm sorry."

I shrugged. Telling me he was sorry for running over my expensive camera wasn't enough.

He put his head back down and lifted the whiteboard again. This time, it read, "I miss you."

My heart palpitated, and I wasn't sure why. Was it because I missed him, too? But how could someone miss a person they were mad at?

My fingers twitched beside my phone. Something about that stupid sign, so simple and direct but saturated with so many feels, made me realize just how much I missed my best friend. Like a sack of bricks had smacked me in the chest. I wanted to forgive and forget, but dang if pride wasn't a warrior battling logic over this.

In the end, I didn't reach for my phone. Instead, I shook my head, leaned over the desk, and closed the curtains.

My phone lit up with a text notification from Yash—a sad face emoji.

I bit my lip, tempted to respond.

*Nope.* Delete notification.

How was I supposed to avoid him for an entire weeklong trip with all four parents and a sister trying to push us together to mend the friendship we'd been sworn into since birth?

I returned to looking for a camera repair place but with no luck. My thoughts kept going back to Yash with the urgent need to talk to someone about him. My family couldn't be trusted, because they would all say I was overreacting. My friends would either be anti-Yash, which came with too strong of a hate filter attached, or tell me to simply get over it and move on. Tamara was tired of hearing me complain about him, and she wasn't holding back on telling me so anymore.

Ah, screw it. What were friends for?

**Nikki:** Guess who my parents invited on our trip to Dubai?

**Tamara:** Yo boy Yash???

**Nikki:** How'd you guess? Also, quick reply!

**Tamara:** LOL! Who else would they invite? Some non-BFF of theirs?

**Nikki:** So . . . no sympathy???

**Tamara:** You're going to DUBAI. So, that's a no. I'll be sitting here by my lonesome trying not to fall asleep during trig.

Ugh. She had a point, but still.

I almost told her about the camera, but then I remembered my parents could do surveillance on my phone if they so wished (because the tech was there if they had an uncle to show them).

I decided not to mention it, then tried to distract myself from all the things going wrong by checking online for camera sales and camera repair shops. Tension built and bubbled inside my head, stretching against my skull and pulsating. This accident, which wasn't even my fault, could bite my summer internship plans in the big ole butt. That internship was hard to beat on a resume. Plus, if I excelled and they really liked me, they might invite me for another internship or even a better program, which might open up to an actual job. How amazing would that be?

I groaned out loud, irritated that the internet wasn't faster, more helpful, clearer. It was hopeless!

I plopped into bed face-first. Ugh. I wished the comforter would swallow me right into its sea of muted geometric patterns.

I managed to lift my head, pulling my tablet toward me, and scrolled through WebToon, disinterest and irritation trying hard to creep into the cracks of my thoughts. WebToon was a webcomic platform that Yash had discovered a few years back when he'd briefly considered the possibilities of a career in art.

"That's so cool," I'd said to him, totally in awe over the fact that some episodes came with music; that the entire platform was—for the most part—free to read; and that it offered hundreds of series, each with hundreds of episodes.

"I'd never be able to do that," he'd always say. "Be that good or come up with a compelling story line plus dialogue plus character arcs plus complete panels plus prepare it weekly. That's way too much. And the competition to not only get in as a creator, but to stand out against everyone else? Sounds so stressful. No thank you."

Three, then four, then five different series came and went across my screen. Some were short episodes, some totally not keeping my interest. I hated this feeling of anxiety chomping away any focus.

Until I landed on my favorite series.

*The Fall* by Jalebi_Writer. Not a real name, obvs. But that was the pseudonym at the end of every episode, and the name attached to his social media accounts, the name that popped up during our brief online interactions.

My gaze landed on the masterful art of his world in comic form. He had taken beautiful parts of the city and turned them dark and creepy and devouring and just . . . ugh! His series had my entire creative heart. Not only were these sometimes colorful, sometimes black-and-white—broad strokes and sharp lines mesmerizing—but the story line was equally captivating. The pacing was superb and the characterization meaningful. Don't let anyone tell ya that comics are stupid and a waste of brain space. They are art and storytelling and balancing a dozen things at once. And Jalebi_Writer was doing it right.

What was *The Fall* about? Basically, a brown boy decided to start a murder podcast. He always started and ended each episode with a reminder that the murder mystery wasn't real. He wasn't getting a lot of listens, but he was having fun. Then one day he and his friends were visiting a volcano lodge, and after staying a few days, they heard about an awful accident. A bunch of relatives and their elderly grandfather had taken a night walk down a trail on the edge of a crater to try to get a better look at the glow of the caldera. It was dark—no lights except the moon and stars—and they left the grandfather behind without a flashlight. Alone.

Well, guess he slipped and died, and it was ruled an accident. But the boy and his friends weren't buying that. Like, why walk the trail at night with an elderly person? Why leave someone behind without a buddy? Why would the man not follow the trail of flashlights from other people on the path? Why did he stray from the path, and how did he get past the barrier rope? Why did the family wait for hours to notify park rangers?

So now, the boy had a real murder mystery on his hands. His podcast started blowing up, but so did the stakes; because every turn leads him down a dark tunnel of whodunits and what-ifs and, ugh! It was so captivating, so good!

I was living for this twisted tale and hungrily devoured this week's episode.

At the conclusion of a harrowing scene that left the main character sick and delirious, watching a sketchy woman through a window, Jalebi_Writer ended with:

Announcement time! Thanks to all of you readers, the likes, the subscribers, the comments, the purchased coins to early access has all led to *The Fall* becoming the top-rated mystery on WebToon and one of the top ten series in its HISTORY!!

I'm totally blown away! I had no idea this story would take off, and so quickly. I'm humbled, too, because there's so many awesome series here. Do me a solid and keep supporting a young artist! Gotta pay for college, lol! Also, smash that subscribe button and hit like! These numbers help out so much! Thanks!

I gasped, clasping a hand over my mouth to keep from squealing!

I immediately dropped the tablet and reached for my phone to DM him on social. He was probably busy and too popular to even respond, but still!

I clicked on his profile pic, the animated one of a brown boy looking like an Indian teen sleuth, with sharply drawn eyes, dark hair falling over his brows, and jagged lines for a jaw.

**Nikki: Congrats on your big announcement! That's so cool!**

Although I had always secretly hoped it, I had never expected a famous person—or even just someone I admired—to respond to me. I'd never thought in a million years that when I first DM'd Jalebi_Writer all those months ago, that he would read my message, much less respond! But it had happened, and major bragging points for that! He was just so cool and down to earth.

And yeah, I was absolutely aware of all the dangers that could come from chatting with a stranger virtually; but like, there was a bit of trust and accountability with this guy, because he wasn't just any random dude. He was a public figure: a real—and huge—author with a trail of receipts that I'd always kept; and my own account was set to private.

**Jalebi_Writer: Thanks, Nikki!**

What! I almost fainted, my skin thrumming. That was so fast! OMG.

**Nikki:** You're doing so well for a guy who hasn't even started college!

**Jalebi_Writer:** LOL! Took a lot of work and some luck. Still have a ways to go.

**Nikki:** Your parents must be so proud.

There was a pause before he responded.

**Jalebi_Writer:** Ah . . . they don't really know?

I sputtered.

**Nikki:** WHAT! How do they not know?? You should tell them. They gotta be proud of this!

**Jalebi_Writer:** Maybe. Hey. It's nice to hear from you. Thanks for the support.

How you been?

**Nikki:** Good.

Which was the most basic and artificial response. I was *not* good.

**Jalebi_Writer:** You sure? Don't sound like it. I mean, like you usually have a lot of words haha!

I chewed on my lip. He didn't know me or my family or friends, so he shouldn't have any sudden and harsh reactions. He was neutral. Refreshing. Easy to talk to.

Nikki: Well, no.

Jalebi_Writer: What's up?

Nikki: Someone broke my camera.

Jalebi_Writer: WUT! How?

I smiled at his adorable response. He often spelled "what" as "wut" in his episodes.

Nikki: Was on the ground trying to get a shot when the neighbor ran it over.

Jalebi_Writer: OMG. Are you OK? Did you get hurt?

Nikki: No. I was farther away to avoid shadows.

Jalebi_Writer: So . . . they didn't see the camera?

Nikki: Apparently not.

Jalebi_Writer: Sounds like . . . an accident??

Nikki: Yeah, but a bad one. My camera is my life and it's expensive.

Jalebi_Writer: I'm sorry.

Nikki: Thanks.

Jalebi_Writer: You should make them pay for the camera. You know them, where they live. Only seems fair.

I twisted my lip. I explained how I couldn't take payment because one, Yash didn't have that kind of money. Two, he'd have to ask his parents for it, which meant my parents would find out because that was how things always happened. And if my parents found out, then I was going to be in huge trouble. I wanted to at least give them a happy Diwali. And then, I added the general story of what had happened between Yash and me. Maybe that would help him understand that I was already in hot water with everyone, and this incident would just make them . . . I dunno . . . blame me for more.

And. Send.

Ack!

I dropped my head onto the pillow and groaned. Was that too much baggage? Was he like, who TF is this girl just rambling on like he cares? Most authors wouldn't give me this much time, so maybe he regretted ever opening his DMs to me.

Ah! I was so stupid. He was going to think I was some weirdo who talked too much and never respond to me again.

I was about to sign out of my social media account to save myself the desperation of waiting for a response that was surely never to come when . . . *what?* . . . he responded!

> **Jalebi_Writer:** That's . . . a lot. Bet this guy had no idea you felt this much blame from everyone. Did you ever tell him?

I scoffed and replied with as much sarcasm as one could in DMs.

Nikki: I'm sure he had an idea. <rolling eye emoji> I'm not subtle.

Jalebi_Writer: Can't live life assuming others know what you feel.

I scowled. Hey. He wasn't supposed to take sides.

# CHAPTER FOUR

Who thought waking up at the butt-crack before the butt-crack of dawn was OK? I groggily slapped around my bedside stand to find the phone, which desperately clung to its charger, and tapped the shrieking alarm off. For typical days, I used a bubble-effect alarm to gently coax myself out of sleep and saved the shrieking kind for fifteen minutes later in case I slept through the first alarm.

Guess I slept through the first alarm.

2:30 A.M. glared back at me, looking as angry as my brain felt having been snatched away from sleep. Like, WTF?

Dude, I hear ya.

With so much effort—because exhaustion did, in fact, turn your body into mush—I pushed myself out of bed and went through my morning routine. By the time I stepped back into my room to make the bed and triple-check that I had everything, the rest of the family was already downstairs and ready to go. Lilly was bright-eyed with such excitement that it made my heart swell. Our parents fluttered around for last-minute things like fairies high on fairy dust, but their joy was contagious. All right, I wasn't even mad. We were going to freaking Dubai! Bless their hearts for scrimping and saving for this trip. I could not ruin this.

Three large suitcases, black with red paint stroke designs so we could quickly identify them, plus two matching carry-ons, all on wheels, and two backpacks hugged the side window next to the front door. If this were a Disney movie, they'd blink up at me with big doe eyes and wiggle around, eager to get on their first international journey.

Wow, was I sleepy!

"She's ready! Finally! Gawd!" Lilly exclaimed, and shoved a partially opened Ziploc bag of thepla at me. I unwrapped the paper towel inside the plastic bag, pulled out two round flatbreads, and clung to them with my teeth while wrapping the rest back up and zipping the bag.

Savory, spicy, with specs of bitter methi greens hit my tongue. It was, no doubt, the quintessential travel snack. Mummie must've made two stacks last night. One for the way to Dubai, the other for the way back. Whenever we traveled longer than a couple of hours, thepla and (if we were lucky) cheesy, cumin-laced potato pastry puffs were almost always guaranteed.

"Did you guys even sleep?" I asked around a big ole bite.

"Beta, don't talk with your mouth full," Mummie chided.

Lilly shook her head. "How could you sleep, Motiben? Were you not super-duper excited? I couldn't keep my eyes closed. So I looked up all the best things to eat when we get there. Like, we gotta try camel milk chocolate. What even is that!"

I grimaced. "Ew."

"Challo, challo," Papa said, urging us out as he thumbed through our passports.

Mummie flung back the front door and we all bristled at the sudden chill. It was pitch-black, barely three in the morning, but we managed to fit all our stuff into Masa's minivan. My uncle took the bigger suitcases from Mummie and gave us girls a sleepy smile.

Papa did a final sweep through the house and checked all the locks before we buckled up and headed to the airport. He sat up front with Masa while Mummie, Lilly, and I sat in the middle row of seats. The back row had been taken out to make room for all the bags.

Between the cold, the conversation, and the frenzy of excitement percolating through the air, it was easy to wake all the way up. My eyelids weren't as sore and my body not as slack.

"You'll be right at home," Mummie assured Papa. "UAE has a very large number of Indians living there. My cousin in Abu Dhabi—we're going to Abu Dhabi, remember, girls, to meet some cousins?" She glanced at us.

We nodded. Yes, yes, who could forget that when she'd been talking about them nonstop and forcing us into her WhatsApp video calls with them?

She went on with Papa, but sort of talking to all of us, "My cousin says there's many Indian residents and Indian food. We can always find something familiar to eat. Samosa and pani puri and vada pav vendors are everywhere. But surely we can try so much more?"

Papa tentatively nodded. He wasn't the most adventurous with new food. He was all about Gujarati cuisine, pizza, and tacos—stuff we made at home.

"The country is a huge melting pot. Lots of Asian, Indian, Lebanese, Persian, and European culinary influences, too."

While our parents chattered away, moving on to Masa checking in on our place and plans for Masi to make us return meals when he picked us up, Lilly swiped endlessly through her tablet. Every picture of food made her eyes go wider than the last until I thought surely they would pop out of her head.

Between the two of us, there was going to be a ton of things we wanted to try. Stuffed dates, Arabic coffee, pizza called manousheh, honey halloumi, sugarcane juice, chebab pancakes, kanafeh and luqaimat and kellaj sweets. OK, we definitely had a sweet tooth.

We didn't know what half of this stuff was, but that was the point, right? While I loved Indian street food, I didn't want to eat exclusively that all week.

Lilly squealed at a picture of a fluffy treat, "I don't know what a gallusette is, but it's filled with Nutella, so yeah, gotta find that!"

While Lilly continued to focus on all the food a kid could want, I started making a list of all the places to see. The tallest building in the world with the fastest elevator in the world, the world's largest mall with the biggest indoor aquarium, the palm-shaped island, the fastest roller coasters in the world, the beaches, the gold and spice souks, the water fountain shows . . . and that wasn't even the beginning of the Diwali sights. Ugh, too bad I had to be tied to the family the entire trip. I wanted to explore instead of doing the basic parent stuff of chilling with family and doing Diwali puja and seeing some Diwali fireworks and eating.

"Are you sure I can't explore Dubai on my own?" I asked, peering around Lilly to look at Mummie. "Like you said, it's the safest city in the world, with the lowest crime rate in the world. It's super clean and easy to navigate with taxis. I promise I'll check in every hour, and you can track me on my phone."

Mummie heaved, letting out a dramatic sigh. But I got it. Asking Indian parents to let their teenage daughter run free in a city, much less in a foreign country, was a monster of a request. Yet I had to try. Sure, my parents were probably going to take us to see a lot of what we asked for, but not everything, and definitely not the entire time. There was just so much to pack into a few days, plus trying to get the right shots (on my phone because I still had to try for that internship), which sort of depended on the time of day. Besides, I couldn't just be cooped up with my mom's big, loud family while there was a fantastic city out there, ready to be explored. Also, maybe I didn't want to be cooped up with Yash, either.

"I'll think about it," she finally replied.

I gawked at her. "Really?"

She nodded once and returned to the conversation with Papa and Masa.

Lilly gave me her huge OMG face, where her eyes widened to the size of saucers and her mouth puckered. We both knew this could be a big deal, for a ton of reasons.

One, it was Dubai!

Two, my parents didn't often let me wander in unfamiliar places alone.

Three, my parents were still a bit pissed at the whole thing about the fake ID and clubbing and helping Yash cover up our car accident and also fighting with him.

Four, I was a girl. There were plenty of horror stories about girls being kidnapped in foreign countries.

Masa dropped us off at the airport and off we went with his well wishes.

With bags labeled, IDs checked, and tickets scanned, we were on our way to Dubai. And per usual for the few times I had flown, I was passed out asleep on takeoff.

\* \* \*

During our layover in Florida, Lilly and I wandered off to get something to eat. There was only so much thepla a kid could take. By the time we returned, our bellies full of pasta, our flight crew was making their grand entrance.

I'd seen pilots and airline attendants every time we went to the airport, but I wasn't prepared for the glamour of Emirates. The women were all so poised with a low bun tucked beneath the infamous red hat with a cream scarf that draped down one side and across the chest to the other side of the neck—not to mention the elegant tan outfit with red pleated skirt, the red heels, and matching red lipstick.

"Wow," Lilly said, gawking.

Like a clique of celebrities, they had every head turning.

As they strolled past, a sign that we were almost ready to begin boarding, familiar, grinning faces sprouted up behind them.

Yash's parents appeared first from around the corridor. Then Yash with his floppy hair, sweatshirt, and jogger pants.

They'd taken a flight out of Houston instead of Austin to save some money, but we would all take the international flight together. Yash's parents were just as eager as my parents, and Yash, by the look of stoicism on his face, was either dead tired or couldn't give a crap.

We greeted his parents with hellos and smiles. Yash greeted my parents and Lilly the same way. I intended to give him every cold shoulder I had when he made it to me. Except this time, he didn't even try to greet me. He took one look at me, nodded, and placed his big ole headphones over his head.

My heart cracked. I wasn't sure why. I didn't want to talk to him, and all the tension between us was thick enough to walk on. And probably—yeah, OK, most definitely—I'd treated him just as indifferently all summer long.

Ugh. Whatever. I just wanted to enjoy *my* trip with *my* family. But our parents had slightly different plans for us.

Out of the corner of my eye, I could see them watching us not interacting. But, before long, the staff began boarding people. We shuffled into line. Lilly and I stood ahead of our parents, followed by Yash and his parents.

We moved past the first-class seats, positioned at the front both for quick access for those who could afford it and to make the rest of us envious. The seats were almost as large as a couch and pulled out into an actual bed. They had plenty of space and were almost all the way enclosed, like a fancy cubicle. I read the two-story version of this plane had a spa with a shower and everything, and a mini restaurant.

Anyway, that was far beyond the likes of us.

We ambled all the way to the second half of the plane as people took their sweet time storing their carry-ons in the massive overhead bins.

International flights were *much* bigger than domestic ones, it turned out. There was a row of three seats to the right, an aisle, a row of four seats in the middle, another aisle, and another set of three by the opposite window.

I checked my ticket and stopped at our row, slipping my mini backpack off as Mummie tapped my shoulder.

"Huh?" I asked.

"Second-to-last row, window seat," she instructed.

"What? My ticket says—"

"I know what our tickets say. You and Yash will sit in the back and start getting along."

My heart began to beat faster as I glanced at him from over my parents' shoulders. He was watching me, but with more of a "what's going on" look. Did he know about this?

I frowned and opened my mouth to argue, but Mummie arched one brow, tilting her head to the side, and shot me that warning look that said I best shut my mouth and do as she says.

She added, "If you want to see Dubai on your own, then Yash will have to escort you."

"*What?*"

She shrugged, as if this wasn't a gigantic ask of me. "I suggest you two hash it out and make this work if you want any chance of seeing more of the city, because we don't have the energy to run around with you. We have family to catch up with."

My eye twitched.

"Exactly. You don't want to sit around with a bunch of adults over cha and nasto talking about real estate and the vast differences of living in the UAE versus the States."

I dramatically threw my head back and groaned, pivoted on my heels, and marched to the second-to-last row, window seat.

I retrieved my earbuds and tablet, dropping them onto the very cushiony seat while Yash helped our parents stash their bags. He then made his way toward me, his jaw clenched and cheeks flushed. Maybe he hadn't known this was the plan, either.

I stood on my tiptoes to shove my backpack into the overhead bin, getting frustrated because the guy who was in front of me had stuck his bag inside all wrong, but I was too short to fix the heavy thing.

"Here," Yash said, moving one side of his earphones off his right ear and reaching up to adjust the other guy's bag and then mine, his armpit almost in my face.

"I didn't need your help."

"Really?" he asked, his upper body still stretched over me.

"Thanks," I grumbled, escaping the close proximity of his body to slip into my seat.

"It's what tall guys are for," he added, looking back at his family once more before heaving out a breath and sitting beside me.

I crossed my arms and looked out the window, ready to fall asleep on takeoff and not wake up until we landed. Which, of course, wouldn't happen because the flight was, like, fourteen hours long.

I nipped my nail, thinking of a million ways to avoid conversation, when Yash readjusted his headphones, covered his head with his hoodie, stuffed his hands into the front pockets of his sweatshirt, leaned his head back, and, I assumed, closed his eyes.

Oh, well, that made it easier.

But what should've been a moment of relief turned into a queasy sensation in the pit of my stomach. Why was he mad at me? Or . . . had Yash finally moved on from our friendship the way I'd kept telling him to?

# CHAPTER FIVE

I woke up, startled, to the sound of snoring. *My* snoring! OMG.

I sucked in a breath, hoping no one had heard that awful sound, and moved with a crick in my neck. The plane was dark except for aisle lights and the calming glow of little specs like stars on the ceiling.

Rubbing my neck, I stretched and slowly looked over to make sure Yash hadn't heard me snoring.

He was watching me, a tablet on the pull-out tray and a stylus in his hand.

"Were you watching me sleep?" I muttered.

"No. That's creepy. I just happened to look over because you woke up. Bro, you snore so loud, you woke everyone."

I gasped and hit his arm.

He feigned pain and laughed. "What? It's not my fault that you snore."

"Shut up."

He straightened up and went back to his tablet. "You got drool on your face."

I quickly ran the back of my sweatshirt over my mouth, and yep, there it was, a trail of my spit. Gross. This was not happening to me.

"Can I get out? I need to use the restroom."

Yash put his tablet away, letting me out of our row as he raised his hands to reach toward the ceiling in a long stretch.

After using the restroom and making sure there was no evidence of ever having drooled, I stood at the back of the aisle. Behind me was a sizable area where the flight attendants made coffee and warmed meal trays and had stacks upon stacks of snacks.

Had they passed out drinks and snacks while I was busy snoring?

"Do you need any help?" a flight attendant asked. She had removed the famous Emirates red hat and cream scarf. Guess it was only for looks and probably uncomfortable to work in for long hours.

"Are there any snacks left?" I asked.

"Sure thing." She handed me a big handful of cookies and trail mix and added, "You're welcome to come back here and take whatever snack or beverage you'd like if we're busy."

I grinned. Noted. Free food and soda!

I returned with my stash, plus a Coke, earning Yash's envy. I'd have shared, or at least let him know what the flight attendant had said, if he'd only, ya know, said more than a few sentences to me this entire time.

He didn't utter a word, though the crooked scowl on his face said it all.

Once situated, with the pull-down tray leveled for my treasure, I perused the mighty selection of entertainment on the large screen attached to the back of the seat in front of me. Wow. This flight had hundreds of shows, movies, and music to choose from. Truly the stuff of legends. Good snacks, tasty meals to come (pizza plus all sorts of desi multi-item full meals with the best chocolate desserts), all the soda I could handle, and catching up on entertainment.

Yet I found myself glancing to the left. The seat at the end was empty, so why was Yash sitting next to me? And what was he working on? His brows furrowed, and he kept pinching his lips together the way he did when he was deep in study mode, but I knew he wasn't studying from the way he was using his stylus. Broad strokes and narrow scratches and a hundred taps.

Every time he caught me trying to look, he paused and side-eyed me and I, like a squirrel, quickly looked away. Was he drawing again? After he'd given up creative pursuits last year when his dad told him to stop wasting his time when he should be studying for SATs?

My heart squirmed. I wanted to ask why he hadn't told me, because it would've been a huge deal, but then I remembered that *I* was the one who'd stopped talking to him. I'd never let him get far with any attempted conversations.

I mean, I could just ask. Right?

I rubbed my hands against my pants. Why were they so clammy all of a sudden?

I could do this. But by the time I mustered the courage to break the wall established by yours truly, he asked, "Where did you get all the snacks? They didn't give me any."

He patted his belly.

"Bro . . ." I slid him a package of cookies. And not the kind on domestic flights that were two small, pathetic pieces, but a six-pack of buttery cookies with raspberry jam in the middle. His favorite.

His face lit up. "Thanks."

I shrugged. And his smile fell.

A few minutes went by, or maybe a few hours—time really had no meaning on an international flight when everyone was snoozing away—when I leaned forward and stretched.

"Ugh. My back hurts. Why aren't planes any faster?" I grumbled to no one.

"Parents all snagged their own rows. Bet they're stretched across multiple seats, passed out."

"They did this on purpose, putting us together."

"No crap," he mumbled. "I'd move over and let you put your feet up on my lap, but as I recall you don't like me anymore, so I won't."

"Well, dang. Don't hold back."

He flashed that side-eye again, his lips stern.

"Why . . . why are you so mean to me all of a sudden?" I muttered, glancing down so he couldn't see my worry. I didn't understand why I was feeling this way. I was the one who locked him out, but this felt so jarring. Just the other day he was trying so hard to talk to me.

He twisted toward me and asked, "*For real?*"

I nodded once.

"You're the one who gave me the silent treatment the entire summer. And blew up at me for the camera. And then ignored me when I tried to text you. I mean, what do you want, Nikki? Because you treating me like crap for so long ain't cool."

"You're the one who ratted me out to my parents. Who, by the way, barely regained any trust in me after that. I was grounded *all* summer," I hissed back.

"That's your fault. You told on yourself, remember? Was I supposed to lie to their faces when they asked me right after? There was no point of pretending I didn't know anything."

I crossed my arms and slammed my back into the seat, huffing. "Don't talk to me like that."

"Am I just supposed to be quiet and take it? Grow up."

I seethed so hard that my teeth could've cracked through my jaw. I wanted to snatch back the cookies but instead just glared at whatever TV series was on.

* * *

About three episodes later, I got up to pee and walked up and down the aisles. This time, the flight attendants were nowhere to be found. Of course they were still on the plane, but the back of the plane had long compartments that looked like they could've been bunk beds for sleeping. Maybe that was where all the flight attendants were, except one down in first-class and one fixing something in the very back that I could see.

I grabbed more snacks, eyeing the cookies that Yash liked. He was being a true pain in the butt, but I also needed his help if my parents were going to let me get farther than ten feet from them in Dubai. Taking a few cookie packs and a root beer, I slowly walked back to our row. Which wasn't a long walk, even if I *was* doing lunges to get some of the ache out of my body.

He'd just popped up to go to the restroom himself, letting me into my seat first. And when he returned, he sat in the empty seat at the end of the row.

With a sigh, knowing I had to try harder if he was going to help me out in the slightest bit, I lowered the tray for the middle seat and placed a handful of cookie packs and the soda on it. After a second, I slid them closer to him just in case he didn't realize it was an offering.

He slowly tilted his head, as if taking the treats meant signing over his soul or something. Then he dragged his gaze up to meet mine.

The words "I'm sorry" teetered on the tip of my tongue. I knew I should apologize. Our tension had gone on long enough; and more than that, I needed us to chill out for the next week. But I was stubborn and, yep, still petty. But also, was I ready to have a conversation? I'd been simmering over this for months, and we really needed to. So why then, did my body feel like dead weight even thinking about it?

I cocked my head toward the back. "They said we can get whatever we want whenever we want off the snack and drinks cart if they're busy."

He nodded. Wow, it was hard to read him when he was this unhappy with me.

"Do you still like drinking this soda when you're playing on your tablet?" I asked quietly.

He nodded.

"Are you . . . um, drawing again?"

He nodded.

I pressed my lips together and let the confession rush out. "Listen. I really want to see the city and, ya know, not be locked to my parents and distant family once they meet up. They're just going to eat and talk the entire time, and I can't believe we're flying halfway across the world and not seeing more of Dubai. So . . . the thing is, well, my mom will let me sightsee but not alone. And they're not big on doing a bunch of stuff in a short amount of time, much less stuff I want to do. They'll let me go if I can convince them that we're OK and talking. And if you come with me."

For a few long seconds, Yash didn't move, and I was sure he was going to bark out a laugh right in my face and say something cruel, like, "Payback's a b—." Or at the least snicker because he had the upper hand.

Instead, he shoved the hood off his head, crossed his arms, and sat back. "Why should I? You've labeled me an enemy and won't even talk to me, except now, when you need something from me."

"You're right. I do need something from you. How about you help me out?"

He listed his head to the side and thought for a few, unnervingly long minutes. "Well, we need a deal then, don't we?"

"What are you thinking?" I asked apprehensively.

"I can pretend we're OK, and I'll go around the city with you . . . *if* . . ."

Oh boy. What would his big demand be? What did he want for his incomprehensible leverage? I was completely at his mercy. And he knew it. He could literally ask for anything in the world from me if I wanted this chance to explore the city on my own bad enough.

I tried to play my poker face, and I wasn't even sure what that was, but I hoped it was enough not to scream "desperate to make a bargain."

He locked eyes on mine, and boy was I about to sweat some big, fat droplets. I could feel them pushing out of my pores as his stare grew intense. He knew he had me!

Argh! Just say it already!

"What?" I finally asked.

"Two things. One, I want you to go tandem skydiving with me. And you have to agree to whatever else I want to do."

My eyes went wide with horror and my breath hitched. So random. He . . . wanted me to jump out of a freaking plane with nothing but an instructor and a parachute attached to my back as the only thing keeping me from splattering to my death?

"What! How, why are you even planning on skydiving? I can't believe your parents agreed to that."

He shrugged as if it were absolutely no biggie to plummet thousands of feet from the air toward the earth. "It's Dubai," he said casually, as if that explained it all.

"It's Dubai," I mocked. "Like that makes it normal for you?"

"It's perfectly safe, one of the best, and coolest, spots to sky-dive. Like how many people do you know who've skydived, huh? It gives me major bragging rights at school."

I eyed him. "Who are you trying to impress? Is it Cindy Ortega from calculus?" I smacked my lips. "You're not going to impress her with this stunt."

"First of all, skydiving does indeed impress girls. Every girl who knows I'm scheduled to dive is all over me."

I cringed. Ew. But also, it saddened me to know that he'd told these things to others and not me, all because of our fight.

"And second, why do you care?"

"I don't care. It's just so random and wild and unlike you. But also, why drag me into it? You want to skydive into my vomit? Because that's what'll happen up there. Just me and my hurled-up lunch hanging out in freefall."

He chuckled. "Awesomely gross."

"Why is that amusing? *You're* gross."

"It's part of the deal."

"But why?"

"What better way of convincing our parents that we're getting along than for you to skydive with me?"

"Whatever. You're scared, so you need someone else to do it with you."

He shrugged but didn't agree to or deny my statement.

I blew out a breath. "Fine. But you know my mom will freak out and never let me go."

"We'll see," he replied, cocky. "I'm sure my mom has already told your mom about it, and if one mom is cool with it, the other will probably come around."

"Not when it involves their eldest daughter falling from the sky."

"You can't just ask her. You have to *convince* her."

I rolled my eyes.

"Well, I'm going the morning after Diwali, which is the day our families will be hanging out with your mom's cousins. So . . . unless you wanna be stuck at someone's house for days when Dubai is right outside the door, be my guest. I'm actually giving you a way out of sitting through hours and hours of boredom. I heard your mom has a big-ass family."

I almost spat out my drink. "Oh my god. She does." Her family in UAE stretched from Dubai to Abu Dhabi, and that wasn't even counting her relatives in the US, across London to Paris, and into India. "Fine. But then we go do what I want to, OK?"

"Pfft. You think you're the only one who wants to see stuff?"

"Your parents are letting you run around alone?"

"Yeah. Dubai is one of the safest cities in the world."

"That's what I've been trying to convince my parents of! How did you get them to let you go solo?"

He shrugged. "I'm responsible and showed them everywhere I'll be and when, how to get there and back. Also, hate to say it, I'm a guy."

"Eh." I sat back in the seat and looked at a cartoon dog sprinting across the screen. It was sad but true. Guys felt safer and were safer, no matter where they were in the world. But that also meant being with him would make my parents feel better about me going out without them.

"OK," I finally said. "I'll do it. What's the other thing?"

He couldn't possibly have in mind anything worse than sky-diving.

"That we actually talk about what happened and how we're

going to move forward. By which I mean you need to listen to my side and actually think about it—and not just go back to being mad, because we all know you hold a grudge longer than anyone."

"That's a little mean."

He looked me dead in the eye with an RBF that could've turned skeletons over in their graves. "Nah. Mean is how you've treated me all summer. Mean is not having a conversation like people who know how to use words."

I swallowed. Well, out of all the things he could've asked for (money; food; covering his butt for eternity so he could get away with anything; being his chauffeur if and when I ever got driving privileges back; doing his chores . . . the list could go on), he asked for the most basic thing. Something that I knew we needed to do but—because I'd let my pettiness continue for so long—felt endlessly awkward and pointless by now.

But I could try, right? I could try to be OK with him, listen to his side of the story, and not let on how much I missed him.

For the duration of the trip. For one week. For the sake of getting the right picture to get into an internship (even if it was with a shot taken on my phone) and mending a bridge with my parents.

It was all worth it. If I could put aside my bitterness and put on a smile instead.

For one measly week.

Then I wouldn't have to be trapped next to him. And when college started in less than a year, I wouldn't have to really deal with him again, ever. And it wouldn't hurt.

At least . . . that's what I told myself.

How hard could it be to pretend, then forget about Yash?

# CHAPTER SIX

I'd never been happier to hurry across a giant airport in my life. And I was not one who liked much walking. But there was an insurmountable pleasure in being able to stretch and have room and work leg muscles when we'd been on one plane or another for nearly an entire day. You'd think tech geniuses would've sped up the time it took to fly across the world by now, but nah.

Anyway, I'd always been a tourist. Preferably one with a camera hanging from my neck, big starry eyes taking in everything, and the mighty need to make memories of it all.

"Calm down," Yash joked, apparently seeing it all over my face.

I was practically salivating at crystal chandeliers, immaculate stores with perfectly piled items, blingy jewelry shops so rich that it made my teeth ache, and endless aisles of candy and dates. Everything was so pristine, sparkly, shiny, new, *extra*. I imagined this was what wealthy people saw *all the time*.

"We're still in the airport," Yash reminded me.

"I know! But what a fancy airport!" I replied, trying not to gawk at the traditionally dressed men who checked our passports at customs. They were covered in a long-sleeved, white garment that reached their feet called a kandura and a red-and-white checkered ghutra head garment. There weren't as many women around as men, but the few we could see wore traditional black abaya and hijab to cover them from head to toe. Some men and women were dressed less formally back at the shops in loose trousers or long skirts.

Yet, beneath all that fabric, the Emirati staff moved with elegance.

I grinned up at the man checking our papers, but he barely made eye contact and spoke sternly to Papa and Yash's dad. Um, OK. He probably saw one too many eager tourists every minute.

"Come on!" Lilly said, tugging my wrist in one hand and Yash's wrist in the other.

Mummie, though her eyes were droopy and tired, laughed at us as we made our way to baggage claim to find that our bags were in rough shape. International flights were *not* kind.

Traveling 101: Don't go for the hard case suitcases for international travel. Ours got busted the hell up.

"Looks like we'll have to do some luggage shopping," Papa groaned.

"At least they didn't lose our bags," Mummie said, looking on the bright side.

"One bag looks OK!" Lilly pointed out, smashing my hand into Yash's as she darted for the sole survivor of a luggage massacre. Hopefully it was the one with our fancy Diwali clothes.

At first, I didn't really think much of our hands touching, except that we both felt warm and clammy and needed a wash after traveling. But then, we both seemed to simultaneously realize that we were, literally, holding hands. We froze and stared straight ahead at Lilly before releasing our hold and sidestepping each other.

Yash cleared his throat and ran his palm over the back of his head, while I ran mine against my pants.

I hoped no one saw. For one thing, it was just plain weird. For another, we did some research into our visit, and PDA was frowned upon in the UAE. When you talk about a clean city, this was it. And things like cursing, littering, fighting, and drunkenness were all fine-to-jail-worthy offenses. UAE didn't mess around, which was why Dubai was one of the safest cities in the world.

Yash asked, "Ready to talk?"

"Dude, give me a minute."

"You had months, bro."

I painted on a smile for our watching parents, who were too far to hear our muted conversation. "Are you kidding? I'm exhausted."

"Just remember the deal. I'm going to be on you until we talk, so don't think you're going to slip away," Yash grunted.

He then fetched luggage carts. Once our bags were all accounted for, we checked in for our hotel taxis at the concierge office, and off we went.

Lilly and I were glued to the window as we passed pristine buildings and fancy cars, sharply dressed crowds in both traditional and modern clothes, palm trees that stretched into the desert sun, and beautifully written Arabic signs, many of which were also tagged with English.

"Lovely, isn't it?" Mummie asked from the other side of Lilly. Papa was sitting up front with the driver while our luggage took up the back. Yash and his parents had taken a second car.

"Yeah," I replied in all honesty and with total awe.

Leave it to my parents to find a hotel that was smack-dab in the heart of, for lack of a better phrase, Little Gujarat. We were surrounded by Indian restaurants and Indian expats and Indian visitors, jewelry, and clothing stores, a mandir within walking distance, and yo, was that a pani puri vendor across the parking lot?

Why yes, yes it was, and we would be eating little puffed puri stuffed with lentils, chickpeas, and potatoes, doused with sweet chutney, and dripping with spicy mint water soon enough. I glanced at Papa, who clearly couldn't be happier.

My stomach grumbled hard.

"Are you hungry?" Papa asked.

"We have thepla," Mummie added right on beat.

"No!" Lilly and I both said in unison.

I added in a more leveled, kinder tone, "We love Mummie's cooking, but no theplas, please, for at least a week."

Lilly pouted, dramatically adding, "I need real food."

Mummie hushed her. "Did you or did you not eat a deli sandwich, two pizzas, three desserts, and a salad on the plane? How are you this hungry?"

Lilly pointed in the direction we were all staring. "Pani puri."

Mummie's expression went flat. "I made pani puri two weekends ago and you grumbled about it."

"Only about leftovers. But there's a real street food guy. It's different when it's street food."

I nodded. "It really is. The whole experience is different."

She sighed. "Let's get unpacked and showered, and then we can look into food."

Staff helped pile our bags onto the luggage cart right as Yash and his parents pulled up in a second cab.

We entered an elegant lobby with shimmering chandeliers and a sitting area draped in lush burgundy fabrics with red-and-gold pillows. There was a tourist guide's office to the right, and ahead a tall, golden teapot with small matching cups and a golden box filled with dates.

I wondered if there was tea or Arabic coffee in there. And if the dates were real and for us to eat.

By the time I found the guts to tip the teapot over a cup, my parents called me over and up we went, in a glass elevator to the fifth floor. We shared a room with two large beds. I'd have to sleep with Lilly. I bet Yash got his own bed. Perks of being an only child.

In no time, we'd all showered, and I emerged from the bathroom to both our families waiting on me. Asking if Yash's family was really going to be all up in our space and vice versa wasn't even a question. It was a fact that they would be. Because it had always been that way. But now I didn't have another room to go hide in.

My mom handed me the extra room card and off we went, like one giant family shuffling across the way to the pani puri street vendor. Nothing said comfort and fun like stuffing your face outside while being handed one gloriously filled puri after another.

Yash, because it was such a Yash thing to do, tipped my puri up right as it reached my mouth and made me spill pani all down my chin. I slapped his arm, but he dodged out of the way. Everyone had a good laugh. I couldn't be too mad, because licking the spicy mint water off my lips and chin was still tasty.

The breeze picked up, the sun began to set, and all we'd done was eat, laugh, and eat some more.

* * *

In case anyone ever wondered where I'd inherited such mighty snoring from, it was hands down a maternal gene. Mummie was snoring like she hadn't slept in weeks.

My eye, sore and achy, twitched. I'd never wanted to sleep so badly my entire life. Between Mummie's snoring, Lilly's arms that kept pushing me toward the edge of the bed, and jetlag, I wasn't going to make it tonight.

I sucked in a breath and shoved off the covers. Grabbing the room card, my tablet, phone, shoes, and a sweatshirt, I quietly escaped into the dimly lit hallway.

I snuck into the elevator, tugging the sweatshirt over my head. I wasn't stupid, though. I wasn't going to leave the hotel.

It was quiet with a few staff roaming around or attending desks and a handful of guests moving in and out.

The small gift shop at one end of the ground floor was open, but I hadn't brought any money. I turned the corner, jogged down the steps, around the fountain beneath a sparkling chandelier, finally opened that golden box of dates, and popped one in my mouth. Yum! Subtle sweetness hit my tongue.

I grabbed one of the paper napkins beside the box and plucked out a few more giant dates and wandered in the quiet with a plan to lounge around in the actual lounge when I saw Yash. He was slouched on the many cushions. With the tapestry and drapes surrounding him, he looked like a prince.

Before I could backtrack, he happened to glance up and saw me. I froze. He rolled his eyes and cocked his chin at the other end of the seating area. Thick cushions and plush pillows made up three sides of a large rectangle of a couch.

I traipsed down the three steps into the sitting area and sat at the other corner so that I could lean against the pillows and extend my legs over the seat and look out at the entryway.

"Can't sleep?" I asked.

"Nah," he replied.

"Drawing?" I jerked my chin toward his tablet.

He didn't look up from it and neither confirmed nor denied. He went quiet, and I fell into silent thought, hating the tension between us, but, man, did I miss just being near him.

Without a word, he slid a bronze box of chocolates toward me. Without looking at the box, I took a piece. I unwrapped it and popped the square into my mouth, side-eyeing him as he smirked.

"What?" I asked around the bite. Smooth chocolate melted in my mouth with a slightly chewy center that tasted like gritty, creamy pistachio.

"Is it good?"

"Yeah. It's really good. Wow."

He clamped down on a laugh.

"What?" I asked, snatching the box and reading: Al Nassma assorted pack of gourmet camel milk chocolates filled with nougat, pistachio, and espresso.

I immediately gagged.

He laughed. "Don't do that. You said they were good."

"Camel milk! Gross!"

He laughed harder. "It's just milk. You like it. It's not like it tastes different."

I shoved the box back at him. True. The treats were superrich, creamy, and decadent. I kinda wanted more. "Where did you even get these?"

"The souvenir shop."

"Good to know. Lilly wanted to try them."

"I might get more to take home, to be honest." He unwrapped a square, popped it into his mouth, and winked.

I dramatically rolled my eyes, intending to give him sass, but then yawned instead. With the lull of the gently swishing fountain water and occasional staff member walking by, I could fall asleep on these super comfy cushions any second.

"Wanna talk now?"

I pushed out a breath and shook my head. "I can't sleep, but I'm super tired," I replied as I sank lower in the seats, until I was practically lying down. Boy, if my mom saw this, she'd scold me for looking not at all like a proper lady.

"Don't fall asleep down here," he said.

"It's fine. I won't . . ."

"Your eyelids are closing. Nikki!"

I startled upright. "Ugh. Fine."

I turned on my tablet, connected to the hotel Wi-Fi, and logged into WebToon, gasping anew over my favorite series. I found myself mumbling, "Don't go in there," and "Why is the author doing me like this?"

"Bro, what are you reading?" Yash asked, irritated that I was making noise.

"If you must know, I'm reading WebToon."

"I—I thought you weren't into comics."

True, aside from fleeting awe, I hadn't been that much into them when he'd first introduced me to comics. But now I understood what all the fuss was about.

"Graphic novels," I corrected.

"Whatever."

But his snide comment was OK. I didn't mind keeping this for myself.

# CHAPTER SEVEN

Our first (full) day in Dubai!

Lilly and I woke up buzzing to go the next day, even if we hadn't slept much. Day one meant tours, and we had a few family adventures lined up. Our parents walked in the door with a bag in hand.

Papa smiled that big smile of his, as if he'd come bearing gifts of gold. He pulled out two paper-wrapped fruits and proceeded to cut them into slices with a plastic knife he'd saved from the plane.

We sat on the edge of the bed in expectation because one, we were hungry, and two, we could never get tired of mangos.

But when he turned to us to hand over pieces stacked inside one of the hotel room's drinking glasses, I salivated.

"Sitaphal!" I squealed with delight.

My parents' faces lit up as we devoured the sweet, grainy, custard-like flesh of one of our favorite Indian fruits. They were hard to come by in Austin and way expensive to the point where my mom had once smuggled some out of India, past customs, risking facing a hefty fine just to get me some fruit.

My dad, for as far back as memory served, had sliced fresh fruit for us every single morning. We typically had mangos, a house favorite, when in season. Melon at other times. And if we were lucky, this delicious custard apple, crunchy white tamarind, tart jamun berries, or crisp golden dates from the Indian grocery store.

I wasn't expecting him to carry on the tradition while on vacation, but here we were. The dedication was real.

"Where did you get this?" I asked, savoring every plump bite around the black seeds.

"We went to mandir a few streets down, and they had fruit vendors," Papa replied, watching me eat as his eyes smiled back at us.

"Ah! So good!" And thank goodness they didn't make us wake up at daybreak to go worship with them. I really, *really* enjoyed sleeping in.

"Get changed quickly. Have to be on time for the tour bus," Mummie said.

"What about breakfast? Like, carbs and stuff?" I asked, because a growing teen needed more than fruit.

"You both slept in late. No time."

"Why didn't you wake us?" Lilly asked, rubbing her eyes.

"You two were sleepyheads and needed the rest."

"Besides," Papa added, "we did try to wake you. You were knocked out. Don't worry, we're sure to find something to eat on the tour."

My mom went for the mini fridge where she was storing the leftover thepla. Lilly and I caught each other's panicked looks and I blurted, "OK! No worries! We'll be fine. C'mon, Lilly, let's go!"

Papa adjusted his button-down shirt and said, "Don't forget your camera, huh? This will be a great opportunity to get fantastic pictures!"

My stomach churned all that fruit goodness into acidic bile ready to claw its way back up my throat. I didn't respond, instead pretending to have too much crammed into my mouth to reply. I had an excuse ready—that I'd left my camera at home—so why were my hands shaking like I was about to lie to my dad? It wasn't a lie. I *had* left it at home. But if he probed, then I was either going to fall down a hole of lies or brace for his disappointment during a vacation where no one should be angry.

Once we were up and dressed, we met Yash's family at the lounge area, where he bounced up from the red-and-gold sitting pillows as if he'd never left. Dude had great core muscles. I wouldn't have been able to jump up without using my hands.

He casually popped open the pretty case beside the teapot, took a date, and tossed it into his mouth, all while avoiding eye contact.

"We're off to tour the Palm Jumeirah!" Hetal Auntie exclaimed.

And that was when it hit me. For a good portion of this vacation, we were going to be glued at the hip like some freaky conglomeration of seven individuals melded into one touristy monster.

I adjusted my mini backpack over my shoulder, small enough to be considered a purse but large enough to hold water and snacks and, oh, let's say a camera, so Papa didn't ask about it. I made a note to try to always sit/stand/walk behind my parents.

We shuffled out into the desert heat and morning sun. Despite being in the middle of a very large metropolis, it just didn't feel like it. Traffic was bearable, the sidewalks somewhat cluttered with pedestrians, but we weren't simmering in polluted haze. How was the air so clean?

There was a definite hustle and bustle, though, of people on their way to their destinations and others starting work. A man with a mustache and a broad smile welcomed us partway down the block, seeing that other cars had taken up space directly in front of the hotel's welcoming doors where a man in a white uniform opened and closed the glass panes for visitors.

"Bhagat family of four and Amin family of three?" he asked, sweeping his exuberant gaze across all seven of us but finally landing on Papa, who confirmed that we were indeed hopping onto the correct tour bus.

We were. The outside of the short bus clearly stated *DUBAI TOURS.*

I headed to the back, past three other tourists. They seemed to be a set of parents with a teenage daughter who barely looked at us but sat up and smiled when Yash entered the bus second to last.

He gave her a small smile in return, and something unsettling hit my gut, though I didn't understand why. I'd never really had any issues with Yash crushing on or flirting with other girls. Except the girls I didn't like, which was seldom. He had good taste in girls but never dated any of them.

Maybe . . . I mean, was it possible that I was a little jealous now? Because he hadn't genuinely smiled at me in a long time? Even though our estrangement was partially my fault.

In any case, he politely declined when the girl scooted over to declare an empty seat just for him. He glanced at me as he passed our parents, two seats to each side of the bus, and then finally sat next to me. Lilly was parked right in front of us and in her own little world as she ticked items off on the research tabs of her tablet. That girl and her tablet.

My stomach growled something fierce right as he slid into the seat beside me. My cheeks flushed. Nothing like seeing a ridiculously pretty girl who'd made eyes at Yash, only for him to sit beside the girl with gas punching through her guts.

"Didn't you eat breakfast?" he asked—or complained. It was hard to tell.

Lilly turned around in her seat and said, "Only fruit. Bet Mummie has thepla in her purse, though."

Yash grinned at her. "My mom has thepla in her purse, too."

Then they both looked at me. Was I desperate enough for thepla? No, no. Of course not. I could wait until we passed a food place. We were bound to on a tour, right?

"Welcome, welcome!" the host/driver said as he stood at the front and faced us, the door to his left now closed.

We all politely said "Hi" or "Hello" or in the case of Yash, "Yo!"

The girl looked back at him and giggled. Which caused my eyes to roll.

With the energy of an Austin high school football player on game day, the host revved up in a booming voice. "Welcome, welcome to *Dubaiiiiii*! As you will see, we have one of the safest, cleanest, most advanced and most beautiful cities in the world! Do you know why the buildings look so shiny and new? It's because they *are* new! Only three decades ago, our beautiful area was mostly desert. But then we brought in one-third of the world's cranes, and we built all of this. Isn't that amazing? We have the world's fastest-growing city. And we did not stop there!

"We have the world's tallest building, the world's fastest elevator, the world's only seven-star hotel, the world's fastest roller coaster and bullet coaster . . . the list, my friends, truly goes on. And I will show you! Sit back and enjoy our air-conditioned bus. Up front, I have ice-cold waters and juices. Please stay hydrated, my friends. Dubai heat and sun can be intense. I also have snacks, small things, like cookies and crackers. But we will be stopping by places that have great food, so don't worry."

Then he pointed to us in the back. "Ay! Are you here for Diwali, my friends?"

We nodded, and my parents concurred enthusiastically. It always felt so special when strangers knew about Diwali.

He clapped his hands together. "You are in luck! Diwali in Dubai is the best, second to none, I assure you! There will be fireworks and concerts and contests and food. Dress your best and have fun! OK. Off we go to see the Palm Jumeirah. A manmade set of islands that look like . . . you guessed it! A palm tree!"

"Dude is hyped," Yash said, smiling at Lilly. "Heard you were looking for this." He slid the box of camel milk chocolates to her, and she lit up on first bite before gluing herself to the window and pointing out all the things.

All right, so maybe this trip wasn't going to be so bad, after all.

Or so I thought.

Papa twisted in his seat and gave a thumbs-up. Then he made a motion with his hands like he was holding and clicking a camera.

I nodded like an idiot with an idiot smile on my face.

When he turned back to the front, looping an arm around Mummie's shoulders, Yash leaned down and whispered, "He doesn't know?"

I furiously shook my head, throwing death glares at him.

He shrugged and mouthed, "What?" As in, "What does he think happened to your camera?"

I heaved out a big sigh and looked away. There was nothing to say and everything for him to assume. By way of not telling my dad that the camera was broken, or at least back at home, I was in essence lying my pretty little face off.

While the tour guide gave us details about everything we passed, I was totally enamored by how nice and clean everything looked. Which made sense, because, like the tour guide had said, most of this was pretty much new.

Yash was on his tablet, drawing away. I could see that much. His screen was in the early phase of shapes and sketches. I knew from long ago that he layered his illustrations when he drew digitally, starting with rough sketches, then final lines, layers of colors and shading and details, until a beautifully created scene became complete.

I commemorated moments with photography as Yash did with art.

At this point, I couldn't tell what he was drawing, but you better believe that I was using my most nonchalant skills to side-eye pry.

Wow, that hurt my brain.

I found myself checking social media, where Jalebi_Writer had posted a teaser for his next episode—a snippet of a panel—and people were going nuts trying to guess what was going to happen. He made sure to add that those with coins to skip ahead a few episodes shouldn't post spoilers or he'd start blocking them.

"What are you laughing at?" Yash asked.

Oh. Was I laughing out loud? "Nothing. Just checking social."

He glanced over my shoulder. "Who is that?"

"A WebToon creator."

His right brow cocked up and his lips twitched. "Thought you'd be into more . . . romantic ones."

"Because I'm a girl?" I asked dryly. "I can't be into the dark and suspenseful?"

"No. I didn't mean that."

"Yeah, you did."

He sighed. "You're always into the romantic subplots of movies. Just figured you'd be into the romantic main plots, too."

"Oh. There's one or two that I like, but this is still among my faves."

He nodded, as if he had anything to do with me liking non-romantic stories.

I wasn't sure why I felt the need to brag, but I did. "This creator is super popular."

"Oh yeah?"

"Yep. And he chats with me. Most soon-to-be-celebrities wouldn't do that."

"What do you mean you *talk* to him?" he asked. "Do you—do you know who this guy even is?"

I scoffed. "I'm not stupid."

He swallowed, clenching his jaw into a blade that could cut glass.

"It's DMs, OK? No phone calls or emails, nothing to trace back to me. He doesn't know my age or where I go to school or where I live. He doesn't even follow me, and my account is private. There is no personal information being exchanged. It's fine."

"That's good, then."

I rolled my eyes.

After a minute of silence, he muttered, "You don't even know if this guy is a grown-ass man."

"Oh my god. He's a teen."

"How do you know that if you've never met him, hmm?"

Why was he getting so upset? This was starting to feel like the many small arguments we'd had leading up to the big one. But I wasn't going to let this ruin my vacation.

I replied coolly, "Because he was featured on WebToon as an up-and-coming teen creator. They vet their creators."

He didn't respond, just kept working.

"I kinda like him," I admitted.

"Be careful. Meeting people off the internet and you don't even know who they are."

"I *do* know who he is. He's a big WebToon artist, and I have receipts in case he tries anything fishy. He won't risk ruining his burgeoning career," I stated with grand gesticulation.

"*Burgeoning?*" he scoffed.

"Yes. Meaning: increasing rapidly. Catfishing or child endangerment would ruin him. So, chill out."

"You talk to him but not to me?" he asked bitterly.

"You know it's not like that."

"Ready to talk now?"

"No," I snapped, but then jerked my chin toward his tablet. "Are you drawing?" Wow, I had *not* meant to keep my temperamental tone when asking that.

He seemed surprised that I'd notice, almost like he'd been caught doing something wrong. It wasn't a big secret that his parents didn't particularly favor him spending so much time with a creative pursuit when they, much like my own parents, wanted him to concentrate on school and college applications. Anything creative—be it art or photography—was considered a hobby or, at best, a side hustle.

I was fortunate that my parents encouraged my creative side, even supported my desire to minor in photography. I guessed it had something to do with them being OK with my pursuit of journalism, since photography sort of went hand in hand with that.

But Yash? His parents were another story.

He stammered, his face flaring up and his ears reddening. I quickly said, "I mean, it's cool that you're back into it. I won't tell anyone."

He nodded, his chin dropping toward his tablet as he scribbled away.

"Can I see?" I asked timidly, even though we both knew I didn't have a right to ask.

"Uh, just keeping this to myself right now."

I swallowed but nodded—not that he could see me when his gaze was locked on his screen. I didn't really expect him to let me in after all this time, especially when he was so private about whatever it was that he was working on.

After some thought, I came to the conclusion that maybe he sat in the back not so much to convince my parents that we were cool but so he could escape his and delve into his art.

"Your parents still don't like it?"

He was hunched over his work and cast a glance at his parents up ahead. "No. They want me to get into engineering. Which is fine." He shook his head and let out a rueful chuckle. "Not like art will take me anywhere."

I wanted to tell him that he was an amazing artist. I wanted him to know that he had support. That he didn't need to take the path set out before him because his parents were pushing it or because it was what was expected from him. Because let's face it, every auntie, uncle, and college-aged person at mandir would throw in their two cents, not that anyone asked for it. But let it be known that our community was not big on anyone pursuing creative careers. It was too much of a gamble with futures and incomes and prestige.

Didn't Yash know that he would succeed in anything he tried? That any magazine, publishing company, or brand would be lucky to have him on their team?

Yeah, all these were things I wanted to tell him. But I didn't. I couldn't. I just didn't know how to be normal around him again.

# CHAPTER EIGHT

When the tour guide said that the entire Palm Jumeirah had been built on sand, we sort of all held our collective breath. Because looking out, we didn't see a few delicate palm trees and crowds that may or may not cause sinking. We saw towering metal and concrete buildings, multilevel condos, fancy houses, an Airbus, and so many cars. How in the world did this entire thing not sink back into the sea?

The tour guide pointed to a tall, unique structure with a tall pole-looking structure at the top and a curved side, declaring, "Ah, the beautiful Burj Al Arab, the world's only seven-star hotel. You can see it's shaped to resemble a sail, unique architecture. It has penthouses and a helicopter pad and draws the world's celebrities for a stay. Yes, it is very expensive, but I hear quite worth it. You won't be able to see the inside unless you go inside. There are no pictures advertising it. They have restaurants, but they are booked out for months. So, if you intend to visit for a meal, I suggest you have made a reservation three-to-six months ago."

He laughed and we laughed with him. His laughter was infectious, big and robust and coming from the base of his diaphragm.

We got out here and there to take pictures and wander around shimmering buildings and mosaic pathways. The beauty took our minds off of how hot it was. Thank goodness I'd brought my shades, though I was wishing I'd brought a hat, too.

The girl who kept trying to catch Yash's eye had brought her hat—a big floppy one. Lilly snickered every time the girl looked back at him.

"Who does she think she is?" Lilly muttered, but it didn't seem like anyone else heard her.

"Shh," I told her. "Be nice."

Not like the girl was going to hit it off with Yash so well that he'd become obsessed with her and have some long-distance, epic romance and we'd have to see her again. She'd probably return to whatever preppy place she was from and forget all about him soon enough.

We stood beneath palm trees as Lilly and I tried to get selfies making silly faces while still capturing the buildings and water behind us. Lilly returned to our parents, leaving me alone as I scrolled through pictures, deleting every third one that didn't come out right because *of course* a phone camera wasn't going to capture the best light distribution or angle or composition or any cool effect. Ugh. No way any of these would get me noticed for the internship, but they were family memories and that counted for a lot.

The girl from the tour bus approached me.

"Hi!" she said, super cheery with a gigantically fake smile plastered on her smooth face. She looked like she had a blur filter on, which had me wondering if she was wearing foundation, and if so, what kind.

"My name's Cindy," she introduced herself.

"Hey," I replied, not offering my name because, well, I didn't want to. One didn't need a reason aside from that.

"Your brother is really cute. How old is he?" She cocked her chin where Yash was standing, his back to us as he snapped a few pictures of his parents and then both sets of our parents. They were cracking up about something. Lilly was sipping her third water bottle and I knew she was going to have find a bathroom in the next five minutes or her bladder would burst.

I scowled. "We're not related."

"Oh, sorry. I thought you were all related since you boarded the bus together. You look alike."

"No, we don't."

She shrugged.

I felt a stoic expression fall over my face like a mask. Micro-aggressions and assumptions like these were getting on my last nerve. Part of me typically let these sorts of comments go, because I didn't want to hurt the other person's feelings or make them feel awkward or stupid. Part of me realized that they either said this knowing it was offensive or had no idea and really needed to get woke on the matter.

"Seriously," I added with deliberate words so that she paid attention and got it. "Aside from black hair and various shades of brown skin, we look nothing alike."

"You kinda do, actually," she replied indifferently, her gaze flitting away as if she'd suddenly lost interest. But the truth was this: She couldn't give two craps, and she was only talking to me to ask about Yash.

"You just think all brown people look alike, huh? It must be confusing for you, walking around Dubai, then."

I looked her dead in the eye when she whipped her head to glare at me, her jaw dropping. She stuttered to respond.

I said, "Eh. He doesn't like racist white girls."

Lilly's eyes went wide for a flash of a second, because my sister had impeccable timing and had wandered close enough to catch that tail end of our conversation. Lilly hooked arms with mine, snickered, pivoted on her heels, and walked me away. God, the sass on this little girl. I loved it.

Yash had finished taking pictures long enough to see us approaching. He asked, "What's up with that?" He cocked his chin at a surly Cindy, who stood with crossed arms and fumes practically venting from her ears.

Lilly took Yash's hand in hers and pulled him away. "C'mon! We have things to see and food to eat."

"I have thepla!" Mummie crowed from out of nowhere. I swear, the woman had superhuman hearing and an uncanny sense of when her children were hungry.

"Nah, man. I can't do another thepla," I muttered, and hurried after Lilly and Yash.

"Bathroom first, please?" Lilly said.

"You drank half the water bottles, didn't you?" Yash asked her.

"I'm not going to pass out from dehydration."

The tour went on, and Lilly and her acutely intimidating don't-mess-with-me-or-my-people did a fine job of keeping Cindy from even looking at Yash. And Yash? Dude seemed totally unaware of this girl pining over him or the intense, albeit silent, war brewing around him.

"What's so funny?" he asked as we stepped off the bus at the famous Atlantis hotel with its spade-shaped center.

"Huh?"

"You're cackling like the Joker."

"What! Whatever."

"Tell me, since we're supposed to be talking," he said, tugging on my sleeve.

The slight, yet sudden, pull had me tripping up the curb. Yash caught me in his arms like we were starring in some rom-com meet-cute. But probably no one got headbutted in those.

Yash clutched his nose while I rubbed my head. "God, hard-headed is an understatement. What is that? A rock skull?"

He proceeded to gently knock on my head while everyone was watching us and finding this quite amusing. Smirks and giggles and clucking tongues descended all around.

I shoved him away. "Diamonds are the hardest rocks in the world, so if you're saying I'm a diamond, then yes, I am. Thank you."

We left the mugginess outside, despite being right on the edge of a gorgeous aquamarine ocean, and were met with a blast of AC. Shimmering gold-rimmed oil paintings, cascading chandeliers, mosaic ceilings, and glass tiles greeted us through the halls of the Atlantis, the décor interrupted by expensive-looking boutiques.

One could tell who was visiting on a tour bus and who was actually staying there, because the resort guests were dressed nicely with hair and nails done and fancy jewelry on and were just generally looking extra. Must be nice to be rich.

"Feel free to wander and explore," the tour guide said, giving us details and history here and there about the hotel. "We'll meet here in two hours. This circle of fish," he said, grinning down at the mosaic tiles at our feet. We stood in a giant, red circle composed of colorful fish, octopus, and coral art.

There was a lot to do, from swimming with dolphins and jet skiing to scuba diving and visiting the impressive indoor aquarium.

But first, we ate. And then had ice cream at a Cold Stone Creamery where they mixed whatever we wanted into any flavor of ice cream they had.

Finally, we were admitted into the darkness of The Lost Chambers Aquarium and transported to the depths of the sea. Sharks and bioluminescent jellyfish and creepy eels. The sliding double doors looked just like the artifacts from an Indiana Jones movie, or ya know, the Atlantis movie. The blue glow beyond made everything feel so otherworldly.

A cylinder of water greeted us upon entry, filled with a school of fish, and it was just all so . . . hypnotizing. I'd never been so lost in an aquarium, in the beauty and awe.

OK, so this place was awesome. I took in every detail of fountains that looked like ancient pots; the glowing red, blue, and purple jellyfish floating in mesmerizing dances; spotted eels slithering in and out of holes in the wall; ancient-looking scuba suits; creepy crustaceans straight out of horror movies; abstract glass sculptures; gray fish bigger than my dad; and coral filled with colorful fish, and then we ended at a giant pond in the middle of a room.

I leaned over in the low light of red bulbs overhead when Yash crept up behind me and pretended to push me into the pond.

I. Almost. Screamed.

"Yash!" I hissed, backhanding his chest, his laughter vibrating against my knuckles.

"They're not real. If you can't handle statues, how you gonna skydive, huh?" he asked, lifting his arms out.

"I haven't even asked my parents."

"I did. They said cool."

I gasped. "No they didn't! When did you ask?"

"Yesterday."

When he leaned over the lip of the pond, a small, rigid, partially submerged crocodile suddenly moved and Yash yelped, jumping back.

I laughed so hard. "How you gonna skydive if you can't handle statues, huh? They're not real," I mocked in his tone.

"Oh my god. Wait, are they?"

"I'm not trying to find out," I replied, and hurried around the enclosed pond, giving it a wide berth.

*　*　*

After a long day of tours and food and traveling and more food, I crashed into bed to message Tamara all about Dubai even though she was probably asleep. I found myself smiling because, well, things felt normal again, like Yash and I could get through this somehow. Maybe now that we'd had some laughs and been around each other without trying to rip the other's head off, it would be easier to talk.

Lilly was taking her time in the bathroom and our parents were in the lounge making arrangements to visit Mummie's cousins in Abu Dhabi. It was nice of them to send my cousin—second cousin? uncle? whoever my mom's cousin was to me—to pick us up. The next few days would be full of relatives, and if we knew anything about my parents, it was that they could get rambunctious when in close proximity to family. My eyes were already drooping at the anticipated hours and hours of conversation and eating and probably napping on their couches because that's what we did, for some reason.

But, I had a plan to get out of it, as long as Yash kept up his end of the bargain. There were plenty of things to do in Abu Dhabi, if we ended up going there, and I was certain my parents would release me if Yash was attached.

I lay on my stomach, my ankles crossed and in the air behind me, while I perused WebToon. I tapped on *The Fall* the instant the panel appeared with a little green indicator that said UP. A new episode!

"Yes!"

I took in the majestic strokes of artwork, some sharp lines, some watercolor effects, of a big city glowing with blue and white lights from buildings beneath a star-speckled sky as the main character panted in the cold, running from whoever had been watching him. Eek! Was this finally the episode where we learned who the mystery stalker was?

And . . . END.

No, I supposed it couldn't be the most anticipated episode just yet. All right, there were some slow episodes, but not every single one could be high intensity, with heart-stopping cliff hangers. There was this thing called world-building and characterization and arcs and yada, yada. Those seemed like obvious elements to a story, but it wasn't until Yash had pointed them out as an explanation for why creating webcomics would be so hard and stressful that I'd fully appreciated them. It was why he'd never tried his hand at comics. It did seem like a lot, which was even more reason to be in total awe of the creators who pulled it off so well.

I groaned, scrolling past the fade-out of the final panel. I liked to read the comments, but this time, the author had posted a note:

Hey readers! Thanks for supporting *The Fall*. I'm beyond grateful and hope you'll continue with me. Heads up! I'm taking a short break for the holidays (Diwali) but will be back in two weeks! See ya then!

If it were possible to simultaneously frown and sport a short smile, that's what my expression would be doing at this moment. Bummer that *The Fall* was taking a break, because I lived for this world, but supercool that Jalebi_Writer was celebrating Diwali. I wondered if he was desi, as his handle suggested, or whether he just liked Diwali or was celebrating because of friends, family, or location.

I didn't know this guy well enough to ask, but I sent a message anyway, slightly giddy. I was borderline fangirling right now.

I hit SEND after some brief deliberation. I didn't want him to think I was getting too chummy. I wasn't sure why nerves got to me every time I messaged him. I'd messaged several of my favorite author/illustrators; I should be used to it. But thinking back, messaging them was just as nerve-racking as this.

It occurred to me: What if I was ever in the public eye for my art? In the future, I could have my photos everywhere, and it would be really nice to have fans message me. It would make me feel connected and seen, to know people saw my work and liked it and related to it. I double-checked my message for signs of awkwardness.

**Nikki:** Supercool that you celebrate Diwali! Do you have anything special that you do on your side of the world?

Was he glued to his devices? Maybe he was working, and I was interrupting.

**Jalebi_Writer:** Hey! Thanks! Nothing special . . . I mean just the usual. Fireworks, rangoli, puja, fancy clothes, and oh yeah . . . lots and lots of food! How about you? You celebrate?

**Nikki:** Yes, and same! Guess it's typical where there's enough desi to put on a show?

**Jalebi_Writer:** That's cool! Doing anything special this year?

**Nikki:** Normal Diwali stuff, but I guess in a fancier way? Well, fancier to me. Meeting some extended fam. Maybe skydiving?

I wasn't sure why I added that last bit, but as I typed it out, it brought a big smile to my face. Saying that I was going skydiving had me feeling cool, even though tons of tourists went skydiving here. It was a true flex. Like I was fearless and doing something few people I knew had done.

No wonder Yash had told everyone. I totally got the appeal now.

> **Jalebi_Writer:** That's cool. Excited about all that? And skydiving? Damn, that's wild. I've never done that. Think I'd chicken out TBH! Heard it's amazing if your stomach and head can keep it together.

I cringed.

> **Nikki:** What do you mean?

> **Jalebi_Writer:** Don't eat much beforehand. And maybe have some headache meds nearby for afterward. Anyway, don't think too much about it. For sure, still do it!

> **Nikki:** Yeah. You're right. Hey! While I've got you, you wouldn't happen to be able to give any hints on *The Fall.* 😊 Hehehe . . .

He replied with nothing more than a laughing emoji with tears and I knew that was all the answer I'd get. Well, couldn't fault a girl for trying.

# CHAPTER NINE

Whenever the parents wanted to go to mandir for pre-Diwali stuff, Lilly and I dragged our feet. We'd somehow assumed that being in Dubai would dismiss the need to go, yet here we were.

"Can we stay at the hotel?" I asked apprehensively. While we enjoyed mandir during festivities and attended for worship every Sunday, we simply weren't into it as much as the parents were.

"You really should attend mandir at least once while here. It's such a conveniently short walk," Mummie said, fresh from a shower.

We all needed a shower. The first day in Dubai had been filled with tours and had us sweating an ocean.

"What's so important at the hotel, huh?"

"Well," I admitted, finally ready to take the plunge after how things had felt so normal with Yash today. If not now, then when? The ice had been broken and maybe we could move forward. "Yash and I were supposed to have a talk about . . . what happened."

"Finally," she said flatly. Thought she'd be happier. "It took you long enough."

"I needed time. I didn't want to be pushed into talking."

"We pushed because you wasted too much energy on negativity. The longer this awaited mending, the harder it would be to mend. Don't throw out a good friendship because you're stubborn."

"Stubborn?" I retorted.

She clucked her tongue and tugged on a blouse as Papa emerged from the bathroom. She told him, "The kids are going to stay here while we go to mandir."

Papa wiped the beads of water dripping down from his hair and quizzically looked from Mummie to me. "Why? What's so important here?"

"Nikki and Yash want to talk."

"Oh," he said as if that explained it all. Maybe it did.

"Make sure you both say everything you have to say and move forward," she told me.

"OK," I muttered, taking my clothes and disappearing into the bathroom.

Well, at least this round of reprimands had been abbreviated.

When I emerged, Lilly was dressed to go in a set of clean clothes. "I thought you were staying with us."

With brows raised high and a curt shake of the head, she replied, "I do *not* want to be here for *that* conversation."

"I thought you were Team Yash and wanted us to hash it out?"

"Yeah, but this is going to be awkward, and I can't handle that." Then she walked past me and patted my arm, adding, "Good luck, though!"

Everyone had left in a rush, and they would probably be out for at least an hour, if not longer. My parents loved service, especially during Diwali. There was sure to be food and sweets and the opportunity to mingle and socialize, and my family was *all* over that. Honestly, it made them so happy.

My family had been gone for five minutes now, so Yash must've been totally aware that our time was approaching. He hadn't texted, though, which was strange, seeing that he'd been bugging me nonstop to talk. I paced the hotel room, clenching and unclenching my fists and then playing with the hem of my cardigan. My heart was racing, and sweat poured out of my forehead and armpits. Gross.

I let out a pent-up breath and finally texted him. It was best if we met in his room; that way I could leave whenever I wanted if we had another big fight . . . because who didn't like a good storm off? But, more importantly, if things got heated like they had last time, then Yash didn't need to see me cry.

**Nikki:** Hey, you wanna chat?

**Yash:** Yeah, give me a bit. Have to finish something.

I perused social media, then went to messages to tell Tamara what was about to go down. She hadn't responded to my last message, and my DMs would definitely be flooded by morning.

As I hit SEND, an achingly raw thought occurred. What if . . . Yash had decided he didn't want to try anymore? That too much time had passed and our friendship was really over? More than that, did I still *want* to be friends? Because real friends would have to get over this and truly forgive and forget. Which, ironically, meant *I* hadn't been a real friend all summer. Crap, I was a horrible person, wasn't I? Or was he totally wrong? Ugh. I couldn't tell anymore! Did it even matter at this point?

**Yash: I'm ready. Where do you wanna meet?**

**Nikki: I'll come to your room.**

I took a few breaths to calm down and stop the jitters, to coach myself into being chill. Wrapping my cardigan around my body, I went one room down to Yash's. After two knocks, he pulled open the door and offered a weak smile, prompting me to come in.

We'd been alone plenty of times, but it had never felt like we were alone. It had never been weird or intense, but this was as awkward as I'd ever been around anyone.

The door automatically clicked when he closed it. I sat on a chair in the corner, pulling my right knee to my chest, while Yash planted himself on the edge of one of two beds. His room mirrored mine, but he got a whole bed to himself.

Water trailed from his spiky, wet hair down to his neck. He wiped it away and cleared his throat, his eyes darting from me to the floor.

Silence.

For some reason, I thought about Tamara. She had three objectives in life: ace her classes and get into the university of her dreams to pursue human resources (WTH kind of teen yearns to be in HR?); be an unstoppable badass in gaming by stomping out all the boys who thought girls couldn't keep up; and get some alone time with her secret boyfriend. Unlike my parents, who were OK with me dating if I ever wanted to so long as they met and approved of him, Tamara's parents were old-school and didn't think she even noticed boys.

Tamara had all sorts of plans for getting her boyfriend alone in her room, if ever her parents were out of the house when she was there. Her boyfriend had two brothers and shared a room with one, so getting privacy at his place wasn't going to happen. In her desperation, she had crafted pretty elaborate plans. I wasn't sure what she intended to do, because it seemed like the mere idea of fooling around gave her anxiety; but bless her heart, she sure did try.

And here I was, totally alone with Yash. In a hotel room.

I giggled, startling both myself and the boy on the bed. I slapped a hand over my mouth. This so wasn't a funny moment.

He gaped at me quizzically, mouthing, "What?"

I shook my head, cleared my throat, and lowered my hand. "So, you wanted to talk?"

He folded his fingers over one another and then unfolded them, over and over, when he asked, "Do you even want to be friends anymore?"

My heart rammed into my chest. Was not being friends truly an option? And now that it seemed like it was, a new level of horror filled me.

My breath caught in my throat. The thought was like a set of serrated knives thrown haphazardly at my soul, but the level of suffering in his tone sort of ripped me apart.

He scratched his head, fluffing the still damp hair so that parts of it stood up. He didn't look at me when he talked, just at the floor or at my feet or the window to my left. "I don't want to throw out our friendship. I mean, we were best friends. I thought."

"We were," I mumbled, not understanding why my entire body had gone rigid. I wasn't angry. Yash deserved to feel whatever he felt and to decide whatever he wanted. But I was . . . sad, terrified, *panicked*.

"Friends don't act the way you did, Nikki. For an entire summer, we weren't friends."

I swallowed, nodding in agreement, but he wasn't looking at me.

"It didn't happen on purpose, you know? We were arguing about the whole club thing, and you were getting louder, so I got louder, and neither one of us knew that your parents were there. It was over. The fact that you got pissed at me for not lying to them. You really thought if I lied to their face, after they heard you tell on yourself for sneaking out, that they'd believe me? Maybe you were entitled to be mad at me, even though it wasn't my fault—"

"But it was," I finally said, breaking his monologue.

He dragged his eyes from the window to me, his brows slightly raised in a way that made him look so hurt.

I swallowed and went on. "You brought it up. You were arguing with me and wouldn't let it go. If you hadn't kept arguing, we wouldn't have gotten so loud that my parents heard. I suppose I told on myself, but we were fighting because you wouldn't let it go."

Yash pressed his lips together, watching me watching him. He clucked his tongue. "Nah, man. You were doing something you weren't supposed to be doing. You knew your parents would be mad if they found out, that you were jeopardizing your freedom and internship if they found out. Stuff like that doesn't fly in our families. It wasn't like you. I was worried. I don't get along with all of your friends, and that's fine. But these new friends came out of nowhere and you started lying to your parents, to me, and going to shady places. Forget that those girls ditched you at a club. What if something had happened to you, huh?"

His voice was getting higher. "How the hell would anyone know where to look for you when you usually go to *Torchy's* and *Top Golf*? You were pissed that *you* got caught, and you took it out on me. And on top of that, you threw me under the bus for something totally unrelated that you promised to keep secret. You did that crap out of pettiness. And then stayed mad at me. Not at yourself or the situation, but at *me*."

He lowered his voice and wiped the water beading down his neck, adding, "You gave me the silent treatment, walked away, never acknowledged me, avoided me like I had hurt you. But you know what? You hurt me. You never just talked to me."

His tone shifted from quiet and pained to upset. "You always get on people for hurting your friends for this and that, but here you were doing that to me. So while you were pissed and being petty, I suffered."

"You were mad at me, too," I reminded him. "All those times you clenched your jaw and rolled your eyes. Passive-aggressive reactions are mean, too."

"Yeah, I was mad. I was mad at you for letting it go on for so long. I was mad that you ratted me out just to deflect attention from you getting in trouble. I was mad that you could treat me that way."

"What did you expect?" I shot back, my voice rising even though I didn't mean to.

"I dunno," he said sharply. "For you to talk to me like you always did? For you to listen to what I had to say, even if you didn't agree with it, because that's what friends do, that's what *we* always did. We got into trouble all the time, sometimes together and a few times because of each other; but damn, Nikki, you never severed us. And I would never, ever have broken us."

I froze beneath his glare and heated words, tears filling my eyes.

"You wanna know why I was really mad at you for sneaking out? Forget the fake friends and your parents finding out. You know what happens to girls in those places? To kids who don't pay attention? Take one wrong drink or walk by one wrong car."

His jaw clenched. "What if something horrible had happened to you? You wouldn't even listen to me, or let me tell you about this stuff going down in that club. You just wanted to do something and for once, I dunno why, not think about reality."

I blinked away tears. It was getting hard to breathe. I'd only been thinking about having fun and not getting caught. I hadn't been thinking about some of the awful things that had happened in those clubs in the past year. The realization of his worries made my stomach turn sour.

Silence devoured us. Yash returned to fiddling with his thumbs and looking out the window. He chewed on his lower lip.

My parents had grounded me for the *entire* freaking summer and forced me to sit in on family meals whenever we ate with Yash and his parents, which was often because their lives went on despite my issue. Because of our falling out and the fact that he'd damaged my parents' car, my parents had told his parents everything that had happened. Another thing I blamed on Yash, which he, in turn, blamed on me.

It was humiliating enough being treated like a child, but then to know that Yash's parents knew everything on top of that and were probably judging me for it made for some very embarrassing meals.

I'd been so angry. It was easy to be angry, but now I saw all too well the pain in my childhood best friend, and it hurt my heart.

Yash groaned from across the room, snapping me back into the now. Our eyes met when he asked, "What are you thinking about? Your jaw is so tight, looks like it's about to crack through your face."

I relaxed, not realizing how aggressively I was clenching my teeth until now. The muscles in my jaw ached. "Just thinking about our fight."

"Yeah?"

"I was just wondering . . ." My voice trailed off.

"What?"

I let out a breath and just went for it, went for what I'd wanted to ask all summer: "Does everyone hate me?"

I didn't give him a second to answer as the words flooded out of me, or maybe I didn't want to hear the truth. "Do your parents think I'm a bad influence? That you're perfect and good and probably damaged my parents' car because of me? Am I the villain? That's how I feel. Everyone is blaming everything on me and taking your side and I've never felt so betrayed, not just by you but by everyone. And I felt all ragey."

His mouth dropped. "No, Nikki, my parents don't think you're a bad influence. No one thinks you're a villain. No one hates you. Everyone still loves you. I still love you—"

He froze as if he hadn't meant to say that, as if maybe I'd take those last four words the wrong way.

He stretched his neck and glared at the ceiling. "You know we all care about you. You let it blow up in your head, didn't you?" He lowered his head and watched me.

"You know I did," I mumbled, chewing on the inside of my cheek. "I know this should've happened a long time ago, but I'm sorry Yash, for everything. I really missed you, and that's my fault. I didn't mean to hurt you."

He leaned over and twiddled his thumbs, his gaze on his socked feet. His words trembled when he spoke. "I . . . was depressed, to be honest. I wasn't just feeling hurt. It was hard not being friends."

My heart sank into the pit of my stomach and broke into a dozen pieces.

"I was struggling, but I talked it out with some other friends and older kids at mandir. They gave me advice and let me vent, and then I went back to drawing and it helped me cope."

"I'm so sorry." I shuddered, wiping away my tears.

He dragged his gaze toward me. His expression was solemn, exhausted. He held the back of his neck. "I don't have anything else to say, really. Do—do you?"

"I'd like to be friends again. If that's what you want, too," I said, hopeful and holding my breath.

He cracked a smile. Kindness and relief pushed away the weariness in his eyes.

# CHAPTER TEN

Today was our second (full) day in Dubai and the first day of Diwali (technically, the first day of five main festivities and two days until actual Diwali). Traditionally, we'd buy something new for the occasion. Silver, gold, jewelry, clothes, or at least sweets. We had a full day planned, which ended with the latter half spent browsing the famous shopping areas. Since we were on a tight budget and in a different country, chances were unlikely that we'd buy much to haul back home.

"Hey," Yash said the next morning in the hallway on the first floor, behind the elevators, as our posse shuffled toward breakfast.

"Hi," I said, shyly, for some reason. I thought the awkwardness would go away and we'd be back to our normal selves. Maybe this would take some more time.

My parents seemed giddy at the concept of hotel food, but who was I kidding? We all thought it was fancy. Hotel living was not a common thing for our family, and it meant more than thepla and cha. Thank god.

A massive load had lifted off my shoulders. Lilly stood beside me and grinned. Maybe she knew Yash and I had made up, or maybe she was excited about a buffet and that fake mummy coffin at the end of the hall. Tall and wide, dusted with gold and blue paint, it looked so much like the real thing. Well, if I'd ever seen the real thing. Also, if the real thing was still new.

A host greeted us at the door to the right and we filed into a giant double room. Our mouths dropped. The hotels we'd been at before had nothing on this place. And it wasn't like this hotel was super fancy or expensive. It was just Dubai!

I think at some point all the rulers and politicians of the UAE must've gotten together and said, "Bro, we gotta level up with all this oil cash we're sitting on. We're going to build the biggest, the bestest, the fastest everything in the world. So everything will be new and sparkling luxury for common tourists but, like, totally normal for our peeps. Hotels will be no exception. Forget Paris and London. Dubai is gonna be lit."

And then they all laughed and agreed and did the dang thing.

Everything in this place was on par with an Egyptian theme, from the bronze walls and sculptures to the tapestry and arched windows. The restaurant smelled so good and was filled with mouth-watering food.

The host walked us to a table in the adjacent room, since the first one had smaller tables and settings for two to four people.

Lilly, Yash, and I slowed down as we passed the refreshments table with typical morning beverages like coffee, tea, water, and juices next to the usual fruit trays of melons and berries. But it was the vast pastry table that we immediately attached to. Platters of all sorts of bagels and turnovers and croissants and star-shaped pastries oozing with what looked like jam. Platters of square-cut cakes and brownies and maybe cheesecake and tarts? I didn't know! What I did know was that the three of us would be circling right back to this corner.

"Here is your table," the host said, extending a hand to a seating of eight. The moms automatically hung their purses on the extra chair.

"This restaurant is buffet-style. You will find all beverages, fruit, pastries, and dessert in the room we just walked through. At this side, along the wall, we have main courses, soups, and sides. We provide new choices daily. There are waffle servers and made-to-order omelets. Please help yourselves. Enjoy!"

He nodded with a smile as our gazes hungrily took in the far wall of many, many choices.

We kinda went wild. The parents had their fill of spicy potato and pea-stuffed samosas and spinach pakora and tangy dhal. Tomorrow would be idli day! I didn't think any of us were expecting full-on Indian food to be so readily available, but it made sense, given that Indians made up a large population here. Our parents were instantly at home.

I took Lilly to get our waffles made, cute ones in the shape of hearts. She had hers with chocolate chips, mine had blueberries, and Yash's was plain. We each took a samosa and herbed breakfast potatoes and buttery biscuits. First, we ate the "real" stuff, eyeing the sugary goodies as we filled up on water and juice. Then we giddily tried almost everything at the dessert table. Yash went for a bagel, too, and I grabbed a chocolate croissant. The rest of our "seconds" plate was filled with sugary, tart squares of goodness.

My parents' eyes went wide when we returned, but they just laughed. Whew! We wouldn't have gotten away with this at home! And, as per usual, we'd returned to three bowls of fruit. Papa winked at us. The daily morning fruit dedication was real!

Everything was delicious and decadent and so much better than American hotel breakfasts!

Lilly and I blew out a breath and sat back, patting our bellies. "We won't be able to fit into our Diwali clothes at this rate," I remarked.

"I don't even care," she said. "We can wear sweats, right?"

I laughed. Diwali was one of the few times we went all out with dressing up. Sparkling new lehengas with assorted bangles to match, gaudy jewelry, cute hair and makeup, and lots of joy. We only made this much effort at weddings, and only if the couple was close to us. Otherwise, this was our one time of the year to be new and fresh and extravagant.

Once the dads finished their coffee, we walked out into a balmy morning. The sun was already so bright it had me squinting the second we left the hotel. One of the valets motioned toward a row of taxis, waiting to take any of us anywhere.

This time, we managed to get an SUV so we could all travel together. Lilly, Yash, and I crawled into the very back. Moms and my dad in the middle row, and Uncle up front.

Lilly sat against the window and glued herself to the sights, talking about this tidbit and that, and checking off her endless list of notes about the city. She was a walking tourism website.

I adjusted my mini backpack on my lap and looked out her window.

I didn't know if it was the smooth roads or the purr of the vehicle, but within seconds, my eyelids drooped. I'd been wide-awake, high on sugar, minutes ago, and now I struggled to stay alert. Like, hard. And I wasn't the only one.

In my bleary-eyed state, I noticed Mummie's head droop, and then Auntie's, and even Papa's. Hopefully Uncle was awake at the front of the car.

In another second I jolted awake, my breaths coming fast against Yash. Our shoulders were crushed together, my head bent at a horrible angle against his shoulder. I quickly wiped away drool, hoping he didn't notice, then leaned way over toward Lilly, who was now asleep against the window. Were we really so dead tired that we'd just fallen asleep in a random car in a foreign country on the way to who knew where? Yes. Apparently, we were.

I stole a glance at Yash to see if he'd caught me drooling. He was fast asleep.

Yash could fall asleep anywhere, anytime, and in any position. Now he slept sitting upright, as though awake with his eyes closed in meditation. But his finger twitched, and his lips parted—telltale signs of a deep sleep.

I mindlessly watched him. Maybe because I was still drowsy and fighting the incomprehensibly aggressive need to fall back asleep, maybe because he was just nice to look at.

His nose twitched and I stilled. Was he awake? No. He continued to sleep, and my gaze honed in on the freckles across one cheek and the mole on the other. He always joked about being the only Indian with freckles; for the first time, I realized it was an unbelievably attractive trait.

I yawned and sat back, startled to find Lilly observing me. I blinked, mortified. Her blank expression melted into a cunning one, complete with a smirk and glossy amusement in her eyes. Oh boy. She was going to tease me forever about this one, wasn't she?

I tilted my head to the side and bit my lip, on the verge of asking for her mercy, when we pulled into our destination and everyone, one by one, woke up. I'd been so sleepy and distracted that I'd nearly forgotten our plans for the day.

We were at *the mall*.

Yeah, sounded like an ordinary weekend trip with the family back home and I wasn't expecting to be dazzled. I mean, a mall was a mall.

When the taxi pulled up to a behemoth of a building, the driver asked, "Are you visiting for the first time?"

"Yes," Uncle replied.

"Excellent! You will enjoy the Dubai Mall. Make sure to tour the Burj Khalifa. It's the tallest building in the world, you know? And behind the mall is a wonderful water and light show that happens every thirty minutes. Even better at night!"

Uncle laughed and thanked him for the tips.

We crawled out of the cab, still half sleepy.

From afar, the mall was unassuming. One could tell it was extremely large, but it looked practically miniature in comparison to the Burj Khalifa, which towered next to it. The tallest building in the world pierced the sky with gray and black metallic beams, glass, and the extraordinary sheen of a brand-new construction. A typical wide base shot up into points, getting narrower as the levels went up so that it looked like the universe's biggest spire. It was an architectural feat.

We stood at the entrance of the mall, and if I craned my head all the way back, I could see the top of the Burj Khalifa.

"He thought we didn't know," Papa said with a chuckle. As if we hadn't done some research, because riding to the top, or even the midway point, required a ticket. We would go there first.

Inside the mall, I shivered in the sudden chill of the AC, calling to mind wintry pastimes and reminding me there was an indoor ski resort in Dubai. Unfortunately, we didn't have time to visit it. Not that any of us skied or snowboarded, but tubing was a thing, right?

Everything was opulent and clean and orderly. The shops looked too pricey for us to even think about buying something. But we hadn't come to shop.

We stayed close together in order not to get lost in the shuffle of the crowds. Music, conversations, laughter, and the click-clack of heels against what was probably marble floors trilled around us. I held Lilly's hand and followed our parents with Yash close behind. Even though he was practically an adult, I kept checking over my shoulder to make sure we hadn't lost him. Our parents clearly had the same idea—they were checking for us every few seconds.

We followed the signs to the Burj Khalifa. Staying on track was easy. Well, until we walked into the atrium.

We slowed, marveling at the multistory aquarium set beneath a ceiling of shimmering lights that resembled stars. Bigger than a department store, the atrium stood like a glowing blue wonder.

"Are those sharks?" Lilly whispered, her feet inching toward the aquarium feature like magnets.

"We just went to an aquarium yesterday," Mummie said. Her words may have sounded unimpressed, but the twinkle in her eye said otherwise.

"We have to get to the elevator," Papa said, corralling us back in with the primary mission for the morning. Still, we slowly walked past, ignoring the infinitely long line for admission into what I assumed was a walk-through archway.

We left the crowds behind, showing our tickets and walking into an even longer hallway.

"That's a long-ass line," Yash muttered as we settled into its tail end.

The wait consisted of almost an hour of shuffling forward in increments of about ten people, but it was hardly boring. The walls came to life with shimmer and animation as a colorful video expanded across the entirety of the walkway, telling the history of the building and boasting of its mighty architectural achievements—like how it had fifty-seven elevators. It looked like it cost a pretty penny, which was likely why we had to front quite a bit just to ride an elevator.

"You think it'll be worth the wait?" I asked Yash, getting restless despite the changing colors of neon pink and green and blue flashing across the walls around us.

Yash swiped across his phone with one hand, the other tucked into his jeans pocket.

Lilly wiggled next to me, no longer holding my hand but blatantly watching us.

"You texting your girlfriend?" she teased him.

Yash glanced up at her, partly amused, and I wondered how much he could see through that curtain of dark hair falling over his eyes. His hair was so long it was curling at the ends.

"Maybe," he said, his voice teasing but his expression serious.

And . . . something in my chest cracked. Not in a my-crush-was-crushing-on-someone-else sort of way, but in the way pain felt all-consuming when a person who once told you everything now told you nothing. We were strangers starting over.

# CHAPTER ELEVEN

The attendant called up the next batch of people. We stepped into what was basically a futuristic elevator. The walls were matte metallic, pristine but cold and sterile. The elevator doors closed, and the operator pressed our floor. Way, *way* up.

The doors turned into the same retina display the walls in the hallway had been, showing images of the building and then flitting away to numbers as we ascended. Fast. I felt it in the tingles rippling through my belly, but it wasn't jarring like most elevators.

Going up one hundred and forty floors in one minute at twenty-two miles per hour was surprisingly smooth. How did I know that info? Because the retina display on the doors said so. I bet no other elevator in the world had a kph/mph next to the rapidly jumping floor number.

We shuffled out, murmuring with great awe, into a giant gift shop, *of course*, where every item boasted that we had gone to the Burj Khalifa and paid a bunch of money to prove it with a lousy souvenir.

There had to be at least a hundred people walking around and even more outside. The sun was bright in the glass enclosed deck overlooking Dubai. Dozens of people gathered here and there in the spacious area. There were a lot of selfies and group pictures going on.

"Over here!" Lilly said, hopping toward a spot on the right, claiming a portion of the glass wall that happened to open up.

"Perfect!" I said, glancing out at the desert and the oddity of the metropolis situated in the middle of literally nowhere. Sand stretched as far as the eye could see.

Right below us were other buildings and the turquoise waters of massive pools, probably where the water and light show would take place.

"Group pictures!" Hetal Auntie exclaimed, waving us in to get closer.

She stopped a passerby to snap a few pictures. Then she rearranged us, and then my mom rearranged us, shuffling back and forth with shoulders knocking against other shoulders until we stood as thus: fathers on the outside, then the moms, then Lilly with Yash squished against me with an apologetic expression.

"Smile!" the passerby said.

Click. Click. Click.

Then we took turns with family pictures and couples (parents) pictures, and then Lilly and me and then just Yash, and then with all of us kids.

There was too much of a rush to get pictures—while we had the cooperation of a stranger to help out—to acknowledge the ache in my chest every time Yash's arm brushed against mine. There was too much shuffling, too much commotion, too many directions about where to stand and how to smile and participate.

"Where's your camera?" Papa asked.

The blood drained from my face as everyone looked to me expectantly.

"This would make for great pictures!" Mummie added as Auntie nodded her head in agreement.

Lilly wandered off nearby to snap shots of the city below, glued to the glass and so close to the invisible edge that my heart palpitated. The deck was perfectly safe, the walls perfectly durable, but that didn't totally erase my fear of one of us falling to our death.

"I haven't seen you use your camera since we arrived," Papa remarked.

I gulped, my eyes darting to the right. Yash looked up from his phone, landing a gaze on me and then on my dad. Why was he on his phone so much, anyway?

Maybe he saw the panic on my face, because he seemed to panic, too. Please, dear lord, don't let him ruthlessly confess the truth. It wasn't just about him owning up to an expensive accident, and he knew that!

I harnessed all the Jean Grey and Professor X mutant powers that I could scrounge to telepathically plead with Yash. My words tumbled over themselves trying to find something to say to Papa, anything!

*I'd left the camera at the hotel*? No, no. That wouldn't work because Papa would just keep asking about it.

*I'd left the camera at home*? Which was true. But then he would probe into why I'd left such an important device for a budding photographer on this epic trip.

*I broke it*? Too much.

Sweat sort of bubbled out of my forehead and my panic turned into unnerving dread, the sort that sank my insides into my legs until my entire torso was puddling at my feet. OMG, why was I so scared? It wasn't like the car accident or trying to get into a club.

I sucked in a breath. They were waiting, and now even Auntie and Uncle were listening in.

"I . . . um . . . just using my phone . . ." *Please don't ask why I didn't bring it! Why I'd be missing opportune moments to capture on the expensive camera made for this!* I *wanted* to look away, but I *couldn't.*

"Our spot opened up!" Yash blurted.

We all looked at him quizzically, and it was as if he'd absorbed my not-so-super power of freezing up with no words to utter. There had to be a word for this.

He broke me out of the catatonic state and pointed to the other side of the deck where spots around the observation glass had opened up.

"We better hurry to get that selfie you were talking about!" Yash said unnaturally loud. He grabbed my wrist and tugged me away, muttering, "Sorry!" back to our parents.

I tripped over my feet trying to keep up with him. Our parents probably took this as a sign of us mending our relationship. What was better proof than taking selfies together?

Telepathic mutant powers activated!

Yash squeezed through a small crowd, stopping at the glass, looking down more than one hundred stories. My belly did flips, my head a little dizzy as my toes pressed against the clear glass. Oh, that was a long drop, like staring death in the face.

"Imagine skydiving," Yash said, as if he'd read my thoughts. He was looking straight down and grinning, clearly too excited to consider freefalling to his teenaged demise.

I immediately stepped back, catching my breath. "Not funny."

"Think of this as a warm-up?"

I blew out a breath and took in the amazing aerial view, trying not to imagine plummeting toward the ground. How was I ever going to get the nerve to skydive if I couldn't stand here without my guts rampaging and my thoughts screaming to safely step back?

"Thanks for that," I said. "For rescuing me back there."

"We have to get the pics, right?" he said instead of his usual "That's how we always do."

He turned away from the glass and aimed his phone camera selfie-style, holding it just higher than his face to capture the backdrop, the buildings, and pools below.

"What are you, an auntie? Why are you holding the phone so high?"

"You better smile and get in this picture with me," he said instead, grinning at the camera he held up for our selfie.

Oh yeah, our parents were still watching. I stood closer to him, but only half of my face was in the shot. Eh, good enough.

"Closer," he said.

I grunted but slid closer, looking up at the screen and smiling, and doing my best not to adjust his ridiculous angle.

He took a few snaps, including one where he made bunny ears over my head.

I pushed him away. "Stop. Delete that one."

"That's getting sent to the parents," he said, tapping away on his phone.

"Don't send that!"

"Already sent! If I know my dad, it's about to get WhatsApp'd to everyone." He laughed so hard that his head fell back, flashing the sharp tips of his canines, obsessively amused with how our dads sent poorly taken, random pictures to all the uncles. But the fact that they did it with pride! Like they were good pictures! And how all the receiving uncles agreed, like *what*!

"You're so dumb," I grumbled, but was overwhelmingly pleased to see his real smile after so long.

He shrugged. "Hey, you want me to get some pictures of you for social?" He motioned toward a girl posing with one leg out, her sneaker-clad toe pointed like a ballerina while her friend snapped away. "Post or it didn't happen, right?" he said wryly.

"Sure. Thanks. My parents still don't know how to take a decent picture."

I looked up #BurjKhalifa to get some ideas of location, poses, and angles until we wandered back toward our families, who were in the best spot to get as much of the aquamarine water as possible.

Yash wasn't the best with camera angles or complementary light and shadow, so every shot he took, I'd take back my phone and critique the picture. We had to get it just right, seeing as we might never get this chance again.

"Is that one OK?" he asked on his twentieth try.

"God, you suck. Can you like wait until you stop moving so it's not blurry? And my eyes aren't closed?"

"You're too picky." But he took the phone and shot a few more.

Finally! It only took thirty tries, but Yash captured a decent shot where I looked good at the optimal angle and enough of the background was visible to tell a story with one frame.

"Do you want me to get one of you?" I retrieved my phone while holding out my free hand for his.

"Sure," he said, and stood by the glass pane.

I scowled. There was one thing that hadn't changed about Yash, and that was his hilariously awkward photo stances. The boy could be fluid when doing anything else, but put him in front of a camera and he turned to stone. Deadweight. Tense shoulders. Stiff neck. Impassive expression. And arms that didn't know what to do with themselves.

I choked back a laugh. The sound that came out of me was more of a . . . squawk.

"What?" he asked, frowning.

"Oh my god. Some things never change."

"Huh?"

I shook his arms. "Relax. This won't hurt."

I pressed down on his shoulders. "You're not going into battle."

I gently cupped his face, unprepared for the tingles in my fingers when our skin made contact. If he wasn't frozen before, he was now. I pushed through the sensation, and my eyelids fluttered as I struggled to maintain eye contact. His eyes were glossy, reflective pools of amber specks against dark brown hues, outlined in unfairly long lashes.

His cheeks and jaw were warm to the touch as I moved his

head left and right, stretching it and loosening up that thick, stiff neck. The thin, gold chain hanging from his throat glinted in the sun.

Then I tilted his chin down, my thumb lingering way too close to his lips.

My heart blasted against my ribs, and I wondered if he'd felt that, if he wondered why I was still touching him.

*Move! Move your hands!* my brain screamed at me.

"Are you gonna kiss?" Lilly asked, suddenly at our side and staring at us with a hefty dose of speculation, concern, and just plain grossed out.

Leave it to little sisters calling you out in public, loudly, in the middle of a crowd, not far from your parents, to promptly unstick you from a boy.

Yash and I cleared our throats and immediately parted. In fact, I stepped so far back that I walked into someone, muttering apologies to the woman behind me.

"Hold that pose and try to stay loose," I ordered Yash, but he just stiffened.

"God, you're still so bossy," he mumbled, but did as I instructed.

"Someone has to tell you. Don't you ever notice yourself in pictures?"

"No, because I don't care," he huffed.

"You're so clueless."

"You're too into this. You're a photographer, so you look at details literally no one else cares about."

I groaned, planting my hands on my hips. "You want a nice picture or not?"

He deadpanned when he replied, "Of course I want a nice picture."

We were shaken out of our argument by nearby giggles. Our parents and Lilly were watching, and my first instinct was to walk away, because screw Yash, he got on my nerves. But then I remembered that the least I could do was force him into a nice picture that he would complain about now, forget about later, and fondly look back on in his old, crabby age.

I turned to Yash and politely asked, "Can you listen to me?"

"Sure," he said, and loosened up. He stood right where I instructed so that the light wasn't too harsh or in his eyes. He tilted his chin down and to the side just a little. I had him look at me and away and all sorts of other things for all sorts of pictures.

I knew how this was going to go. My pictures of Yash were going to be incredible, artistic, and people would wonder if he'd gotten into modeling abroad. Yash's pictures of me were blurred and I had triple chins and a shadow beard and closed eyes and the "good" ones would have to be edited to look remotely OK. Because that was how it was between us. Yash totally sucked at taking pictures and I was super meticulous about taking them.

Yash was looking pensive in the current pose when he suddenly cracked up. When he laughed like that, his smile reached his eyes. Wrinkles crinkled at the corners. Most of his teeth showed. He had nice teeth, including several pointed ones that were sort of cute. Long creases lined the edges of his mouth, from his nose to his jaw like narrow dimples, totally transforming his face.

I caught those moments, mainly to spite him—I knew he hated having pictures taken when he was full-on cackling.

"Hey!" He swatted at the camera.

I took a step back. Then another. "What are you laughing at, weirdo? You're attracting all kinds of attention."

People were throwing amused glances our way; luckily, our family had stopped paying attention.

He stepped closer and closer, and I moved farther and farther back.

Yash stopped laughing, and we stood at the far side of the deck again with as much space between us and our family as possible. They were busy taking pictures on their phones, most likely WhatsApping the experience.

Ugh. I really missed this. I really missed him.

He shoved his hands into his pockets and said, "Hey, can we sneak off when we go back down?"

"What for?"

"I got something to show you."

"What?" I pressed.

"No questions."

"You know me, right? I don't like surprises." I let out a ragged, nervous laugh.

He took a long breath and stretched his neck, his gaze landing on the view below. "Just come with me."

# CHAPTER TWELVE

"Yay or nay?" Lilly asked, pushing aside one magnet after another in the gift shop.

"What?" I asked, distracted by a pretty glass sculpture. The price tag on the underside said it was sixty dirham, which was like, what . . . uh. "Carry the one and add four . . ." I mumbled, trying to do the math in my head.

Lilly glanced at the price and said, "About seventeen bucks."

"How are you so good with math? I at least need a pencil and paper, preferably a calculator."

"You know you have a calculator on your phone."

"Ha. Ha. I can't always rely on tech."

"Wow, you sound like Papa. 'Back in the day, calculators were bulky and luxury and teachers didn't allow them to be used during most classes,'" she said, deepening her voice to mimic his.

I laughed, putting the souvenir back and sorting through some stuffed animals, which were even more expensive. I wanted a cute souvenir from all these cool places, but then I thought about how I'd just lost several hundred dollars' worth of camera, and my stomach spasmed. Ugh. Just asking for a twenty for something that wasn't going to get used made me sick. At least the camera brought joy and sharpened my skills—and was, apparently, Papa's pride and joy as much as it was mine.

The stuffed animals stayed put. I shoved my hands into my pockets and walked around, not touching one more thing.

"So, what's up with you and Yash?" Lilly asked again.

"Nothing. Why?"

She tilted her head to the side and grunted. "Please. You guys had the big talk and we didn't press for answers, but now?"

I smirked. "I think we're good, or at least on the way to being good."

"Awesome! Also, finally. Geez."

Behind us, Yash and our parents looked at postcards and candy and T-shirts and whatever else. But no one bought anything.

When we shuffled into line, Mummie ran a hand over Lilly's hair and said, "I'm sure they have cheaper souvenirs at the shops if you girls want. This is a tourist trap."

"Always look for the good deal," Papa added.

They had a point, except the second the idea of buying anything frivolous sprouted in my thoughts, my stomach began to churn.

On the ride down the still fast-as-anything elevator, we were oohing and ahhing all over again. We were back inside the mall in a matter of minutes.

"Let's go see the fish!" Lilly said, pointing at the glowing blue aquarium.

Papa and Uncle checked out the ticket booth and returned moments later. "I have a great idea! Instead of seeing the fish from the bottom, let's go see them from the top."

He cocked his chin at the surrounding levels of the mall overlooking the atrium of the aquarium.

Lilly and I smiled, nodding, but gave each other knowing glances. Sure, it was cool to see this behemoth aquarium, filled with so much water that if it burst, we'd surely wash away. But the truth was, our dads weren't about to fish out (no pun intended) another ridiculous amount of money when we'd seen an aquarium yesterday.

"Let's go!" Mummie called, snapping my attention back to the family.

"Um, is it OK if we explore the mall?" Yash asked, jerking his chin at me.

Everyone paused and blinked back at us. I blinked back at them and then shrugged. "Yeah," I added dumbly.

Our moms snapped out of their daze first, complete with big ole hopeful smiles.

"Of course! Go!" they crowed.

Our dads grinned with approval and Lilly smirked.

"Message us in half an hour. We need to see the water show, then head to the shops in the afternoon," Papa said.

"OK! Cool! Thanks!" Yash said, taking my wrist and leading me away.

I stumbled after him, dumbfounded. My heart raced at the warmth of his hand.

We took the escalator to the fifth floor like he knew where he was going. We passed glass displays of fruit tarts and bakeries that smelled of fluffy cheesecakes and wait . . .

"Is that a Cheesecake Factory?" I asked, leaning back to check out the aisle even as Yash was tugging me forward.

I jogged to keep up and he released my wrist. We turned down one of many super-clean corridors into yet another long hallway. We'd left the smells of coffee and food behind.

"Where are we going? How do you know where we're going?" I glanced behind us, already lost in a mall big enough to fit a small town.

"I downloaded a map?" Then he pointed all around at the signs and interactive mall maps. "This place is high-tech. No way you can get lost here."

I watched his back as I followed, noticing the way he'd held my wrist at first and now was frequently checking for me over his shoulder. He was making such great efforts at decency when he could've easily opted to be the jerk I'd been all summer.

I clenched my eyes shut as he abruptly stopped. I walked right into his back. "Ow! My face!"

He chuckled. "Watch where you're going, then."

He went to cup my face, where my hand was already holding my cheek and nose dramatically, as if his shoulder blade was made of barbed spikes. He paused, then quickly retracted his hands, pivoting to scratch the side of his neck.

"Your big nose hurts, you know?" he grunted, massaging the back of his shoulder.

I seethed. "Your face hurts . . . to look at. Now why are we here?"

"First off, are you still mad at me?"

I stilled, my words sloshing at the back of my throat. "Huh?" I finally said, confused about what he was referring to. "No. I miss you. Like a lot. I miss joking around and eating together. I miss teasing you for how much you eat and how much you sweat in the summer."

"Is this an apology? I'm confused."

I pouted. "I miss your fake, shocked reactions at how gross I can be."

"I mean, you can burp the entire alphabet, and your room is always a mess."

"I miss being near you and not even having to say or do anything. Instead of this awkwardness." I wanted to hug him so badly, aware that my entire body was shaking.

"I missed you, too. But I was kinda talking about the camera."

"Oh." My cheeks flushed super hot. "Of course. What about it?"

His shoulders deflated. "I've been so stressed over it. I felt terrible and I know how much it meant to you."

"Look, I panicked and overreacted. I know it was an accident. Don't feel bad, OK? I don't want you feeling bad about anything because of me. I shouldn't have left it on the ground without paying more attention."

"Your dad keeps bringing it up. You haven't told him?"

"No! I get sick every time I think about telling him. You saw his face, right? All happy about the camera. He knows how much it meant to me, and I know how much it meant to him. I'll have to tell him, but I'm too scared. Plus, I don't want to ruin this trip. I just want everyone to be happy and have a good time. I'll worry about it when we get back."

Yash's hands clenched and unclenched at his sides. If we'd been all the way back to normal, he'd have hugged me right now. Or pushed my forehead with a finger and told me to suck it up, but in a way that made me slap his hand away, and we'd end up briefly fighting, then laughing, and I'd feel better. Instead, he checked his phone and then shoved it, and his hands, into his pockets.

"Why are you always on your phone? Don't tell me it's Cindy Ortega. Or the other Cindy."

"Huh? How many Cindys are there?"

"Oh, right. You didn't talk to tour bus Cindy."

"I'm not texting anyone. I'm checking an order. It's here." He lifted his chin toward the store to his right.

Before I could ask, he added, "I really need you to not argue with me. For once. I know. I know." He rolled his eyes and sighed dramatically. "That's a big ask of you. But for the love of god and emotions and this trip, can you just accept this?"

"Accept what?"

He smiled and said, "You'll see in a minute. Don't move. For real. You get lost easily, and I can't be yelled at today."

"Whatever. Just go."

"All right." He jogged into a storefront.

I waited for him near a bench, wondering what was so important that he had to sneak off like that.

Yash emerged from the store a few minutes later holding a sizable box. He walked toward me, grinning. For the first time, I squinted at the store signage. It was an electronics store.

Then it clicked (no pun intended). Had he ordered a camera for me when I'd told him not to?

My heart was beating so fast that I was sure I would puke up my sugary breakfast all over this expensive mall floor. Before he even made the offering, I shook my mouth, muttering, "No. No. No."

"Yeah," he insisted.

"This is too much."

"Oh my god. Just take it. Please."

"It's too much. You don't owe me."

"Bro, not everything's about you, OK? I don't need to feel this bad. So . . . just do me a favor and accept it, so I can sleep again."

"You slept just fine in the car."

He threw his head back. "I'm just going to open this myself and at the hotel be like, oh, Uncle, looks like your daughter forgot about her expensive-ass camera that you lovingly bought her. And he'll take it and scold you and then make you carry it around anyway."

"Savage."

"Desperate times call for desperate measures."

"So dramatic, dude."

He clucked his tongue. "You know you want to take it. And it's OK to let down your pride and be happy about it."

Yash leaned toward me and whispered, "You know you miss taking pictures with a real camera with all the lens capabilities and buttons and, I dunno, zooming and other features probably."

I laughed. "So did you even read which camera this is before you bought it?"

"I know it's similar to the one you had before; that exact model isn't available anymore. Hopefully he doesn't remember it too well."

"He doesn't know anything about cameras. He just bought what I asked for."

From the specs on the side of the box, I could tell it was similar in size to the broken one. The same color: black. We could, theoretically, pass this off as the original. A secret I was willing to take to my grave, or at least, ya know, keep until post-internship. But a year was a long time.

My parents had bought my refurbed camera because it was the one I'd picked out after weeks of research. I was practically an expert by then. I'd watched tutorials beforehand, so when we got home from the electronics store, I'd ripped open that box and dived in like a pro.

My parents had joyfully laughed at me and thought it was so easy. Nah, man. It was because I'd taught myself first, but a lot of it was natural. The way I held the camera and adjusted the lenses and sought lighting and darkness and contours and color schemes. I'd never felt as complete as when I was holding that camera.

"I was able to piece a lot of it back together," I confessed.

"Seriously?" Yash asked, his voice cracking with disbelief.

"I thought I could fix it."

The corner of his mouth hiked up. "That's not how it works."

"I know!" I slapped his arm, and he feigned pain.

"I know it's not the same. I can't replace the one from your dad. But this is the next best thing to get you back on track with photography."

I eyed the offering, tempted to accept it, but I was reluctant to take such an expensive gift. "How did you afford this? Where did you get the money from? Did you ask your parents for money? Oh my god. You *did* ask them! Did they ask why you needed that much money? Of course they did, but did you tell them?"

"No. Calm down. I didn't ask them for anything, and they don't know anything. No one knows."

"Then how did you get the money?"

He grunted beneath his breath and didn't reply. He just stood there, off to the side from passersby, holding the box.

I eyed him. "Are you doing something . . . shady?"

"What? No!"

"Gambling?"

"No."

"Sold your soul?"

"Well, that escalated."

"Tell me."

"Why? *Why* do you have to know? Just, please accept the gift. I ran over your most prized possession. Of course I was always going to replace it."

"Did you use your savings? The money from your parents and grandparents across all major festivities?"

He slumped his shoulders in exaggerated defeat. "No. That piggy bank is intact."

I snickered, imagining Yash's antique pink piggy bank. Yeah, it was real. He'd said that he liked the antiquated use of it as a visual reminder to save and hustle. I didn't understand how he hustled. Unless doing yard work around the neighborhood counted. Which, maybe it did.

"How many yards did you have to mow for this? How many ant armies did you have to annihilate?"

"Don't worry about it."

I watched him watching me. I even put on my best and most formidable RBF, but Yash didn't crack. He didn't waver or blink or avert his gaze.

"Not going to tell me, huh?"

He snickered. "No. It's a gift."

"I can't accept it."

"Yes, you can." He shoved the box into my hands, and I fumbled for it.

I pushed it back into his arms and he pushed it into mine until finally, he took a huge stride backward, hands in the air and said, "Not it."

"I've taken quarter gifts from you and ones as expensive as fifty bucks on occasion. This is way too much."

"My conditions for forgiving you," he blurted.

I groaned, looking at the camera in my hands, and bit my lip. "God. Fine."

He blew out a breath. "Thank you."

"On the condition that I'll pay you back."

"No."

I shoved the camera into his chest, but he wouldn't hold it. "Then I don't accept."

"Why are you so stubborn?" he asked, his voice rising, hands now behind his back.

"Why are you?" I shot back, my voice rising, too.

"Just take the gift. I owe you!"

"Just let me pay you back. It's too much!"

We each glared at the other, our nostrils wide and flaring, our lips pressed into determined and unforgiving lines, our brows furrowed. I was certain passersby were watching our public quarrel, and if we weren't careful, we might get escorted out by security.

He gritted, "OK. You're making me play dirty. If you don't take this stupid camera, your parents will find out."

"If you don't accept my money, my parents will find out."

"God! Fine!"

I blew out a breath.

"But I probably won't accept it," he argued.

"I'll pay you back. The internship pay will cover it."

He smiled, his shoulders slackening. "I'll pretend to take it, then leave it in your room."

I laughed. "And I'll put it back in your room."

"And we'll just push around that wad of cash until we're a hundred and forget what the hell it was for."

"May our future kids and grandkids keep up the tradition."

"It'll be the reason our future families will feud for generations to come," he added.

"It's a deal."

"You want to be forgiven or what? Plus, you can't get the internship without the shot."

"*Yash* . . ."

"OK," he said quietly. "I'll accept the money. But you need this now. So . . . take it off my chest. Literally."

I stepped back and held the gift with reverence, my hands shaking with anticipation. It was an updated version of the one my dad had gotten me and at least the same brand, so it wouldn't be too suspicious at a glance. I opened the box right then and there. This time, Yash took the box while I pulled out the camera and oohed and ahhed, spilling details about all the specs into ears that had no idea what I was going on about.

I held it to my chest. "It's perfect."

"I wanted to get it to you before we left, but the stores in Austin didn't have it and the order wouldn't have arrived on time. So, I just ordered here. And it's universal with the chargers and adapters."

"Even after everything I put you through?"

"You're a giant pain in the ass sometimes."

OK, I gave him that. He was right.

"But I wouldn't ever leave you hanging like that. Not when it meant so much to you and your dad, and for the internship. Anyway, it was seriously messing with my head, so it's not all about you." He shoved his hands into his pockets and shrugged.

Overcome with appreciation and relief, I nearly hugged him. Instead, I pinched his cheek and said, "Thank you, Yash. I love this gift."

"OK. Let's charge the battery before we have to head back."

We sat down, plugging the charger into a USB port on the side of the bench because . . . Dubai. This was how they rolled.

# CHAPTER THIRTEEN

I wonder if they have Arabic coffee here," I pondered aloud, trying to fill the stagnant silence between us as I rested one knee on the bench to face Yash.

He was facing the wall, bent over his phone.

"You're going to have a hunchback sitting like that."

He scoffed. "OK, *Mom*."

"You can go check out the mall if you want. You don't have to waste your time by sitting here with me."

"And spend the rest of the day trying to find you when you get lost?"

I rolled my eyes, but I was glad to have him here.

We watched people walk by with shopping bags, and I wondered how many were tourists and how many locals actually shopped here. I supposed there had to be quite a few locals here, because who else would be buying furniture and rugs and TVs?

Many questions weighed heavily in my mind, ones that started to form on the tip of my tongue. But my heart raced at their audacity.

Ah, forget it. Yash was expecting me to smooth our issues and go skydiving, so why should I feel awkward asking my former best friend of eighteen years a few questions?

I cleared my throat, dragging a nail over the bench at my knee, and came out with it. "So . . . what's new?"

When he didn't respond, I glanced up, expecting him to be back on his phone. Instead, he was observing me. Not angry or indifferent seeming, but . . . pensive? It was hard to tell with Yash sometimes.

He shrugged.

"Nothing? That can't be true. What did you do all summer?"

He shrugged again.

"How are classes? Playing sports? Clubs? New friends?"

"Nothing much."

"That's all? At least tell me what your mom makes you for lunch before I die jumping out of a plane."

He huffed. "You know my mom doesn't make my lunches anymore."

"Do *you* make your lunches? My, how much you've grown."

"I drive off campus for lunch."

"Oh, no wonder you drive so fast."

"OK, I bought you an expensive-ass camera. You gotta let that go."

Someone strolling nearby gave us a look.

"Calm down," I muttered to him.

"You make up your mind about skydiving yet?"

I groaned and fiddled with the camera, but we had a deal. "Seriously, what's up with you and skydiving?"

"It's a momentous thing to do. I might never be in Dubai again to try it. Will you?"

"Probably not."

He checked his phone. "Does it have enough charge? We gotta get back."

"Yeah, I think so."

"Got what you need from the box? Gonna toss it out."

"Yep."

I set up the camera before turning it off and fitting everything into my mini backpack while Yash got rid of the new-purchase evidence. My bag sagged on my back, and I hoped my parents wouldn't notice the change in density, the difference between a water bottle and snacks versus a camera.

"OK, let's go." Yash led the way back down the halls and yeah, that sure was a giant Cheesecake Factory just hanging out in Dubai Mall. We took the escalators all the way down and back to the aquarium where our parents and Lilly were standing, still marveling at the sharks and sea turtles and a mini ocean of fish.

"What did you kids do?" Papa asked when he saw us approaching.

I shrugged. "Talked."

Yash nodded.

"By the way, it's cool if I go skydiving with Yash in a few days, right?" Yash said he'd cleared it, but I was still so surprised they'd allowed it that I wanted to double-check.

"*What*?" Papa balked, looking from me to Mummie.

Mummie waved him off. "Oh, the kids want to skydive. It's not a big deal."

Lilly's eyes went wide. "Since when are you brave?"

Auntie added, "It's perfectly fine. Yash did all the research and we looked it over. They have strict guidelines for those wanting to skydive and their company is one of the best in the world."

"I don't wanna go," Lilly stated, not that Auntie was suggesting it. Anyway, you had to be eighteen or over, so it wasn't as if Lilly could tag along even if she'd wanted to.

Mummie told Papa, "I agreed to Nikki going. Yash wants to take her, and Hetalben already paid for the ticket."

I choked back a cough. Oh my gosh. Mummie was on board and the ticket had been paid for? And dang, she didn't even ask my dad? My stomach twisted. I had no choice now. I had to go.

"So let them do this *together*," Mummie said to Papa, hitting on that last word as if skydiving was the spark that Yash and I needed to rekindle our friendship. Nothing like jumping to your conceivable doom to make you reevaluate your battles and forgive people.

"I want to see all the information and regulations," Papa said to Yash.

Yash immediately sent him links on WhatsApp to scrutinize. "I'll think about it," he said.

Mummie rolled her eyes. See? That was where I got it from! She had that look on her face, like: *Whatever, let him think he was making a decision, but you go ahead, daughter.*

Ah. I was sorta hoping Papa would put his foot down and declare how dangerous it was for his barely of age daughter to be flopping off a plane with nothing but a prayer and a parachute to keep her out of Death's hands. But nope.

Did my parents think skydiving with Yash would solidify our reunion? Or were they so Team Yash that they'd pretty much let me do whatever he asked of me?

"Let's get to the water show," Uncle said.

"Ready?" Mummie called back.

Everyone had already started moving toward the side exit of the mall, in the direction of the Dubai Fountain. Except Yash. He waited between the rest of our families and me.

When I started walking toward them, he said, "You really think our parents would let us do this if it was that dangerous? Do you really, truly, not want to? Because, yeah, I want you to go with me and we had a deal, but I won't force it."

I sighed, tapping a finger against my leg. "No. It seems pretty amazing to brag about later."

I scowled at him. He took a comical step backward with hands up.

"I think you *really* want to skydive, for some reason, but are too scared to do it alone. I'll hold your hand. But seriously. What girl are you trying to impress, huh?"

His cheeks flushed and he immediately walked away.

"Yash!" I hurried after him, and we followed our families into the blazing day. No wonder the aquamarine water looked so prominent against all the buildings and features from so high up. The massive fountain was bigger than a football field.

We kept going until we found an unobstructed spot.

Crowds of people waited for the show, taking group shots and selfies. Some weren't even facing the fountain. That was when I realized that we were at the base of the Burj Khalifa.

"Whoa," Lilly said, craning her neck all the way back and shielding her eyes.

"Whoa indeed," I muttered, following her look up, beholding all one hundred and sixty-three glorious stories of the Burj Khalifa.

Sunlight glimmered on the glossy metallic blue-and-gray structure that seemed to be made entirely of glass. It spiraled high in the air and pierced the cloudless sky, dominating the skyline.

"No way we can get that all in one pic," she said.

"We can try," Yash said, nodding at me.

Right! I had a camera now! I whipped my mini backpack from around my shoulders and pulled out the camera, snapping pictures and trying to find the best angles, but man, trying to get the entire building into the frame from this close was near impossible. I was even squatting and pointing the camera up at an angle. Better yet, upside down to be inverted later. It minimized the angle, allowing me to capture everyone and everything, and cast the flash lower to offset the shadowing so the building wasn't glaring. Epic.

"Finally! The camera appears!" Papa said, beaming as he gathered everyone into a picture with the Burj Khalifa behind them. "Watch how she makes a masterpiece out of these pictures."

I grinned. Papa was so cheesy sometimes, but I loved it. I loved how much he supported my creative pursuit, even though it pained me knowing that this wasn't the camera he'd worked so hard to buy me.

For now, I greedily, giddily captured everything I could, from the gleam off metal structures to the triple-story-high advertisements on the side of the mall in glimmering lights and the iridescent water glistening in the afternoon sun.

Then the water show started, and a notable excitement shimmied through the crowd. We found our spot near the fountain, my camera at the ready.

Beautiful Arabic music started up, flowing from unseen speakers, loud and smooth as if we were at a concert. Keeping the rhythm in perfect synchronicity, lights followed rows of bursting water, flashing one way, then another, until they hit our end of the pool in a towering cylinder of gushing water. No wonder it was touted as the world's highest water fountain.

Some of the sprouting fountains made the water wave and dance and delighted everyone. Crowds were cheering and oohing and ahhing.

The music revved up, along with the speed of the water show and changing lights. I tried to capture as much as possible while my family took their own pictures and videos.

I hurried away from them, aiming to get the water and light in the forefront with the Burj Khalifa in the background. I had to walk pretty far and didn't even think to tell my family. The combination of visuals and sounds moved my soul to capture the most I could in a single shot. I wasn't the only one pursuing the perfect composition. Lots of photographers were out. Cameras of all kinds, from cell phones to professional tripod setups.

I breathed in the air and felt the mist touch my skin. Everything just seemed magical, and I bet this place was even better at night.

When the music hit a crescendo, water exploded across the fountain at its highest, most magnificent burst.

The water fell and the music abruptly ended, but there was a roar of applause.

The Dubai Fountain water show was definitely a highlight and something worth seeing. Maybe twice.

I rushed back to my family before they worried, gripping the camera and all the solid shots I hoped I'd gotten. I'd have to look through them later.

"Where did you go?" Mummie chided. "Don't walk off like that."

"I'm sorry!" I said. "I couldn't help it. I had to get better angles. Wait until you see these!" I began to show her some of the shots from the other side.

She gasped at the beauty.

"Right?"

Yash and Lilly crowded me to look but then parted for Papa.

"Oh. So professional. Wow," he said, patting my head like I was still a kid. "You missed taking these kinds of photos earlier and yesterday, though?"

"I know. But this was worth it." I glanced at Yash, who gave a short smile, and I was so glad to know there was still something there for us to rekindle.

*  *  *

After taking a regular taxi, we ended up taking a *water* taxi to get to the souks that afternoon. These markets were world-renowned for the best gold, spices, fabrics, and even souvenirs. It was supposed to be an experience.

But the water taxi was cool, too. There were about fifteen of us siting on an open boat, half to one side, the other half on the other, facing the water, the driver at the front. The breeze off the water was cool and refreshing, but the sun was getting higher and hotter. Had none of us thought to bring shades or hats or sunscreen? Ugh.

My camera devoured shots of the scenery, capturing my family as they enjoyed a breezy ten-minute ride.

"So nice," Mummie commented.

We carefully exited the boat, finding our footing on solid ground again, and checked Maps. The area was decorated here and there for Diwali with strings of marigolds and lights, but not enough to impress the parents.

"India would be covered in decorations," Auntie said, tsking.

"We can still make it," Uncle joked.

Mumbai was about a three-hour plane ride away, so we *could* make it.

We meandered through crowds, which dispersed for a bit between the water taxi deck and the souks. Something to the left caught my eye: one of the most nostalgic drinks ever.

A small vendor was surrounded by coconuts and sugarcane; there seemed to be nothing more Indian than this.

"Coconuts!" Lilly exclaimed as I snapped a few pictures of luscious green coconuts and sugarcane sticks.

Everyone was suddenly thirsty. The problem? Who could possibly decide which drink?

I swore we spent half the afternoon debating when, finally, all the guys got coconuts and the girls got sugarcane. That way, there was some trading in between. Best of both worlds!

A guy deftly cut open coconuts while a woman in a gorgeous red hijab pushed whole sugarcane into a press, extracting murky green juice. The moms took their frothy drinks with a hint of masala and salt, while Lilly and I went pure.

I held up the drink against the mound of coconuts and sugar-canes for a social media shot on my phone. Nailed it.

First sips were always the best. Sometimes, the Indian grocery stores back home would have enough sugarcanes to press juice, but it wasn't like this.

Floral, grassy, mild sweetness hit my taste buds. My eyelids fluttered. Mmm! So good!

The parents shared their drinks, and the coconuts were drained in a matter of minutes. The vendor cut them open and made a spoon from the cuttings so we could all eat the thin flesh. Which was the best part, to be honest!

Yash kept eyeing my drink and I kept eyeing his split coconut.

"Want some?" I asked, offering a taste.

"What took you so long?" He grinned and handed me his entire coconut in exchange for some of my drink.

"Here," I said, giving half of the coconut back to him after sharing the other half with Lilly, who slurped the last bit of translucent coconut meat.

"Nah. You can have it," he said.

"You don't want any?"

"I know how much you love that stuff," he said, and drank more of my juice.

"Bro, I didn't give you my entire drink."

He cocked his chin at the heavy coconut in my hand. "Only fair."

"Get your own drink, then!"

He shoved me away with his elbow. "I'm not thirsty now."

"Replace my drink, then."

Ugh! Fine! I finished the rest of the coconut since he insisted, but also before he drank the rest of my sugarcane juice. "Thanks," I said, snatching what little remained of my drink back. "Gimme that."

"You kids want more?" his dad asked.

"No. It's too sweet," Yash said, then burped. In. My. Face.

"Gross!" I said, shoving him.

He laughed but didn't apologize. I was the queen of burping matches, but my parents probably wouldn't want me out-burping him in public.

Off we went to the Bur Dubai Souk, decorated in garlands and strings of lights as big as a canopy that said: HAPPY DIWALI. Now we were getting festive!

Sweet and savory scents wafted through the air. I was a sucker for coconuts, orange-colored chum chum, and nutty peda with hints of saffron.

There was nothing like eating from vendor carts, a little of everything, during festivities. The crowds were robust and excitement shimmied through the air as people kicked off the five days of Diwali by purchasing something new. Maybe a thin gold necklace or petite ring. A silver utensil? New clothes to wear for Diwali? A box of sweets for family and friends?

Renewal and freshness tingled all around, and as I glanced at my family and then at Yash, I knew how badly we needed to start over to fully partake in Diwali. And I was glad we were getting off on the right foot.

New beginnings. After all, that was what Diwali was all about.

# CHAPTER FOURTEEN

I had never walked so much in my life. My feet ached, but I was happy to rest on the evening of the first day of Diwali. It was nice to chill out for a bit in Yash's room. I was sitting on the edge of his bed, with Yash tucked away closer to the headboard, and flipping through one of a dozen hotel brochures for tourists, my right knee tucked into my chest in what I called "peak Asian sitting style." I got it from my dad and realized it was the only true comfortable sitting position for me.

Our parents said they'd be right up, and Lilly had hung back with them.

"Can you believe they still use paper?" I asked.

"Hmm?" he muttered, barely looking up from his tablet.

"I guess not everyone has QR readers. I do, on my phone, and it still doesn't work half the time. Like, whenever we go to restaurants now, they have touchless menus. Almost always have to ask for a menu. My parents always do. They don't like squinting at my phone."

"Same." Yash swiped across his tablet in delicate, artistic strokes with a stylus, and I knew he was drawing.

"Can I see what you're working on?" I asked, twiddling my thumbs. Maybe he'd let me see. And if he let me see, then maybe that meant we were back to full-on normal best friends again.

"Nah," he replied casually.

I frowned. "Really? What's so special about it? Is it a secret?"

I leaned over and he shrugged one shoulder to block my view. "Stop," he said with a chuckle.

"Let me see. Are you drawing erotica?"

"What!" He laughed even harder, shoving his shoulder so high it had to be hurting his neck.

"Obviously something you're really into. I've seen you drawing all the time on this trip."

"You think I'm really into erotica?" he asked dryly.

"I dunno what you've been into since spring."

His shoulder dropped. "Yeah, if you'd talked to me since then you'd know I'm not into erotica."

"Puppies?" I said.

"How the hell did you go from erotica to puppies?"

"Tell me what's so amazing."

"You assume it's amazing," he said, twisting from me so that I only saw his big head instead of any part of the screen.

I gently tugged a tuft of his hair. He needed a haircut. Who let him walk out the house like this? "If you're drawing it, of course it's amazing."

He paused and glanced back at me. "Your tactics won't work."

"What tactics? I'm being honest. Your drawings were great before you stopped. You're drawing again. Which means you've been practicing, and practice makes art better. So, yeah. Amazing," I added with a smile. A genuine smile, because there was one thing we could all agree on, and that was how fantastic of an artist Yash was. He could go places with his illustrations. Maybe do cover art for books or get featured in major magazines or commercials or—gasp—work on animation. Maybe he'd get his dream job at Disney.

Whoa. My heart was beating out of control with exciting possibilities.

"Lemme see!" I said, and went for the tablet, snaking my arm over his shoulder when he shrugged and caught my wrist between his shoulder and cheek.

"God, woman," he blurted, dropping his stylus and tapping on the screen to either save his work or close out or both.

"Did I mess you up?" I hoped I hadn't accidentally erased his brilliance.

"No! I turned off the tablet so you can't see or mess up my work!"

I steadied myself on my knees, leaning against his back. "Why won't you tell me what you're working on? I promise I won't tell, and I wouldn't criticize it."

He laughed beneath me. "No. Forget it."

"Please?"

"Nope!"

I tickled his armpit until he relinquished his neck grip on my wrist. I went straight for the tablet on the bed beneath him as he laughed under tickle fire.

"How are you so strong?" he asked between bursts of laughter.

"My dad cuts me fruit every morning, that's how," I said, trying to crawl over him to get to the device.

He reached behind to tickle me, his fingers brushing my hip and sending both a jolt of electricity across my skin and an unbearable tickle that had me jerking away. It was enough for him to twist beneath me so that I fell over his chest. But now the tablet was snug under his weight, and there was no way I could wiggle my skinny fingers underneath his back.

We were a battle of tickling offense and elbow defense, and if we weren't careful, there was sure to be a repeat of our tickle fight from sophomore year where he almost busted my lip and I'd bruised his side so badly he couldn't wash it for a week.

"Dude. I will bruise you the heck up," I warned.

"That happened once because I was being gentle. You want me to not be gentle?"

Before I could fathom a comeback, he lifted me! Actually lifted me above him like he was bench-pressing a few pounds, and then he managed to tickle me. I toppled in his wobbly hands and nearly tumbled off the bed because this was not some graceful balancing act. Yash was struggling.

I fell. Hard. Right onto his chest. An ache sprouted across my ribs and chin.

"Ow! My chest!" I wailed, instantly splitting his attention between his own pain and concern over mine.

When he turned to check on me, despite the snarling ache, I snatched a corner of the tablet from beneath Yash, yanking it from underneath his weight with all my might, and toppled backward. He stopped himself before he was touching my, um, boobs.

His cheeks turned rosy and mine were on fire. But as I fell back against the bed, ignoring the pain in my chest and chin, I laughed. I'd won.

Except, when I fell back, Yash came with me, kneeling over me, his hair a wild mess, and his face flushed. His knees dug into the mattress at my side, the compression causing me to tilt toward him. He staggered forward, as if he couldn't stop the momentum, his hands landing on either side of my head. His thick, fluffy hair fell over his brows.

I heaved, clutching the tablet to my chest as butterflies tore through my insides in some maddening rage.

Two thoughts instantly flung themselves at me.

One: I didn't have his passcode, so I hadn't actually won anything.

Two: This felt a lot like some romantic moment.

Alone in a hotel room, on the same bed, Yash looking kind of . . . cute? OMG. Was I crushing on Yash? Was I actually attracted to him?

No. No freaking way.

But butterflies did *not* lie. And the swarming horde in the pit of my belly was yelling that either Yash, or this moment, was crushworthy.

Yash parted his lips as he watched me. It was hard to read his expression. Was there the slightest chance that he was attracted to me? That he thought this was a moment, too? That, maybe, perhaps, in some surreal alternate universe, he would lean down and kiss me?

And what would I do? Did I even want that? Maybe? God, I didn't know! But like, it wouldn't be the worst thing, right? Because Yash was cute. I'd always known that. And he was nice, and just a good guy all around.

Goosebumps skittered across my skin, from my neck down my arms to my fingertips. The fingertips that were the only thing separating us.

He let out a breath through those parted lips before pressing his mouth into a line. He took the tablet and sat back.

The device slipped through my fingers, just like the moment had. He coldly said, "You can't do that."

My smile slipped as I pushed myself onto my elbows. "Huh?"

He sniffed, looking at the tablet in his limp hands. "You don't need to know everything."

I blinked up at him.

"You can't take something that's private because you want to be in my business. I said no, and you gotta respect that. It's personal."

I swallowed hard, my throat parched, the butterflies in my stomach thrashing but not in a good way. I felt like I was about to puke.

I sat up, pulling my knees to my chest. "You're right. I'm sorry."

I let out a haggard breath and blinked away any tears that dared to sprout. His words cut sharper than a blade and lodged themselves into my brain. I didn't need to know everything, but there was a time when he shared everything with me anyway. Any other time, I'd shrug it off and apologize and we would be good. So then why did this hurt so much?

He watched me. The fleck of anger in his eyes dissipated, as if he regretted his words. But he was right, and he shouldn't be the one regretting any of this.

Yash opened his mouth as if he were about to speak, but I spoke first. "I should go get ready for dinner before everyone gets back."

He moved aside when I scuttled off the bed, searching the floor for anything that belonged to me, but really just to keep my gaze down. Because if I looked at him, I might lose it. I might cry, something emotional and raw, and I didn't want to do that in front of him. His simple, respectful requests had never made me feel one way or another, so I wasn't totally sure what the heck was happening right now.

Was it because I thought we were having a moment and he was just annoyed?

Was it because we weren't best friends like before and might never be that close again?

Was it because all the damage I'd done to us was surfacing?

"Nikki . . ." he started, but then he didn't add anything else. There was nothing for him to say, and no reason for me to stay.

"It's fine. Don't feel weird. I'm OK." I stumbled into my shoes and was out the door, leaving Yash on the edge of his bed as his hotel room door clicked shut behind me.

I shuddered out a breath and looked toward the ceiling. My eyes burned with stupid tears. I hiccupped on my next breath and went to my room right as our families walked out of the elevator.

My parents and Lilly immediately honed in on my watery eyes. Mummie asked, "What happened? Are you OK? Why are you crying?"

"Nikki is crying?" Auntie asked.

Yash opened his door. His mom looked past me, to him, and then back at me.

I forced a chuckle, glancing at the carpet to somehow indicate that I'd tripped or done something clumsy.

"Oh no! It's nothing. I just hurt myself trying to get back before you guys."

Mummie held a hand to her chest. "Oh my goodness, beta. Did you stub your toe or twist your ankle? You must learn to not hurry so much. One of these days, you might hurt yourself beyond repair."

She told Auntie, "You know she cries over a paper cut and is fine in another minute. My beta is so sensitive."

"That's dramatic," I muttered.

"Are you ready for dinner?" Papa asked, eyeing Yash and his parents as they disappeared into their room.

"For sure, let me wash up."

I went into our room, afraid to glance back, afraid to know whether Yash had heard my mom mention me crying, afraid to see if he'd heard any or all of that; because, how mortifying.

As I washed my hands, my thoughts chaotically tumbling over what Yash had said, my lips trembled. Tears streamed down my face like a big ole crybaby. I silently bawled. And not just a few sobs, but a hundred. A magnitude of emotions I'd kept in for months. An avalanche of what I'd been feeling since being mad at Yash, since he told me he'd been depressed. A wave of relief when we decided to move forward. And now this little ask for privacy that was *normal*?

What was I doing? Why was I crying? Why did my heart hurt?

I heaved to catch my breath.

Mummie knocked on the door, asking, "Beta? Are you OK? Do you need more time?"

"A few more minutes? Washing my face!" I called out, hoping to sound as cool as possible. But moms always knew.

"OK. Did you hurt yourself that badly?"

"What? No. No, I'm OK." Lies tasted rancid.

"Take your time," she said in that motherly tone that meant she knew I was lying, that I was probably crying because my feelings were hurt and I didn't want her to know, but that it was OK. Which, darn it, only made me cry more.

All right! I had to get over this right now. Everyone was waiting for me, and there was no fury like a ravenously hungry desi family waiting on a slowpoke to get ready.

I washed my face and glared at my reflection until my eyes were no longer watery, no longer showed any signs of having sobbed. I didn't want anyone's pity or concern, or for them to think I was fragile in any way. And I definitely didn't want anyone to know that Yash had anything to do with this.

When I emerged, acting casual, Mummie hugged me and asked, "Are you sure you're OK?"

"Yes," I replied. "Where are we going to eat? Please don't tell me Indian food. I'm so tired of Indian food. *Papa.*"

"Eh. You can never be tired of your motherland's food," Papa said.

I rolled my eyes. "I can't take this much sauce and spice and fried dough. Like, can we get a salad? Or some noodles? This hotel has a really good Indochinese restaurant downstairs! You can eat Indian food and I can eat something not Indian food."

Papa laughed. "Hah. If it's agreeable to everyone, we can go there."

As we shuffled back out the door, Lilly tugged at my sleeve and wagged her finger toward her face. I leaned down as she whispered, "Are you OK?"

"Yes," I said with a genuine smile. Lilly was so sweet.

She furrowed her brows and looked up at me with her serious face. "I heard you crying."

I gulped. "Oh, you heard that?"

She nodded. "We all did."

I blew out a breath and stood upright. "I'm fine. Thanks for asking."

# CHAPTER FIFTEEN

We met everyone in the sitting area of the lobby before heading to dinner. Auntie and Uncle were standing around, thumbing through their phone—pictures, I assumed—while Yash was sitting on a plush pillow.

He was biting his nail when he saw me. He often did that when he was anxious or pensive. His nails were shredded when he was both. My eye twitched when we locked gazes. Awkward.

I wished I was wearing a jacket so I could thrust my fists into the pockets. Instead, my arms dangled at my sides and my hands didn't know what to do with themselves. Ball into loose fists, tight fists? Tap my thighs? Rub against my pants? Just hang?

Our parents had been talking, but then they got quiet. When I finally looked over at them to see what had happened, I realized everyone was watching us.

"Everything all right?" Papa asked.

"Yes," I replied.

"Are you sure nothing is going on between you two?" Papa eyed Yash.

Wow. Nothing like a dad going from friendly uncle to protective papa in two seconds flat. He was *not* about to let a boy hurt me.

My instinct was to lie yet again, because I hadn't mastered accepting my faults, but man, lies created webs and I was getting stuck. So I braced for everyone's reactions and, for once, told the truth.

I turned to Yash and said, "I'm sorry."

He cautiously eyed our parents.

I explained to everyone, "I was trying to pry into Yash's business, even when he kept asking me to leave it alone. So, he got stern with me and I took it personally. But really, it's not his fault. I just got emotional because I realized I wasn't respecting his boundaries. Just, ya know, some stuff I'm working through."

I pressed my lips together and nodded, wholly embarrassed yet somewhat relieved to get that into the open so we could all get over it.

"Ah! Is that all?" Mummie said, clucking her tongue at me. "Beta, you're maturing. It's OK—as long as Yash is OK?"

He nodded. "Yeah, I'm fine."

Heat prickled up my neck and I didn't have to look at him to know that he was staring at the back of my head.

Papa chortled. "OK! Let's put that behind us and eat!"

Everyone laughed in agreement, and I forced a smile all while Yash stood at my back and Lilly cast me a worried look. I tousled her hair, and she gently pushed me away.

"I'm fine," I reassured her.

Then Yash walked to us and flicked her collar. "You can beat me up later for making your sister cry."

I froze. Crap. So he *had* heard my mom?

He shot me a somewhat sorrowful expression, and those sad eyes killed me. They'd killed me when we fought last spring and with every conflict and revelation since, and they were killing me now.

Lilly ran after Yash and our parents while Papa slowed his pace to match mine. Since I couldn't walk any slower without it being comically absurd, I couldn't evade my father. He clasped his hands behind his back, his chin held high, but didn't turn toward me. Instead, we walked side by side, past the elevators and small dessert shop, to the door at the back of a long hallway. One would never know there was a restaurant back here if not for the sign and arrows.

"Is that all that happened?" he asked.

I nodded. "Yeah. It was dumb."

"Hmm. Nothing else happened?"

It took a moment to catch on. I scrunched my face, mortified. "Ew. No."

"Ah. Good. Good. Because you know I would have words with him if something had happened. Decades-long friendship with his parents or not."

"Oh my god. No. Papa. Nothing physical or romantic or anything other than me trying to make him tell me what's new with him since our big fight happened."

"That's good. I mean, that a boy didn't try to push you into anything."

"Oh my god. Everyone knows Yash isn't like that. And definitely nothing between us. Again, ew."

"Hah. Ew indeed. But also, good that you're taking interest in him again. It'll take some time to mend your friendship, but one thing I've learned is that good friends are hard to find. We have superficial friends, acquaintances, people who shouldn't be trusted at all, passersby, and then we have true, honest friends. And those friendships, beta, are like fine gold. We go out of our way to collect them, bring them securely into our lives, cherish them, protect them, maintain their beauty. It takes appreciation and work."

"Yeah. I get that. I'm working on it."

He smiled, still looking straight ahead as we passed a seven-foot-tall, wooden mythological bird painted in gold and bronze with red and green accents. "All it took was a trip to Dubai, huh?"

I groaned. "Yeah. Guess hardheaded runs in the family," I jested.

"Hah. Your mother's side," he replied, without missing a beat.

"Ow. Burn. I'm telling her."

We laughed, rounding the corner, and met the rest of our group waiting at the hostess desk.

"What's so funny?" Mummie asked.

I grinned so hard that I thought my teeth would pop off.

"Nothing," Papa said, snaking an arm around her waist before a woman in black slacks and a white button-down shirt escorted us to a table where our parents ate—surprise, surprise—Indian food and we kids enjoyed Indian-Chinese fusion.

While they had their curried vegetables and freshly baked paratha, Yash, Lilly, and I shared portions of noodles with cauliflower doused in a slightly sweet sauce called gobi Manchurian.

We had dumplings and sweet and sour soup and salad with sesame dressing.

"What is this?" Lilly asked, rigidly pressing a finger onto the menu.

I balked. "What is chocolate dosa?"

"That doesn't even sound good," Yash commented.

The parents shook their heads in disdain, as if smothering a crispy crepe made from rice and lentil batter with chocolate was an affront to our kind. OK, it quite possibly was. But we ordered it anyway because chocolate was our love language. In peak dosa fashion, the giant crepe came folded into threes, almost three feet long, and hung precariously off the plate.

"I bet it's Nutella," I commented as Lilly and I ripped it apart.

Unlike savory dosas filled with potatoes and veggies, this one wasn't served with chutney and dhal. But it was good all on its own. It was like eating very thin and warm wafer-type flatbread with Nutella spread. The edges were crispy with butter and the center a little thicker, a little chewier.

My eyelids fluttered. "This is good."

"So good," Lilly concurred.

I passed the plate around and everyone, albeit reluctantly, ripped off a piece. At first bite, they scrunched up their faces at the odd combination, but they liked it.

"Surprisingly good," Yash said from his seat across the table from me.

I pushed the plate toward him like a peace offering, and he partook. He flicked his second piece down with a "thanks" and sent a dollop of chocolate spread right at my face. It splattered across my lip and eye, which I'd closed just in time.

Yash's shoulders shot up. "Oops."

Lilly gasped, catching the parents' attention. Everyone froze.

I licked as far as I could and asked, "Did I get it?" I turned to Lilly with one eye closed tight, the sticky weight of chocolate heavy on my lashes.

"Wait," she said. She ripped off a clean edge of the dosa and swiped it across my face and ate it.

"Ew!" I cackled, wiping the chocolate off my face. But we had a good laugh.

After dinner, Yash and I led our party out into the hall and got into an elevator full of other people. Our parents waved us to go on ahead. So we did. Lilly stayed with them.

Yash walked me to my door in spiraling silence.

"I'm sorry I made you cry," he said, twisting his mouth and shoving his hands into his pants pockets.

"You think so much of yourself that you thought you made me cry?" I scoffed.

But he wasn't buying it. Not with those imploring eyes.

My shoulders deflated. "You had something personal, and I was pushing it. I'm the one who's sorry."

His lips twitched. "I kinda wanna hug you right now."

I rolled my eyes, but of course I wanted that, too. "It's been so long. Do you even know how to hug?"

He gave a small laugh and turned to walk to his room. I stopped my brain from overthinking and grabbed his arm, pulling him back.

Yash turned around to face me as I took a step. Suddenly, we were half a foot apart and he was standing over me with his hair falling over his brows.

I hugged him before I changed my mind. Maybe my ungraceful embrace stunned him; if not that, then me hitting my temple on his chin must've, because he jerked. It took him a quick minute to hug me back, but when he did, I felt warm, safe, snuggled, like an entire childhood of amazing memories wrapped around me.

"I kinda wanna hug you, too," I mumbled into his neck.

His arms tightened around my waist. I felt his head tilting down and his breath against my hair. Chills raced down my back, but in a really amazing way.

"I know," he finally said. "You get that look when you want to hug me."

"What look?" I muttered.

"Cross-eyed, Disney princess look."

I laughed. "Shut up. I do not!"

He flinched. "Calm down."

I didn't let him go, but instead gathered some of his shirt into my fists at his back and pressed my forehead into his shoulder. A wave of timidness washed over me, and my skin flared hot, my stomach doing flips.

It was much, much easier to admit this when my brain shut off and I didn't have to look at Yash. Also, how mad could he be if he was hugging me?

The words spilled out. "I'm really sorry for what I did."

He took a second to respond, "I know. Just don't try that

again? I mean, you don't even have my passcode, so not sure what you were going to do."

"I don't know, either."

I found myself clutching onto him even harder. Maybe so he couldn't pull away and look at me. Maybe I just wanted to hang on to him a little longer because man, I missed his hugs.

He eventually pulled back, but was still holding me.

Yash was looking down at what I assumed was the top of my head, and now I was thinking that I hoped I smelled OK with him hugging me for this long and that the hotel's shampoo and conditioner were embrace-worthy.

I stared at his chest.

His hold around my waist went slack.

We stood like this for a long minute before I said, "Did you turn into a statue, or . . . ?"

"Can you look me in the eye?"

I sucked in a breath and looked up at him. Boy, was his face close. The amber specs in his eyes looked more like swirls in this lighting. His forehead was totally covered by fluffy hair. The brown tint of his skin had gotten darker during our many Dubai excursions.

Why were there butterflies rocking out in my guts again? Oh no. The last time I had these butterflies, Yash had made me cry.

I maintained hardcore eye contact and asked, "Now what?"

"Nothing," he said after a beat.

My shoulders deflated. "Is that all you're going to say?"

He shrugged. His gaze dropped to my mouth, and I stilled. Well, except for the huge gulp that was quite possibly audible. Oh my lord, what was wrong with me? Seriously, what was going on?

Maybe Yash was thinking the same thing, or maybe my reaction was freaking him out, because his skin flushed and he swallowed hard, too.

"Oh my god, are y'all gonna kiss or what?" Lilly asked from three feet away.

I yelped and both Yash and I jumped, stepping away from each other. "You scared me!"

She shrugged. "You're just standing there, holding each other, looking into each other's eyes for, like, a whole minute. Kiss or don't kiss, but that's a long hug."

"Oh my lord," I muttered, trying not to look at Yash as he cleared his throat and said, "We were just talking."

"Who talks that close?" Lilly countered. "I don't talk that close to no one. Seems very uncomfortable."

I rubbed my arm. Meanwhile, Yash flicked her ear and said, "I've seen you talking pretty close to a certain boy in your class after school."

"What!" she barked. "You have not!"

By the way her cheeks reddened and that serious scowl, I'd say my little sister was hiding a crush from me.

"OK, now you have to spill," I said, even as our parents wandered down the hall, chatting as always.

She huffed and crossed her arms at Yash, snickering. "I can't believe you saw that!"

"So? Who is he? Do I know him?" I asked.

"No. Maybe."

"C'mon. This is what sisters are for."

She side-eyed Yash. "Then what's he doing here?"

Yash raised his hands in surrender. "All right. All right. I get it. No boys allowed in this conversation. Fine. I gotta go catch up on homework anyway."

"Bye," I mouthed to him as he threw a peace sign and walked to his door.

We walked inside our room.

"So? You and Yash? Y'all like each other now or what?" Lilly asked, point-blank.

"No, I don't think so. We're trying to move past our fight. Back to you. Who is this boy?"

She pushed up her glasses, but even my little sister's stern face couldn't keep it together when thinking of her crush. And I was here for it.

# CHAPTER SIXTEEN

The following morning, on our third full day in Dubai, I absentmindedly replied to Tamara's questions, which she'd sent over while I was sleeping.

**Tamara:** Any hot guys?

**Nikki:** Um, no, sorry.

**Tamara:** Taking good pics? Can you send any or do I need to wait?

**Nikki:** Lots! And yeah, you'll have to wait unless you want the basic ones taken on my phone camera.

**Tamara:** Good food?

**Nikki:** An entire book series written for that answer!

**Tamara:** How's it going with Yash?

**Nikki:** Good, actually. We're working on it.

"It's the second day of Diwali!" Mummie crooned.

We practically squealed. One day closer to the actual day of Diwali but definitely the day for food. Back home, we'd be cooking all sorts of treats in preparation for tomorrow. Our mandir would have literal steps covered in food, something(s) made by each family. It was common to see every sweet imaginable, from buttery barfi to color-speckled boondi ke laddoo to silver-foiled kaju katli. Someone always made loads of bright-orange jalebi, entire chocolate cakes, platters of cupcakes and cookies, and mounds of festively decorated Rice Krispies treats. Others would make fried, crunchy, and spicy snacks . . . just really whatever could be shared and celebrated.

This all had me wondering what today would be like here. How was it really celebrated in Dubai? Would my mom's family take us to a mandir? Would it be as extra as ours? As extravagant? Or were we just going to chill at someone's house and call it a day?

We started with breakfast in the magnificent Egyptian-themed restaurant downstairs with Papa hand-delivering bowls of fruit.

Yash gave a small smile, jerking his chin toward the stack of heart-shaped waffles, endless tarts, and pastries. I really wasn't planning on fitting into my Diwali clothes, was I?

We didn't talk much to one another, but listened to our parents make arrangements for the day. Every time we asked what to expect, what to do, how to act, my parents brushed it off as if it weren't a big deal.

"They're family, you'll be fine," Mummie said.

"But we've never met them," I replied. "Aren't there cultural and social gaps to be aware of?"

"Are you planning on getting drunk in your underwear while singing offensive lyrics?" she asked so seriously that we all busted up laughing. She smiled. "You'll be fine, beta. Just be yourself."

I nodded, looking to Lilly as we reined in our giggles. The absurd imagery!

Still, I wanted to know. Did they hug or kiss cheeks or shake hands (no to all three for me, by the way)? Were they uncomfortable with girls who showed leg and arm? Did they expect us to be religious and speak perfect Gujarati and/or Hindi? I mean, *what*?

There was no use in trying to figure it out. I'd been in social settings my entire life, so this was no different. We'd been to new schools and different mandirs and huge festivities before, and this was basically the same thing. Family or not, they were just people. Yet, I found myself caring about what they thought of us.

In the States, we were almost always aware that we were Indian when around others, whether in a negative or positive way. We were different and some people expected us to be religious or closed-off. When we visited India, we were always aware that we were different, and people assumed we didn't speak the language or were wild Americans. We were perpetually foreigners no matter where we were. And it bothered me. I just wanted to be normal, like I was with my immediate family, and not be othered.

Would Mummie's family other us, too?

Our first outing for the day was a tour of the Arabic desert. It was pretty cool to be in a vehicle that could go really fast on sand dunes. Yash and I took turns sitting in the passenger seat to get the best view. I was hypnotically tied to my camera . . . when I wasn't yelping and giggling over the jumps and heart-pounding downward slopes. How did the vehicle not turn over? How did the mounds of beige sand not swallow us whole?

Needless to say, no good shots. Yash just recorded the whole thing.

The driver made small talk about tourism and the event, but we were all pretty much glued to an endless desert around us. It was mind-boggling to think an advanced metropolis like Dubai or Abu Dhabi could sprout up from what looked like nothing but parched earth. Not even land, really. Just dunes and rolls and hills of sand. No trees. No animals. Nothing. Even with the Gulf not terribly far away, how could anything survive this place?

We were let out in the middle of nowhere, I kid you not. But there was a caravan of vehicles and small clusters of tourists climbing out of or getting back into cars.

"This is the magnificent Arabian desert," the tour guide announced. "Please, walk around, take pictures, enjoy the moment. We will continue in twenty minutes."

Twenty minutes was all I needed, well less than the time it took to get family pictures. The Arabian sun climbed high into a blue-painted sky streaked with wispy clouds. The beige dunes were crossed with wavy lines of sand pushed into elegant ripples over time by the wind.

I walked onto the highest dune to capture as many shots as possible, and while it was perfect with the light slanting just right and nothing to create horrendous shadows, these weren't the right shots to land the internship. They were good, but not amazing. Something was missing, but I couldn't pinpoint what it was.

We climbed back into the vehicle with Yash in the passenger seat now, and suddenly the driver became more animated as he told us what to expect. Banquets of food and drinks, decadent desserts, a meal by the light of the flames as we watched dancers, a mehndi booth, camel rides, sandboarding, and so much more.

When we arrived, we all hurried out because my parents seemed to think we needed to secure the best seats and get to the food first.

We passed a train of camels on the left and several men on the far right in front of the mother of all dunes. Whoa. Was that where we could sandboard?

We were still in the middle of the desert without a building; smaller structures comprised of rooms and platforms, all surrounded by walls of tapestries like a gigantic square tent, loomed ahead. A pathway lined by small pools and fountains where water flowed from ancient-looking pots showed us the way.

Upon entry, we saw the restrooms to the left, and ahead lay a table where a golden platter of very large dates greeted us beside golden dallahs, just like the teapot at the hotel with a long, slender neck that had convinced me whatever it poured tasted better this way. Matching cups and saucers waited beside it, begging us to give it a try. Was this finally Arabic coffee?

I giddily poured steamy, dark brown liquid into a cup and tasted.

It was, according to the item card. And wow, was it good. Rich. Smooth. Earthy. With a hint of spices.

I wasn't a coffee connoisseur, but my tastebuds knew what was delicious, and this was it.

"C'mon!" Lilly said, dragging me away from the table.

"Hey!"

She'd almost made me spill the coffee over myself. But that didn't stop me from grabbing some dates first!

Yash was right behind us, doing the same. He was balancing a very full cup of coffee and at least six dates on the saucer around the drink. He shrugged and mouthed, "What?"

I mean, yeah. Our parents had paid for all of this, so might as well enjoy as much as possible.

As soon as we turned the corner into the sprawling room of colorful tapestries, the mouth-watering aromas of food filled the air. A buffet was up ahead. One long table for meats, another for veggies, yet another for soups and breads, and of course drinks and desserts had their own tables. To the right were six women sitting on a rug directly on top of the sand, armed with mehndi cones in front of a row of sitting pillows.

The moms cocked their chins toward the mehndi artists, and Lilly and I made eye contact, knowing that was where we were going first. Maybe dessert first, then mehndi, then food. Yes, that seemed like the logical order.

The area to the right opened into a large room situated around a low stage, because the tables around it for our dining experience were also low. There were no chairs, just broad, thick sitting pillows in muted tones of red and faded gold streaked with blue.

"So cool," I breathed, bending to set my cup and saucer down at the nearest table.

The tables had lamps whose flickering flames cast an ambient light. Even though it was bright outside the tent, the tapestry walls and roof were thick enough to create a dimmer, almost romantic atmosphere.

My parents felt it as they giggled against each other and took selfies. This was a moment to capture.

The pics came out beautifully. There was something heart-warming about seeing my parents clandestinely smiling at each other, with my dad tilting his head down for my mom and my mom shyly tucked away against him with the blurred lamplight flickering behind them set against the cloth walls. The low lighting created a flushed, golden glow that illuminated their skin.

Auntie and Uncle, on the other hand, had gone straight for what they assumed would be the best table and staked their claim. It was close to the stage for an optimal, unobstructed view, but in between speakers to avoid being taken out by migraines.

"Hey," Yash said, bumping my shoulder with his.

"Hey," I said, fixated on my camera.

"Nice shots," he commented.

"Thanks," I replied, grinning. All thanks to his gift, which I was going to one hundred percent pay back.

Since our falling out, Yash had been the one to always make the first move, the one always trying to connect and smooth things over. It was time I started doing that for him.

I nudged him back with my shoulder, our arms still touching, and said, "Listen, I know I was acting like skydiving is a real pain in my butt, but I'm pretty excited to share that with you. So, thanks for making me hold your hand."

He rolled his eyes toward the sky.

"How about we share sandboarding, too?"

"Let me think about it," he teased, ruffling my hair so that masses of it scrunched up from my ponytail.

"Hey!" I shouted after him, fixing my hair while he checked out the endless variety of food.

I walked around taking pictures and absolutely forgot about the coffee and dates.

We all met at our dining table when background music started, adding to the experience. The moms giddily headed over to the mehndi area, where a couple of other tourists had already started getting designs on their palms.

"We have to hurry before it gets too crowded!" Hetal Auntie bellowed.

"Wait for me!" I called.

But they were gone. Dang. Nothing like the anticipation of mehndi to make grown women act like schoolgirls and forget their children.

"Oh, but we gotta try out the rides outside," Yash interrupted, coming to stand in front of me.

"Don't stand between a girl and her mehndi," I warned, leaning around him.

He stuffed his hands into his pockets and cocked his chin toward something behind me. "You agreed to my terms. Whatever I want this trip, remember?"

I grumbled nonsensical grunts.

He pulled me away and I moped, "Wah! But mehndi! And cake!"

# CHAPTER SEVENTEEN

Never had I ever seen a guy want to ride a camel so badly. What was the appeal? A horse, I'd understand. An elephant seemed cool. An ostrich sounded terrifying, but definitely a bragging point. A tiger would be a total badass move, but probably wasn't a thing that happened. But a camel?

Camels sounded tame, unassuming, an animal easily over-looked; but when you came face-to-face with them, they were kind of formidable. Like, huge and muscular and capable of stomping me into the sand.

"Ugh. No . . ." I muttered, staring at one who stared right back like it was daring me with a "Come at me, bro."

*No, thank you. I do not want to come at you, bro.*

Every camel was tethered to the camel in front of it in a circle. They had cloth mouth coverings like socks in stripes of dull yellow and brown, matching the cloth blankets on their backs. The camel I was staring at suddenly swerved its head, and I jumped back, yelping.

Yash cracked up so hard that others started staring at us.

"Not funny!" I said, backing all the way into Yash, my hands groping behind me while I kept focused on the camel.

"It's just . . . a horse with a hump . . ." He snickered, bracing for impact because I practically walked into him to push him out of my way. He took my wrist. "Hey! Where are you going?"

"Not there."

"Dude!" He pulled me back. "We are *not* losing our place in line. We're up first! We have to go."

I turned to him, my gaze darting to the camel. "*Nope.*"

"You'll regret it if you don't try."

"I'm not regretting anything."

"Well, you're going to regret it when I tell the entire school that you were scared of a camel."

I narrowed my eyes. "You *wouldn't.*"

"It'll come out naturally. What did you do out there? Rode a camel in the desert. Cool! Did Nikki ride, too? Nah, man. Why not? She was scared. And then they'll be like, what! She went skydiving though. She's supposed to be the GOAT of the school for that. We gotta take that back. Ain't no GOAT afraid of camel rides."

I groaned and briefly covered his mouth with my palm. "Oh my lord. How are you this vicious?"

"I'm not! It's the way conversations will go. What am I supposed to say, huh?" He tapped the camera hanging from my neck. "And we need proof. So, I dunno, at least just sit on one?"

My shoulders deflated.

"And you agreed to do whatever I ask you on this trip, so . . ."

"Frigging hate you," I muttered.

"Nah, you don't."

A few girls behind us in line squealed with delight. Yash enunciated, "*Little kids* are riding them. Without anyone holding their hand, even. Maybe we should ask them where they get their mighty heroism from? That great intrepidness required for this expedition that isn't a kiddy ride *at all*. Maybe if we can borrow some? We'd give it right back—"

"All right, smart-butt," I said, cutting him off even as he grinned down at me.

"I'll hold your hand," he teased, jerking his chin at the girls. He meant it to be a joke, 'cause ya know, they didn't need anyone holding their hand, but maybe I did? But the second he actually held my hand, our fingers interlocking, a strange embarrassment hit, and I wondered if Yash felt it, too.

He was so warm, and his touch had my skin tingling. I swallowed hard and couldn't manage to look at him. Was he staring at me? Realizing that he was holding my hand like a child? Or realizing that he was *holding* my hand? Like a boy holding a girl's hand because that was what we were doing.

More importantly . . . why did I like it? Why did this feel so different from the millions of times he'd held my hand before?

There wasn't much time to dwell on WTF was happening right now and why it was suddenly so weird—had to be the desert heat—because one of the camel guys waved us over. We shuffled ahead, and for some reason, we were still holding hands.

I found enough calm to glance at Yash when he looked at me from over his shoulder, expecting some wide-eyed glare of equally awkward wonderment of his own WTF was happening. But to my relief, he was hard to read, and that seemed easier to take in than if he was fully aware that we were holding hands the way I was, because surely, I was overthinking.

"You look like a kid again," he commented, and yep, I sure was overthinking this. "Remember when you were afraid of Rollerblading, and I had to coax you into it? You ended up kicking butt at it and Rollerblading at lightning speeds doing circles around me because I never got past point one mile per hour."

I scoffed, watching the caretaker smooth down the blanket on the camel's back.

"And soon you'll be skydiving. Out of an actual plane."

I cringed. "*OK* . . . not helping."

"This is nothing in comparison. If you fall . . . it won't be bone-shattering."

I blew out a breath and then laughed. "Morbid but accurate."

"Don't be scared, it's fine. Look, their mouths are covered so they can't bite or spit at you."

"How are you so fearless all of a sudden?"

He shrugged. "Learned to live life over the summer, I guess."

"Apparently," I mumbled. And instead of wondering if the camel was going to annihilate me, I questioned whether Yash meant he'd changed because I'd pushed him away. What fears had he been tackling that had made him learn to live life?

"Plus, they're tied to one another, so ya know, they can't take off and leave you in the middle of a hot desert."

"Gee. Thanks. That totally doesn't make my dry, scorching death while I choke on sand and heat flash my life before my eyes any more terrifying."

When the caretaker was ready for us, Yash tugged me ahead of him and released my hand to pat my shoulders before getting onto the camel behind me.

The caretaker told me how to get on. The camel was knelt in a sitting position and eyed me, moving its mouth inside the sock-like snout covering. Still massive, wide, and tall.

The blanket wasn't a saddle, so there wasn't a stirrup to slip my foot into and hoist myself up. Just a handlebar sewn into the cloth. I stepped onto a stool, gripped the handlebar, swung my leg over, and adjusted myself, wobbling all the while.

I ignored the strong farm-animal smell and looked over to see Yash barely struggle to get onto his camel. He was settled and ready to go. He gave a thumbs-up, as if this was no big deal.

He made googly-eyes and stuck out his tongue, which had me giggling. The camel grunted beneath me, like some curmudgeon warning me to settle down. I immediately turned ahead and froze.

In the corner of my eye, Papa and Uncle appeared, armed with their phones to either photograph, video, or live WhatsApp this entire thing, oh my god. I felt like a little kid again, except the actual little kid in the family wasn't coming anywhere near a camel. Lilly stood beside Papa and waved.

We rose on the caretaker's commands and clicks. The movement was jarring and jostled me around a bit, to the point where I was sure I'd fall right off! It just added to the list of why I should be terrified of camels.

The camel was much stronger than I'd expected. It felt like pure muscle and strength beneath me. For the moment, I felt like a queen, high above a throng of admirers, elegantly trotting around atop her magnificent beast. Then I remembered to take pictures of my view of the camel, of Yash as my camel made a turn, and of our sandy surroundings.

When our ride ended, the camels dutifully knelt back down to sitting positions, jostling me back and forth until I slid off and, oh thank god, back onto precious ground.

I met Yash at the front as he walked toward me.

I snapped pics of the camels, but the camera seemed to have a mind of its own, gravitating toward Yash, no matter how often I yanked it back to the intended subject.

He looked kinda cute, all tall and lean, his hair disheveled, glancing one way, then another, then at me. His cheeks flushed, his expression going from finally relaxed to how-dare-you-take-pictures-of-me.

"You did it," he declared proudly. "You lasted a whole five minutes!"

He pinched my cheeks, and I fought him off, demanding, "Stand right there!"

"Huh?"

"Beside the camel. I gotta get a picture of you."

He sighed but relented and I snapped some pictures. Then we quickly switched places and he got pictures of me on his cell phone because he hadn't learned how to use the camera. I, of course, threw a peace sign, because that seemed fitting.

"Do you want me to take a picture of you both?" the care-taker asked. "It will be a couple of minutes before the next round of people climb on. Go. Go," he insisted before we could decline.

Yash handed him his phone and then stood beside me.

"Ah, closer?" the guy instructed, sweeping his hand across the air.

Yash inched closer and closer until our arms were touching. Then we gave big smiles for the camera because this guy wasn't going to take some stiff picture and call it a day.

Finally! A picture he deemed worthy. We thanked him and he waved us off as if he was nothing but happy to help.

Yash retrieved his phone while I hurried to Lilly and asked, "Did you see us?"

"Yes! That's so cool!" she said. "I wanna try now. If you can do it, I can do it!"

I laughed. "True. Are you riding, too, Papa?"

"Oh no," he replied, shaking his head. "This is for young people."

"No. I see adults on there, too. It's for everyone!"

He shook his head, patting Lilly's shoulder.

"You'll have fun!" I told Lilly as the line moved forward.

"Do you want to get your mehndi done now?" Yash asked.

I scoffed, the terror of camels replaced by anticipation. "No. My turn."

I removed the camera from around my neck and gave it to my dad, asking, "Could you hold this for a bit?"

"Yes, of course," Papa said.

"What are you doing?" Yash asked as I took his wrist and tugged him away.

"I don't want to risk breaking it."

"Wait. Where are we going?"

We walked to the other side of the tents as I longingly looked up at the mother of all dunes.

"Oh no," Yash said with a shake of his head.

"Oh yes," I insisted, grinning. Whatever fear or dread I'd had from the camel's reign of terror had vanished. Whoosh! Into thin, Arabian air. Because we were doing this.

# CHAPTER EIGHTEEN

Yash didn't like uncontrolled speed, which is why he could never get into Rollerblading when we were kids. He could do theme park rides because they were attached to frames and routes; there was no deviation. Maybe he thought he could do skydiving because it was all falling and nothing else, no crashes or trips. So, getting him to go sandboarding was a major win.

As we walked up, he freaked out every time someone crashed or fell off or went uncontrollably sideways. He got even more fidgety as we made the trek to the top—huffing and puffing because, man, was it hard to hike up sand in the sun—but we made it, and now he was looking down a steep slope and turning into a pillar of stone.

I shook his arms. "At least the boards don't need mouth guards to keep them from spitting at you!"

"Hah, hah," he replied dryly.

"C'mon. We'll take a run and if you can handle it, another one so we can try to video it!"

"How are you this excited?"

"I mean, we're not even going to actually sandboard standing up. We're sitting down! You can do this!"

One of the guides instructed us on how to sit on the board and what to do—essentially, keep your limbs tucked in and turn toward the bottom to slow your descent to a stop.

"OK. Since *you* want to go, *you* go first," Yash decided.

"Oh, big baby."

"Hey."

"Hey yourself. You called me a scaredy-cat, real mature by the way. But that's fine. I don't mind sitting up front and getting the best view and protecting you," I said with a grin as I straddled the board and sat so that each foot was firm in the sand on either side. "Strong girls will shield boys. Don't worry your pretty head off."

He groaned, but sat on a board beside me.

I gave him a peace sign, adjusted my legs onto the board, and off I went! Down a smooth, steep dune with hot sand kicking up into my face, *ouch*, and my stomach roiling from the speed. It was an adrenaline high that had me actually looking forward to the rush of skydiving.

Wind beat against my body and my hair whipped behind me as I hollered. So fast, free, and in the moment. No burdens or regrets or shoulders slumping beneath the weight of my mistakes.

I struggled to turn at the bottom and fell off, laughing and hoping that it was at least graceful and not my-butt-in-the-air-with-my-mouth-eating-sand.

"Move!" Yash yelled as he careened toward me, slowing down and turning in time but still toppling off his board and right onto me!

We face-planted into the ground, the dune's searing sand grains scratching my cheek and chin.

"Ow! Yash! Get off!" I cried out and tried to turn beneath his weight.

"Nikki!" he shot back. Right. In. My. Ear.

He rolled off and I sat up, spitting sand and rubbing the grains off my face. It was everywhere! In my hair, down my shirt, in my bra!

"Are you OK?" He was at my side, holding my face and checking for wounds.

"Yes," I muttered through squished cheeks.

There was a nanosecond where he squinted in the gleam of the sunlight, hovering over me on one knee, and neither of us seemed to be breathing, to be moving. His hold softened and his thumb . . . did it brush against my skin?

I swallowed. Hard. My heart was pounding in my chest and my pulse raged behind my ears. I was sure Yash could feel it through his fingers.

Oh. My. Word. His touch was doing funny, strange, euphoric things to me. His fingers were warm, sending little sparks wherever they made contact. I stilled, not knowing what to do, how to react. We'd just become friends again. I couldn't *like* like him. That could ruin everything, and Yash was too important to lose a second time. But then again, *he* was the one touching me. Was he just concerned, or was he feeling something, too?

Yash sighed and sat back, one arm draped over the knee that he'd pulled to his chest, and looked at me with imploring eyes. For a minute, it was almost as if nothing bad had ever happened between us, as if nothing had changed, as if there was a lingering promise in the air that everything between us would be perfectly fine for the rest of our lives.

But there was also a strange, alien sensation rummaging around my gut, like maybe I wanted him close to me again. No. Definitely. I *definitely* wanted Yash close to me, his touch on my skin again.

Pfft! That was silly! I'd never felt that way about Yash before, unless missing him during our fight was the same. It didn't feel the same. I shoved aside the sensation lingering in my chest, slapped his leg, ungracefully pushed myself off the sand, and got to my feet.

I started running back to the top—well, whatever this effort of dragging a board with me counted as—and yelled back, "Have to get in as many turns as we can! You'd better hurry up!"

The next thing I knew, I was on my board, adjusting my phone in a grand endeavor to video this time, or at least capture some pictures from up top. Then Yash appeared at my side, sitting on his board. He gave a thumbs-up.

"Who's a big boy?" I joked, and off we went.

\* \* \*

We did the dunes a few times, then ate. I managed to get my fill of food and desserts while everyone was engrossed in the live entertainment of dancers.

Lilly was shaking her shoulders and grooving to the beat, and a little blonde girl near the stage was trying to match the dancer's moves, which had stolen everyone's attention. She was probably four and a better dancer than I'd ever be!

And Yash?

I elbowed him and whispered, "Dude, you stare any harder at her and your eyeballs will pop out."

He pulled his gaze away from the dancer, leaning back on his elbow so that he was closer to me. When our eyes met, he held my gaze, and everything around us sort of melted away. In this moment that could've lasted five minutes or five seconds, nothing else seemed to exist.

"You never got your mehndi done?" he asked.

I shook my head. We'd been so busy with rides and food.

"Come on," he said, and pulled me to my feet.

We went to the mehndi area, which was nearly empty now that most everyone was eating and watching the show. I sat on a plush cushion. Since there were more artists than tourists by this time, one lady worked on each hand. They drew large Arabic designs instead of the small Indian ones I was used to.

I smiled giddily, because they had loads of time to draw designs all over my hands. Our moms had gotten theirs done during peak time and had only gotten partial hands. The green paste was cool on my flesh. The gentle gliding over my palm lulled me into an absolutely relaxed state, and the mehndi smelled earthy, clean, nostalgic. I'd always loved the scent.

Yash sat down beside me and took out his phone to take pictures. I rolled my eyes. He always took the least flattering pictures of me. I really didn't understand how, not when the technology was there to do most of the work.

When my mehndi was finished, we took our time walking around as the air cooled. Since my mehndi hadn't dried enough yet, Yash offered to serve me.

I grinned, feeling like a princess as he fetched me Arabic coffee and cake. We ended up sitting at an empty table in a corner far from the others but well within sight of our parents. As he fed me cake, so as not to ruin my mehndi, we got to talking about how weird our summers had been. I'd spent mine mostly cooped up at home and went out only to take pictures or run errands. Yash had spent his mostly recovering from his mild depression by focusing on art.

Despite how much it pained me to know he'd been hurting, I was overjoyed that he was even telling me this at all. Instead of turning away from the pain, I embraced it. I clung to every word, wishing we'd never be apart again. Even if he *was* eating all my cake.

*  *  *

We left our excursion in the early afternoon, satiated but dead tired. We all passed out during the car ride back to the hotel, where I shot for the bathroom first. I needed a shower to get all the sand off me, which meant washing away the mehndi paste. It was fine because an orange stain had already set, and it would darken in the next day or two. There wasn't time for a quick nap, as Mummie hurried us out of the hotel to meet her cousin from Abu Dhabi. But we still called him Mama, meaning my mother's brother. Ankit Mama from Abu Dhabi had a plush SUV big enough for all of us.

Mummie and Papa happily hugged him and introduced him to us. He had a thick mustache and dimples, a noticeable gut, and a chortle that had us laughing along with him. He didn't feel like a stranger—more like an uncle I'd always known.

"So nice to finally meet you!" he said, looking from me to Lilly and handing us caramel candy. "I picked up juice drinks and nasto from my wife, Amina. Not too spicy, OK?"

"Thank you!" Lilly and I said in unison.

Papa sat in the passenger seat, with Pranav Uncle and the moms in the middle row. I was squished between Lilly and Yash in the back; now I knew she was doing this on purpose, but I didn't mind.

The adults gabbed away as Mama pointed out this building and that park and this structure and that monument, excitedly relaying history and facts. From the very back, we couldn't hear a lot of what he was saying until he raised his voice to ask, "Kids doing OK in the back? Too hot?"

"No, we're good! Thank you!" I hollered.

We kids munched on crunchy fafda strips and savory discs of masala puri that Amina Mami had made, passing them back up front so we could dig into the plastic bag of goodies.

"Supercool," Yash said, marveling at the Arabic wording for what was probably apple juice and orange juice and jeera lemonade.

"Ooh! Like Cheetos Puffs," Lilly commented, ripping into a bag of Emirates Pofaki.

We also ate what were a lot like Funyuns and pizza-flavored chips.

We snacked without chatting, as I tried not to be so scrunched up against Yash. We marveled out the window at McDonald's and KFC and Wendy's and Five Guys passing by. But, like, the fast-food restaurants looked so prim and proper and spotless.

I shook my head. Mmm! We'd never be able to enjoy one of the busted versions back home ever again.

Dubai seemed bigger than ever. The stretch to Abu Dhabi was quick, though, dotted with sparse landscapes and lots of billboards.

Mama pointed out the famous Sheikh Zayed Grand Mosque, made almost entirely of lavish marble with mosaics embedded in the pillars, gold-plated crystal chandeliers, domes etched with verses from the Quran in elegant Arabic, and a main building surrounded by sparkling pools. It welcomed more than fifty-five thousand visitors a day!

Lilly perked up at the mention of Yas Waterworld and Warner Bros. World amusement park.

Yash had never been more alert than at the mention of the world's fastest roller coaster at Ferrari World.

But nah, we weren't going to any of those cool places. Just to Mama's house in the suburbs of Abu Dhabi, to meet family and eat some more. Which was fine, because I was exhausted and hungry again, and the car snacks were only making me hungrier. Besides, my parents had taught us about hospitality early on—how important it was to show but also to be grateful for it. It was our language of endearment.

We drove less than two hours before crawling out of the car and being greeted by a butt-load of people. Were these, um, all family?

Lilly clung to me as a mass of aunties came at us with hugs and pinches to the cheek and just as many uncles with their pats to our head and offerings of candy and oh my god. Mummie had said she had some cousins here, not . . .

"A big-ass family," Yash had leaned over and muttered.

Lilly giggled, but she seemed to be in shock, too. She was usually never shy and went right up to people to say hello and whatever.

We stood off to the side and pinpointed a few kids our age, give or take a few years, before the whole family descended on us. As if the heat wasn't enough!

They smelled like candy and spices. I was having flashbacks to times when my parents dragged us all over India to see relatives. So much noise. So many bodies. So many conversations and laughter and gossip to totally consume us. Even though Lilly and I had been young the last time we'd gone to India, age didn't prevent my parents from pushing us onto the other kids to get to know them while they merrily talked on and on.

While Ankit Mama seemed like he was doing pretty well for himself, he didn't live in a big house. But he did *have* a house, whereas most of the family lived in apartments closer to work. Instead of a front yard, there was a gated wall between his property and the sidewalk with a concrete courtyard leading to the house. The windows and doors and small balconies were decorated with colorful string lights.

His modest home sucked us into halls and rooms with arches and smooth walls and efficient layouts. More string lights hung from the arches, paired with garlands of orange marigolds and threads of colorful silk blooms. Sparkling rangoli ornaments in peacock blue and green and gold were attached to the walls in spiral designs.

Slightly cooler air greeted us, along with the telltale aromas of good ole Gujarati cooking. Fried everything was in the air. Spices, both sweet and savory, hit my nostrils. A table near the wall was partially covered with sweets.

Diwali cooking had long been underway.

In an instant, it didn't matter that I'd never met these people before—that they were essentially strangers—because the soft music playing in the background, the vibrant decorations, the massive amount of cooking, the endless horde of people, and the festive vibe had me in full Diwali mode. It was one of those festivities that people couldn't help but bond over, no matter the gap between them. We weren't home, but in a sense, we were.

I took a deep breath and my shoulders slackened. A smile hiked up the corner of my mouth as I gazed out at my family melting into the crowd, my little sister cautiously mixing into a group of kids, and Yash being sought after by the only other boy our age. A trio of teenage girls were waving me over.

I couldn't take three steps without an auntie shoveling food into my hands. I laughed and took everything that was offered, indulging in sugary, nutty, spiced sweets and savory, crunchy, fried nasto. The faint scent of cha erupted from the kitchen, as a new batch simmered in a large steel pot that meant serious business. This family was *not* here to play.

"Come do rangoli with us!" one of the girls said, leading me to her cousins who were in a corner of the hall, hunched over beautiful designs of paisleys and peacocks and hearts made from fine, colored powder.

"Wow! That's gorgeous!" I said, kneeling on the tiles. Their perfectly straight lines, round corners, dips for 3-D effect, and blend of colors made my yearly designs look like a toddler had just smeared nonsense on the floor.

The older girl, maybe eighteen, was Mama's second child. The boy talking to Yash was the eldest. The other two girls were cousins. Basically, they were all my cousins. I dunno, figuring out terms of relation beyond immediate cousins and direct aunts and uncles was confusing, but relatives were relatives. And these ones happened to be super nice.

They spoke Gujarati to the older generation and English with me. They told me about growing up in Abu Dhabi, getting to visit India often, and how different their start of college was compared to Americans. For starters, their curriculum was way harder, and they had to pass an exam to graduate. The girls were very serious about education, and that was cool. It wasn't just because their parents, like mine, pushed education on them but because of how independent they wanted to be.

They showed me how to utilize straws to make rangoli designs, spoons to press down for smoother surfaces with shape, and forks for texture. While I managed to make a purple, white, and green flower, they had finished masterpieces of animals and diya with yellow and orange for the flame.

"Yay!" I said, proud of our work. I whipped out the camera from my mini backpack and snapped pictures.

"Cool! Are you a photographer?" they asked.

I nodded and told them about wanting to become a professional photographer, initially a bit uneasy because I didn't want them to look down on me. My cousins aimed to be engineers and business execs, and here I was in love with lighting. But they never made me feel less than. Instead, they boasted about photography schools there and leading magazines and ad companies that paid really well for talent. Which had me smiling.

This was nice, and I snapped a lot of pictures.

In the spirit of Diwali, we forgave, driving away darkness with light and starting with fresh, strong, optimistic beginnings. This was all my parents asked of me.

I looked at Yash through the lens of my camera, pretending to take pictures when, really, I was just observing him. We'd gone from womb buddies to diaper pals to best friends to this— whatever *this* was.

There went those butterflies, slowly waking up in the pit of my belly. I couldn't really ignore them anymore, but I didn't want to acknowledge them, either. Because what if Yash didn't like me the way that I was starting to like him? That was a big leap, when not long ago he was hurting because of me.

So, whatever new thing I was feeling, I had to keep it to myself.

We started aarti in front of a small shrine. When we were all singing and chanting and giving prayers and asking for blessings as we started anew during Diwali, a warmth hit me. And no, it was not the heat from the kitchen and all the warm bodies, because thank goodness they had AC and fans going strong. I felt content, whole, and utterly at peace.

I glanced at Yash through the corner of my eye as he was praying. We were going to be OK, and that had my eyes brimming with tears.

When we finished, Amina Mami presented to each of us one of her gifts of Diwali—an individual diya. They were small, ceramic candle holders in the shape of a teardrop with a tea light candle embedded in the middle. With each one, we lit our own.

Papa was at my side as we lit ours. The flame flickered against the wick and came to life, dousing us in a soft glow.

He said to me, "Be the light. No matter how much our flame dims over the year, this is a time for renewal. Don't let the negative energy keep you in the dark. Bring your flame back to life, let it roar, and be brighter than ever, beta."

I nodded, overcome with sentiment and longing. I smiled up at him, and he patted my head, a grin of his own radiating down at me.

Across the sea of flickering flames was Yash. He glanced up at me and smiled, little wrinkles crinkling at the corner of his eyes. Then he approached. Had he felt the moment, too? Or did he . . . maybe like me differently the way I was liking him? If so, would he say something on this most auspicious of days?

He grinned down at me, and I wanted to ask so badly. But then he quietly burped and said, "I know I ate a ton of snacks, but oh my god, I'm so hungry."

"Ew," I grunted. "Could you not?"

He laughed and followed the crowd toward the kitchen. Well, maybe that was saying enough? At least about the *sort* of like he had for me.

\* \* \*

Dinner. Was. *Huge.* I'd never seen so much home-cooked food in one house before in my entire life.

"We used to cook like this for weddings," Mummie said, noting my drop-dead stare at not pots, but *vats,* of food. Lilly could probably fit inside one.

They were full of delicious things like jeera rice, different curried veggie dishes, piping hot dhal, creamy shrikhand (that I didn't like because . . . yogurt). There were equally large platters of fried peppers, fritters of onion or potato bhajia, crunchy pappadum, and little, round, fluffy fried puri. That had been an event to watch! Two aunties making stiff dough, one auntie deftly pinching off just the right amount to roll into a ball, another patting it into flour and rolling into small discs and literally tossing it into frying oil, and one more auntie manning the frying. They were like an assembly line, and Mummie was loving every minute of it.

The men had been on cutting and peeling duty, a couple of them mixing and lifting.

We kids were left to arrange disposable plates, utensils, napkins, and cups. Yash and I, with a couple of the older cousins, ended up manning a buffet-style table, filling little cups with dhal, plopping all the fixings into small compartments with a side of sweets because it wouldn't be Diwali without them. Everything from nutty magas squares topped with almond slivers, orange jalebi, and plump and syrupy gulab jamun to diamond shapes of kaju katli, slightly bitter balls of ladvo, coconutty kopra pak, and so much more.

After dinner, all the kids went into the small backyard armed with sparklers.

"Here," Yash said, pushing a sizzling mini firecracker into my face.

I jumped back. "No!"

He laughed. "How are you so scared of a tiny sparkler?"

"Whose fault is that? You burned my eye when we were little."

"I barely singed your eyelashes."

"And I still don't have full growth in that corner of my eye. I'll have to start wearing fake lashes if they don't grow in before college!"

He chuckled and handed me a sparkler, a smirk on his face, his free hand tucked behind his back. There was something incredibly moving about being outside in the dark with only the string lights casting a dull, golden glow across Yash. The entirety of the right side of his face was consumed in shadow, while the left side had soft contours dusted by the luminescence of distant Diwali lights.

"Hold it right there," I told him.

Yash didn't move, as he'd probably guessed I was going for the camera hanging from my neck. He'd been in this situation a hundred times before, where he was in the middle of doing something and inspiration would strike, and he'd have to hold still and wait until I got my shot. Sometimes he was part of the shot and sometimes he wasn't.

I aimed and adjusted the lens and captured the silver light flickering off the sparkler like tiny explosions. Parts of his knuckles were in the frame, and the rest of him was blurred and doused in warm light. There were little orbs of colored light behind him, lens flare that actually looked elegant instead of being a blundered distraction.

I adjusted the lens again, in and out of focus, until I paused, staring into one of the most perfect pictures I'd ever taken. In this shot, the sparkler was blurred, and Yash's face was in focus. More specifically, his mouth. That impish smirk. That mischievous, laid-back partial smile of his rolled into the barest lift of his lips.

My heart palpitated against my ribs.

*No. Don't do it, brain, don't you dare think it!*

But then the butterflies in my gut and the tingles in my skin crashed into one another and my brain clicked. *You like him.* And once the brain admitted it, it was all I could think about.

"Did you get it? Because my fingers are about to burn off," he said.

"Yeah!" I replied.

He laughed. "OK, weirdo."

I'd never been so relieved to have Yash walk away. I caught more snaps of frozen time, particularly loving Lilly's full-on grin where she showed a lot of teeth in pure enjoyment. Those were the best.

In the corner of my eye, Yash slipped out the gate to the front courtyard. I followed, wondering where he was off to in the dark in the middle of a gigantic city.

He knelt beside the raised edge of a garden, pulling his phone out of his jacket. He adjusted and proceeded to take pictures.

I stepped closer, confused as two items came into view. "Why are you taking pictures of toys like you're paparazzi?"

Yash almost jumped out of his skin. "So sneaky." He went back to doing . . . whatever this was—positioning two stuffed cats.

"Whatcha doing?"

He turned the orange cat to face away from the gray one. He looked up at me and smiled sheepishly. "You remember those old cartoons we used to watch as kids? *Garfield and Friends*?"

"Oh yeah. So?" The show was based off a comic strip series that Yash used to effortlessly doodle when he procrastinated.

"You don't remember how Garfield was always, like in *every* episode, trying to ship Nermal off to Abu Dhabi?"

I thought for a second before realizing what Yash was trying to re-create.

"I figured, if we came all the way out here, then we have to rescue Nermal. And then Garfield and Nermal can make up and be buds."

"That's random, but awesome."

I squatted beside him and playfully pushed him aside with my hip. "Let me help, newbie. Poor Nermal."

Yash sat on his butt and laughed. "I took pictures of them at home, to re-create Garfield putting Nermal in a box and taping it up and writing TO: ABU DHABI."

I spoke while adjusting the toys in the dim lighting. "When we were kids watching this show, I always thought Abu Dhabi was a made-up place. Such a cool name, fun to say. I can't believe it took this long to connect the two!"

After we got the right shot, I sat on my butt beside him, slanted on the driveway and leaning toward the gate. Yash nudged me with a shoulder and showed me the pictures he took at home, complete with fake label sticker on a shipping box and everything.

"Who did you do this for?"

"For myself. When am I ever going to be in Abu Dhabi again? I thought it was funny," he said with a shrug.

It was. And also adorable.

"When we go back, I want to get pics of them sitting in an airplane seat, buckled up together to prove to the world that Nermal is safe and sound and forgave Garfield and that they ended up being best friends."

I giggled. "All right, I can get behind that. Oh! We gotta find one of those I HEART ABU DHABI magnets and get a shot of Nermal around town with it."

Yash laughed. "Garfield basically gave Nermal a free trip to a cool city."

# CHAPTER NINETEEN

Later that night, a vibration went off in the back of my throat, all nasally and irritating, startling me awake in the back row of Ankit Mama's SUV. Nothing like getting knocked out on a car ride, drooling and snoring so hard that my own snoring jostled me awake and, oh yeah, to be doing so against Yash.

"Girls are disgusting," he muttered.

I wiped the drool from my cheek and chin. Oh my god, why was there so much? "Girls are awesome," I countered instead of shying away in mortification.

Yash yawned and rubbed his eyes, which meant he'd probably been asleep, too.

When Mama pulled up to the hotel, we all said our thanks and farewells. As we kids started trotting inside, he told Mummie, "You should come to our mandir tomorrow for Diwali!"

I froze and pivoted on my heels. Oh no. We did *not* come all this way to experience Diwali in a mandir. We could've done that back home.

My parents nodded vigorously, because they were so into mandir activities. Their temple was their sanctuary, and that was cool, and even better that they could fit right in at any mandir anywhere, but I wanted to see Diwali in Dubai. Like, outside on the water where the fireworks happened.

The parents looked like they were seriously considering the idea, and I looked at Yash with worry. His brow was creased like he was thinking the same thing.

We knew enough about our place in the hierarchy to know that we couldn't pipe up and speak out against this. Our parents might've let us go here and there, a couple of places, if we checked in often, but no way were they going to let us stay here if they went to a different city.

They took their sweet time saying goodbye, as was the custom in our family to take forty-five minutes to say "See ya."

I groaned and headed upstairs with Yash and Lilly, grabbing a couple of dates from the gold platter box in the lounge, because, of course. That's what it was there for.

Yash scrolled across his cell and Lilly leaned against the elevator wall, looking absolutely tuckered out. Her hair was a mess and her eyes droopy with sleep.

"We should go see the diya display tonight," Yash said.

I gaped at him quizzically.

"I mean, I'm going. Do you want to come?"

He turned his screen to me, showing a marvelous display of little Diwali lights at the same Dubai Fountain where we'd watched the water show.

I smiled. "How are you not tired?"

"I slept in the car and it's hard to sleep at night. Jet leg, I guess? Besides, if our parents decide to go back to Abu Dhabi tomorrow, then we're screwed. We're going to miss all the concerts and fireworks and shows. Even if Abu Dhabi goes all out for Diwali, we're going to be stuck at someone's house and then at mandir. I'm sure it'll be nice and all for our parents, but we're going to miss so much. Maybe I'll come back one day just for Diwali but probably not. You?"

I shook my head. This was a cool place to visit, but visiting again was not a thing I foresaw in my future. Seemed like an awfully big, expensive trip when Diwali was meant to be spent with families, and it was unlikely our family would plan another trip like this one.

"Let's go," I said, finding a new wave of energy and excitement over the idea of capturing some more amazing pictures. And spending time with Yash.

We looked to Lilly to see if she wanted to come.

She yawned and lazily pushed herself off the wall when the elevator door opened at our floor. "I'm so tired. I ate too much."

Lilly couldn't stop herself from eating a full meal plus three helpings of sweets, because she was 85 percent sweet tooth.

"Just us, then?" Yash asked.

We parted to our respective doors. "Yeah. See you in a bit?"

He nodded, and we went into our rooms. Lilly kicked off her shoes and fell face-first onto the bed. "Parents gonna let you go in the middle of the night? How's it open?"

"The website says the mall is open until one in the morning."

She groaned into the bedspread.

I used the restroom and washed up, noting how my mehndi had already darkened into a deep orange color, then met Yash in the hallway with my camera around my neck. "Hope they let us go."

He pushed for the elevator. "I'm sure they will."

"Hmm. Must be nice to be a guy and have parents who let you run around a foreign city all by yourself in the middle of the night."

We stepped into the elevator, and he pressed for the main floor. "Yeah. I keep forgetting my privilege. But this *is* one of the world's safest cities and it's the night before Diwali, so there's a lot going on. Plus, it's only ten. I get home from hanging out with friends later than this."

I stepped out of the elevator first. "Again, must be nice to be a boy."

We met the parents outside. They were still gabbing away.

I elbowed Yash and said, "You ask them. They'll be more likely to let us go."

He asked, and they actually relented. In fact, Ankit Mama offered to drive us, even though there were plenty of taxis pulled up to the hotel, picking up and dropping off loads of people.

"You sure you don't want to see it?" I asked our parents.

They waved us off, and I hoped they weren't sacrificing experiencing more Dubai things because they wanted us to get reacquainted. I knew that look in their eyes, that gleam of unfettered hope that we could be best friends again.

Well, I wasn't going to argue. This was what I'd so desperately wanted, to get out into the city (somewhat) alone (OK, not tethered to parents) and take pictures of everything that inspired art.

We profusely thanked Ankit Mama as he pulled up to Dubai Mall, where celebrations were going strong.

"No problem! Remember to only use taxi service when you go back. You remember your hotel and address?" he asked.

"Hah," I confirmed, sounding like my mother.

"Don't forget to message your parents, huh? When you get to the show and before you leave and where you're going. Are you sure you don't need me to come with you?"

I smiled. "No, Mama. But thank you! And we just messaged them that we got here."

We said our goodbyes, and off he went.

As we walked up the steps of the mall, Yash commented, "Dude's super nice."

Frosty AC air hit us the second we walked through the main doors. I shivered and clutched the camera around my neck.

"I kinda wanted to see the fountain show at night. Supposed to be even better with the lights," Yash said as we walked down a familiar hall toward the fountain outside.

We emerged from throngs of people into what was essentially a concert. Bollywood music played, or was that coming from a live band where larger crowds had gathered?

Yash grinned. "Guess we don't need to go to Bollywood Parks for a concert after all!"

"But the rides!" I contested. "I still want to go."

The air was crisp and chilled compared to what it had been all day. Though the night sky was near pitch-black and speckled with stars, there was plenty of light coming from every which way. Against the wall of the mall were lit mosaics creating the telltale golden diya lamp holder, encrusted with red and green jewels, with a dancing flame on the edge.

To the right, the Burj Khalifa loomed tall in the sky, sleek and dark gray, lined with lights at the corners, with the windows lit to spell out HAPPY DIWALI.

Ahead was what appeared to be a concert well underway.

To the left was the fountain where we'd seen a water and light show just the other day. The water was tranquil, quiet, but upon it were hundreds of floating, lit diya. Little golden holders, in the shape of teardrops, small enough to fit in my palm, swayed atop the pool. On each one was a flame, the light of Diwali, the essence of good triumphing over evil, and the beginning of newer and better things.

The majesty of the fountain took my breath away and I knew in an instant where the perfect shot would be.

"There!" I said, excitedly pointing to the other side.

"Wait!" Yash called, and hurried after me as I weaved through crowds.

I caught my breath, adjusted my camera, and knelt on one knee to capture what I hoped would be the winning picture for the internship: the star-dusted sky overhead, the mightiness of the Burj Khalifa in the distance, and the flickering flames of hundreds of diya in the forefront, their light casting dancing reflections against a still pool. Nothing seemed to capture Diwali better than this moment.

# CHAPTER TWENTY

We walked around, following the crowds, eating and drinking. As if we hadn't had enough food today! And coffee? Why did we drink coffee so late? Because it was Turkish coffee!

Yash scrunched up his face after taking a sip from a tiny cup of thick, brown liquid. "It's pretty, but tastes like sludge. It's so strong. Why would they serve this to kids? At night?"

I laughed, taking another sip, pretending like it didn't bother me. OK, facts: We were American kids who liked our "coffee" sugary with some type of creamy filler, syrups, and loaded with whipped cream and sprinkles. We were not hardcore coffee enthusiasts, but when in Dubai, do what the Emiratis do.

"Not like we're ever going to get to try this again," I said. "Unless you know someplace that I don't."

"I know Starbucks."

"Basic."

He chuckled. "OK, Ms. Loves-Everything-Pumpkin-Spice. *Who's* basic?"

"But it's so good!"

He leaned an elbow against the tall standing table we'd been sharing and popped a pistachio baklava into his mouth. Next came candied dates stuffed with dried fruit. The slightly sweet, chewy taste reminded me of the Tutti Frutti ice cream from the Indian grocery store.

After our absurdly sweet and caffeinated late-night snack, we checked in with our parents. We left the mall and perused stalls catering to the influx of Diwali tourists.

"Hey, look," I said, holding up a magnet.

"The mother of all magnets," he said, taking the metallic slab from me in a sort of reverence. His grin spread across his face.

"Told you we'd find it."

Yash bought the souvenir in a heartbeat. There was no way we were getting out of here without pictures of Nermal with an I ❤ ABU DHABI magnet.

While I went through more items, wondering if Tamara would wear a kaftan top or if Mummie would use a pashmina shawl, Yash wandered off to just outside the row of stalls in the narrow alleyway.

We kept glancing at each other to make sure the other was always in view until I got distracted by decorative oil lamps, the type one might associate with the *Aladdin* movie, but like, extra. These came in all sizes and colors. Some gold, others red, but all encrusted with raised, painted surfaces to look like jewels. The top opened, but the nozzle was closed, so you couldn't really use it, not that it was a real oil lamp. But so pretty. I bet Lilly would love this.

I checked out the price. Eh. Guess she'll never miss what she's never seen.

When I checked on Yash, he was busy on his tablet, scribbling furiously. He was so into whatever he was doing that he didn't see me approaching.

Yash had always been a great artist using various techniques with ever-evolving skills, but he'd stalled on drawing for a long time to focus on grades and clubs and the one sport a year he tried his hand at. FYI, no sport stuck. He simply wasn't a dedicated athlete. But he was amazing with art. Or so I'd thought.

Seeing the digital brushstrokes of the stall and the soft curves of people walking by and what looked like maybe me—or any girl really—in one of the shops made me realize just how much of Yash's life I'd missed. His technique had jumped a hundredfold, from amazing sketches to digital masterpieces, the kind one might see in animation or video games.

He dabbed here and there, swiftly adding a layer and colors and wow, I had no idea that was how digital drawings happened. I really thought it was all done line by line, scratch by scratch like paper and ink.

"That's so awesome," I said.

He startled to find me nearly nose-deep in his tablet. He immediately tapped it off and tucked it away. "Can I help you?"

I frowned, leaning away. "Oh. Sorry, I'm doing it again. Minding my own business . . ."

The rest of the night came and went as we explored what we could, surrounded by music and lights and lots of conversations . . . just none of our own. Yash was as much into his private drawings as I was into my photography.

The quiet of the taxi ride back and the elevator up was deafening after so much raucous noise. I shivered outside my door and wondered if Yash would hug me good night. Or had that last hug been a pity hug, because I'd been crying?

He paused at my side and then said, "Have a good night."

He walked to his door, pulling out his room card, and looked over to me.

I put on my best smile and chastised myself for feeling so heartbroken that he didn't go in for a hug. "Thanks for tonight. It was really cool."

But then he grinned, his smile reaching his eyes so that they crinkled at the corners. It was nice to see him happy. Dang, Yash was adorable.

# CHAPTER TWENTY-ONE

S leep fewer hours, shower in quick bursts, eat copious amounts of food, and do stuff" was our go-to plan for this vacation, and it was starting to wear me down. I felt it on our fourth full day in Dubai. Staying out so late last night had me groggy the following morning, but there was no time to waste because it was the main day, the actual day of . . .

"Happy Diwali!" Mummie crooned as we giddily admired the lush, maroon, mehndi-stained designs on our hands.

We didn't have presents to exchange or a ton of food to prep while we ate. It seemed so weird not to be doing our own rangoli designs in a designated corner near the foyer, or turning on all the string lights, or prepping and lighting diya. But we *were* getting our outfits ready for later, for when we would attend mandir.

Amina Mami had said that many didn't get super dressed up for Diwali here, as it was more casual and spent outdoors with all the celebrations. Made sense. Probably difficult to run around to all the concerts and fireworks in a heavy lehenga, but we were going to do it anyway.

First off, it was a day to get extra. While we looked nice for weekly mandir activities (in what Mummie called "everyday" Indian clothes of salwar kameez), we only dressed up big for festivities, weddings, and baby showers (trust me, Indian baby showers get extra). Matching bangles and costume jewelry for sure. Our mehndi game was strong.

Second, there were few Indians in my circle who didn't want to be extra anytime they had a good excuse.

Third, we were sure to get lots of pictures. It was a yearly tradition to get nice family pictures, but certainly going all out in Dubai meant a lot more pictures would be had.

For this morning, we dressed in nice "everyday" clothes of new jeans and slacks and blouses, but nothing too fancy. Yet.

Diwali, although not to be misinterpreted as a commercial reason to buy expensive brand clothing and turn up noses at who was wearing what, was first and foremost a time of renewal. Maybe Emiratis and expats and tourists here wouldn't dress superfine today, but we upheld the tradition of living the day of new beginnings with clean bodies dressed in new clothes.

As Papa kept mentioning, "Today is a day of reflection. Let us meditate on what makes life worthwhile and wholesome and blessed and get rid of the things that don't help us create that life. We buy new things for today, clothes and food and gifts and whatever else, sometimes small, sometimes big, sometimes inexpensive, sometimes pricey. But the point isn't how rich we look."

We all nodded in agreement.

"The point is to start fresh, to be clean and cleansed. Outer appearances are only so much. Our inner self has to mirror our outer self; otherwise what is the point? May we all unload negative energy and the darkness that perpetually tries to consume us."

Mummie tacked on a knowing look. Even though she spoke to the room as she got ready, her words were mainly aimed at me.

"Releasing negativity and darkness is only good for our souls and our lives. Now is the best time to do so. Otherwise, you not only diminish your own light, but the damage can be long-lasting and harder to correct over time. Once too much darkness surrounds you, it snuffs out your light, and others will see this. Our flame is too precious to let it die, and it's too valuable to let someone else's lack of light suck the life out of ours. Remember this, today of all days, but also every day."

We nodded in agreement and continued getting ready for the big day.

I laid out my lehenga on the bed beside Lilly's. I smoothed out the soft lavender skirt with large gray, metallic blooms. On top, I flattened out the matching quarter-sleeved blouse and all gray dupatta. The nice thing about the dupatta was that if I got chilly, I could wrap it around myself like a shawl.

Lilly's outfit was bright pink with bold geometric teal and blue designs.

Mummie had hers on her bed; dark green with speckles of pink and yellow and blue. It matched Papa's kurta, a solid dark blue with a slightly lighter blue metallic design. All of our evening clothes were ready.

"How was last night out on the town?" Papa asked, giving Mummie a look, like they'd been patiently waiting all of two minutes to inquire.

"It was fun!" I replied. "You really missed a spectacular diya show. And then we tried Turkish coffee and went to some shops. They had music playing and sales and lights, but we didn't buy anything."

"So, you and Yash are getting along?" he probed.

"Yes! It's hard to stay mad at him when we're doing all these fun things."

He cocked a brow.

"And of course, we had a chat, so things are smoothing over." At least I hoped Yash was enjoying being around me.

My parents beamed and I turned from them to ready my camera supplies before they tried to pry for details.

"We're going to meet for breakfast and then start our day!" Mummie announced.

I was helping Lilly brush her hair into a high ponytail with a braid on the side when I asked, "Are we really going back to Abu Dhabi to spend Diwali day with your family?"

"You didn't like them?" Mummie frowned.

"No! No. They were all supercool and we had a blast, but we shouldn't miss all the uniquely Dubai events. When will we ever get to do this again?"

"When will we ever get to spend Diwali with these relatives again?" she countered.

Oh my lord, there was no arguing with my mother if she wanted to do something her way. I couldn't say, "Who cares about people we've only met once!"

All I could sputter was, "But . . . *Dubai*."

"What of it?" She raised her brows as if daring me to offer even *one* argument in favor of ditching her relatives.

I patted the braid against Lilly's head to signal that I was done and turned to Mummie. "Diwali is about family but, like, our immediate family. We saw relatives yesterday and probably will see them again before we leave. But why spend Diwali day in a mandir or at a house when we do that every year? Dubai has so much more. It's not like Austin, where just the people in the community get into it. Here, the entire city is into it. It's almost like India, and it would be cool to experience a place where everyone knows the holiday and everyone is into it and feel like we and the city aren't separate. You got that growing up in India."

I nodded toward Lilly and added, "We never got that. We've only ever been in a bubble celebrating our culture. Here, there's no bubble. We're not . . . *othered*. Not everyone here is the same, but we're part of the whole."

Mummie's expression softened as she confessed, "We're not spending the day in Abu Dhabi, beta."

Lilly and I both blew out a breath. She slapped my hand behind our backs in a low five. Thank goodness.

"I'd love to," Mummie went on, "but we didn't spend all this money and come all this way *not* to experience Diwali in Dubai. I adore my cousins. I can't believe how welcoming they are, but this will be an experience for us all. Diwali is family time, and we're going to spend it together. None of this 'we go here, and you go there.' So, yes, we'll experience the festivities, but we will also attend mandir."

Lilly and I groaned, then snapped our mouths shut.

Mummie gave us a look of warning. "Mandir is part of Diwali. We won't spend all day there or even too long, but we'll go. It's just around the corner. Besides, some of the family might come here today."

"Can *we* at least go to the Palm or Al Seef and see fireworks?"

"The mandir should have fireworks," Papa suggested.

Lilly responded, "Probably not. I read fireworks are limited and only certain places are allowed to use them. Makes sense, it's so dry here."

I added, "Yeah, and it's nothing like fireworks over the water. Besides." I tapped the camera around my neck. "I might never get a shot at photographs like these again."

We thought all was good and handled when we met Yash and his parents in the hallway to get breakfast. But while we stood in line to get into the restaurant, the parents got to talking about mandir again.

OK, look, I wasn't against attending mandir for worship during a major holiday. Going was a given. But c'mon!

Like a switch had been flicked on, Lilly, Yash, and I exchanged panicked glances. Yash mouthed, "WTF," when his parents agreed to spending more than just "a little time" at mandir.

I wanted to cry.

Yash sidestepped to stand closer to me with a nod that said, "I got this."

He cleared his throat to get their attention.

My parents were never going to deny him—he was practically the son they never had—but also they'd been doting on him more than ever since our fight. Yash shouldn't have to rescue me every time, though. That wasn't his job. He shouldn't feel like he had to all the time, either, and I didn't want to feel like I needed him to. Of course, he could've been stepping in for himself. He for sure didn't want to spend the best part of the best day inside, and he probably knew his parents weren't going to let him run around by himself on one of the busiest days of the year.

When our parents turned to us, when Yash opened his mouth to speak, I jumped in and asked, full of excitement and optimism, "What if Yash comes with me to see fireworks? Please, Papa? Then you can enjoy the mandir peacefully for as long as you want, and we'd at least spent most of the day together."

"How about," Mummie interjected, "we all dress in our Diwali best and go to mandir together, early evening, and do puja. Then you kids can escape into the shows?"

"Uh, re-really?" I stuttered, hoping but never expecting her to go for it. After all, she'd always hammered in that Diwali was family time. And with this being the last Diwali before college, it seemed extra special. So . . . what was her endgame here?

"Why don't you come with us?" I found myself asking.

"We always do more religious things at mandir during this time. It feels important."

Oh my god. But OK, that was cool. The fact that they'd even let us go was something else.

"Lilly, you coming with?" I asked her, knowing how much she loved fireworks and how much she loathed sitting still while our parents gabbed on forever with other people.

She bit her bottom lip and looked from me to Yash and back to me when he raised an eyebrow in questioning. There was no reason for her to hesitate. Sweets might've been her weakness, but fireworks were her kryptonite. She lived for them. Aside from the excitement and awe factor, she couldn't just open the fridge when she wanted them like she could with sweets. So, what was the holdup?

"Lilly?" I nudged. Had her thoughts totally wandered off?

She let out a big sigh and smiled. "Nah, I'm good."

Our mouths dropped open. Yash and I gawked at her. Was she feeling OK?

"What? Why not?" I asked while silently praying: *Please, lord, don't let Lilly's refusal to go with us alter my parents' decision to let us go.* On the other hand, it might bode better for us if we couldn't potentially lose my little sister.

"No. I wanna hang out where there's sweets and food," she replied. Sure, that made sense. Sort of. But there was probably going to be food carts galore out there tonight, and who could say no to that?

"Oh. OK . . . well, if you change your mind, let me know. There's still lots of time left. You sure you don't want to see fireworks?"

Lilly grinned, looking again from Yash then back to me. "I'm sure there'll be *great* fireworks."

I looked to Yash and shrugged. "Guess it's just us?"

He scratched the back of his head, his cheeks flushed. "Yeah."

Mmmkay . . . what was up with everyone?

And then it struck me. Wait. *Wait* one hot minute. Were my parents and Lilly essentially setting us up to go out alone?

It wasn't as if Yash and I hadn't spent enough time together on this trip, and we'd had our talk. We'd made bigger strides in the past few days than we had all summer.

But, whatever. I wasn't going to question them and lose what could quite possibly be my last chance at capturing *the* perfect picture.

# CHAPTER TWENTY-TWO

After breakfast, we all went to Dubai Parks and rode all the rides. Then we went to Bollywood Parks at the end of the multi-themed amusement park. There was just something surreal about being in a theme park based entirely on Indian cinema. The rides and architecture were based on Bollywood movies and there was lots of Indian food. The music playing over the speakers were all hit Hindi songs.

Afterward, we sat in the grassy park area, near the water, and watched live Bollywood singers and dancers. The place was packed. So many people came to see performers dressed to the nines in sparkling, colorful kurtas and lehengas, complete with all the blingy jewelry.

Musicians played music.

Singers sang.

Dancers danced.

For a minute, I thought we'd disappeared into a Bollywood movie and were about to bust out in a choreographed dance.

No matter where we went or what we did that day, Lilly attached herself to my parents. The two of us were usually together; she liked my pace better and could do more rides and run faster to the next thing. But I found myself being pushed toward Yash more and more. And I didn't mind it. Not one bit.

As Yash and I sat on the grass in our best jeans and T-shirts, our arms crushed against each other, his faint smell of body spray and deodorant, his hair flopping over his eyes, I lowered my gaze to my palms and smiled, not realizing at first that Yash was snapping my photo.

"What are you doing?" I asked.

He smirked and played on his phone before showing me his screen. He'd posted one of those pictures to his social media, and yanked the phone away every time I tried to grab it.

"Yash! Delete that! You never take good pictures of me."

He laughed. "This *is* a good picture!"

I groaned and went through my phone to see what picture he'd posted. I stilled. Well, dang. For once he had captured a decent shot. It was of me smiling down at my dark-stained mehndi with the crowds sprawled out on the grass behind me.

But the caption was the best part. *Find yourself someone who looks at you the way she looks at mehndi.*

I cracked up. "OK. That was pretty good."

He took my hand, and a shockwave went through me. I froze as he turned my hand over and lightly ran a finger over the maroon mehndi designs. My breath hitched. How could a soft, fleeting touch on my palm make my entire body shake?

"Nice. It turned out well," he commented.

"Yeah," I muttered.

He cleared his throat and released my hand. I immediately

busied myself by snapping shots on my camera. The dads were most likely live WhatsApping the entire concert to a large chat group of uncles. Lilly was glued to the concert, bobbing her shoulders to the upbeat music as she nibbled on food.

One song ended and segued beautifully into the next. Lilly's eyes went wide, her mouth dropping as she slowly turned her head toward me. It was her favorite song from her favorite movie, and I'd picked up the end of the last song during the change to catch her reaction.

My camera was at the ready, focused on my little sister as surprise and excitement engulfed her entire expression.

Snap. Snap. Snap.

She squealed, her fists balled up and pumping. "Yes!"

Then she threw her arms out and yelled, "I love this song!"

We all laughed, even as Papa swerved his phone to record her. She didn't even care enough to grunt at him or tell him to stop. She was on her knees and half dancing. And now the whole family was into it. Forget if we looked silly. There was nothing like an elaborate Bollywood musical number to bring an Indian family together.

* * *

After a long and glorious day at Bollywood Parks, we returned to the hotel exhausted. At least, I was. Since we had a sizable break in the early evening, I hopped into the shower, hoping to wake up and wash off all the theme park, seeing that Yash, Lilly, and I rode *so many* rides and spilled more than one drink and ice cream. I didn't even care if everyone was in our room.

When I emerged, I was expecting everyone to still be talking away. Instead, I found Lilly sprawled out asleep, taking up the entire bed but somehow managing not to disturb the edge where our parents' outfits lay.

Why was she on their bed? Because Yash had passed out in our bed, but he took up a very slim edge so as not to disrupt our clothes.

And where were the parents? They were probably at mandir helping set up because that was exactly the sort of thing they'd be doing.

The shower hadn't woken me up. It had relaxed me, making me feel even more tired. I moved the clothes from my bed and draped them over the backs of two chairs, then walked back to the bed. Dude. Why was he in *my* bed? He had his own. He had an entire room!

Even if I moved the clothes off the other bed, Lilly was too much of a hog for me to slip in anywhere.

I stood over Yash, arms crossed. Did mind-bending work? Did we still have our Jean Grey and Professor X telepathic mutant powers? No. After the longest two minutes of my life in which I willed him to wake up and move, I caved and crashed beside him.

The bed was big enough for two, maybe even three, people. And we'd fallen asleep next to each other before. It wasn't that big a deal.

The room was icy-cold because Lilly and my parents were apparently part yeti. I shivered, hurrying to get underneath the blanket and shimmying into a curled position as quickly as possible, my eyelids already drifting closed.

As I slept, I must've followed the heat source because I was practically face-planting into Yash's armpit. He stirred awake, and I froze.

"Sorry," I mumbled, and went to move away. "No, wait. You're the one in my bed. Why can't you go to your room?"

"Bro. I'm tired. Just sleep," he muttered.

"Don't 'bro' me."

He didn't move.

"Fine. If you're not getting out of my bed." I pulled my knees to my chest between us and slid my hands underneath his shirt.

He yelped. "God. Are you made of ice?"

"I'm coldhearted, remember?"

He pried open one eye and frowned before shifting to drape an arm around me, pulling me into a hug.

My heart nearly exploded. My body was reacting so chaotically, my pulse raging. WTF? My *like* like of Yash was turning into an all-out crush, and I might actually implode if I didn't tell someone. But definitely not Yash.

He mumbled, "You're not always coldhearted, Nikki. I mean, you were since the fight, so like, damn, defrost already, woman."

I pressed my icy hands into his back.

He hissed.

"Shut up and go back to sleep, bed-thief."

"I'm sure there are mittens somewhere. Or we can wrap your ice talons in towels." He quietly laughed, his body rumbling against mine. My stomach did all sorts of flips as I melted against him. Part of my brain tried to stay awake to question reality but the next thing I knew, we were both passed out.

Thank the lord that Lilly woke up first, because if our parents saw us entangled in limbs and sheets in a bed, they might finally realize that maybe Yash and I were getting closer than they'd intended us to.

Lilly was perched on a chair dead ahead, watching us.

I stirred awake, muttering, "Creeper."

I wiped the drool from my mouth before Yash awoke. We sat up at the same time. He scratched his head, looking away. I froze.

Lilly clucked her tongue. "Y'all dating, or what?"

"What?" I guffawed, and Yash had never jumped to his feet so fast.

"People who are dating, or married, sleep together."

"Oh my god. Not exactly true but also, that's not what 'sleep together' means, so stop saying that."

Yash was at the front door, his face beet red, putting his shoes on as I scurried out of bed asking, "What time is it? Where are our parents? I can't believe we fell asleep on Diwali. We probably missed so much stuff."

"Papa messaged that they'll be back soon, and to start getting ready," Lilly said as I checked our family group chat, and sure enough, they *had* gone to mandir to help.

Next to the WhatsApp was a notification from social. Probably Tamara checking in about the trip or homework or whatever gossip I was missing. I'd have to check that later.

"I'll see you guys in a bit," Yash announced on his way out the door.

A sly smile spread across Lilly's face when Yash was gone. "Just admit you guys are into each other."

"What! We just fell asleep, and why do you sleep across the entire bed like that? I didn't have a choice. Why was he in here, anyway?"

"He fell asleep while the parents were talking, and then I pretended to fall asleep to keep from having to go with them. And then I actually fell asleep." She grinned sheepishly.

The things we did to *not* help out.

"We gotta get ready!" I exclaimed, and went to the bathroom to put on my makeup before everyone came back and crowded the mirror.

I managed to apply just the right amount without foundation streaks or lopsided eyeliner or eye shadow dusting beneath my eyes or specs of mascara all over the place. I took a few selfies before I started on my hair and opened social to send Tamara pics.

Except, when I checked my notifications, they weren't from her. They were from Jalebi_Writer.

My heart skipped a beat. Wow! He was messaging me first!

**Jalebi_Writer:** Hey! I just wanted to say HAPPY DIWALI to you and your family!

I grinned extra hard when I replied.

**Nikki:** Hi! Happy Diwali to you and your family, too!

Tamara had also messaged, wishing us a fun holiday and hoping things were working out with Yash . . . seeing that he'd actually posted a pic of me on social!

**Tamara: So, uh, getting close, huh?**

I bit my lip and tapped out of the message. Just thinking of Yash had my stomach tied into knots, but in a really pleasant way. Like a roller coaster. Sorta scary but definitely thrilling. And darn Tamara and her acuteness. All she had to do was see one picture and she just somehow knew.

Well, I was dying to tell someone, and she was the safest bet.

With the infuriating and uncontrollable need to tell someone, anyone, I got onto social to message Tamara really quick.

**Nikki: OMG! Help! I think I'm crushing on Yash!!!**

Ah! That felt good! Even though Tamara wouldn't check her messages until later.

I then glossed over the group family chat in WhatsApp to make sure there wasn't anything important happening, before hopping back onto social to realize the worst thing had happened.

I almost screamed.

I had *not* messaged Tamara, but I had, in fact, messaged . . . Jalebi_Writer.

Oh my lord. I for sure could never chat with him after that. I shook my head, brushing off the humiliation. Ugh. At least he was offline. I hit the "delete message" option, but wasn't sure if that removed the message from his end, too.

Anyway, no time! I hurried to fix my hair and rushed out of the bathroom as my parents came in.

"I have to go!" Mummie said, practically pushing me out of the way.

Lilly was already dressed. I fixed her hair for her. "Two braids, please," she said, handing me ribbons.

My parents didn't take long to get ready, as Papa was just changing clothes and Mummie wasn't a makeup person and preferred her hair to stay in its perpetual, long braid that reached her waist.

Mummie and I slipped on costume jewelry and lots of bangles to match our outfits in alternating bands of color and gold. Lilly didn't like all that, so she waited on the bed, where she was attached to her tablet.

"We brought you something!" Mummie told me, shimmying with excitement.

Papa flashed a smile at us as he handed her a newspaper-wrapped item. From it, Mummie pulled out three long strings of sewn white jasmine blooms.

I. Squealed.

"I know how much you love wearing mogra. The mandir had these. Of course we had to get them for you."

I hopped up and down, clapping my hands, turning from her so she could fasten the string to my hair, to the side that was secured with a sparkling gold clip. Then she twisted another one into Lilly's hair, lacing her braids together. Finally Mummie pulled her own hair into a bun and fastened a string of flowers around it.

I closed my eyes and inhaled the light fragrance of jasmine and twirled back and forth so that my skirt swished around my ankles. Tonight was going to be epic.

Yash and his parents were waiting in the lounge when we went down to meet them. And why yes, wearing a lehenga had me feeling all kinds of princess. There were knowing nods and head bows every time we passed other Indians, which was like every other step. Some were as dressed up as we were, others more casual, but we all knew what this was about.

I had my camera in my mini backpack and adjusted the strap when we turned the corner to the sitting area. The moms immediately gushed over how nice the families looked, the dads armed with their phones to take pictures.

"Yash. Come," Pranav Uncle said.

Yash looked up and did a double take seeing me. His cheeks flushed as he swept his hair away from his eyes only to have it flop back over his forehead. He had my heart beating in a way that I didn't know it could: chaotic and wild.

He stood, wearing the heck out of a dark green kurta with shiny designs in silver and gold. He looked like he'd stepped out of one of many billboards around the hotel of Indian models in nice threads.

Papa asked a staff member to take our picture, and he happily obliged.

The moms pushed Yash and me together, our arms grazing as I sucked in a breath and found myself holding it. We both stilled, and if awkward could be a visible substance, then we were both clearly covered in it.

He scratched his neck and said, "You look really nice, Nikki."

"I know," I croaked. *Smooth, girl, smooth.* "Um, you look nice, too."

"Nice" was an understatement. Yash looked totally crush-worthy. And he smelled the part, too.

"Thanks for putting on cologne or body spray or whatever," I muttered, trying to play it cool but my joke falling flat.

He smirked and looked ahead at the camera phone–wielding staff member in black and white. "I mean, if you're going to face-plant into my armpits again, I guess I have to. I'm just trying to save your life."

I scoffed, feeling a sense of relief in our familiar snark. "Save my life? Yeah, that's the truth. I almost suffocated from the fumes."

He snickered, flashing a few teeth.

I swallowed and swerved my attention to the camera. When had teeth become so sexy?

# CHAPTER TWENTY-THREE

Diwali was in the air. A bit magical. A bit nostalgic. All excitement.

Everything was so enchanting and perfect and heartwarming. I'd never seen so many Indians out and about for the occasion, some dressed extra, some ordinary, as we walked down a few streets to the mandir. Must've been the clothes that had me feeling fancy, because I walked with a strut, my chin high, excitement bubbling through my blood. No hunched shoulders or dragging feet.

Some only glanced our way, but most grinned and waved and shouted, "Happy Diwali!" in passing.

Was this how Americans felt during Christmas? Like everyone just celebrated it, or they assumed everyone knew what today was, and it was thrown around in a joyful, anticipatory atmosphere boldly shimmering with holiday spirit out in the open?

At the end of our little merry parade was a small but brilliant mandir covered in festive decorations of string lights, rangoli designs, garlands of marigolds, and numerous displays. Crowds excitedly met new people and mingled.

Tonight was like being back home, but better. Diwali in Dubai really did feel more universal and less othering. Diwali here felt more welcomed and celebrated by everyone instead of like a niche holiday for a bunch of brown immigrants. So much so that I didn't mind aunties asking about everything from grades to college majors like they were sizing me up for their sons' future wifey plans. I didn't even mind a long service of worship and an even longer service reminding us of the meaning of Diwali.

The day's speeches stuck with me even as my thoughts kept wandering to Yash.

"Diwali, my friends, is a time of reflection and renewal, a time to rediscover all the things that are truly important to us. This is a day designated for recommitting to upholding those precious things. I'm not talking about money and cars and houses. Yes, we can be thankful for our abundant blessings, but take a deeper look. Whether it's health or family . . . or friends . . . Diwali is the time to rekindle our light, find our strength, and bring ourselves back to what's vital.

"Throughout the year, we stray from our paths, don't we? We get ambushed by stress and unfortunate events. But we must be the light in the world. Therefore, we cannot let our flame die. And nothing, my friends, kills our flame faster than anger and hate."

Those words brought back what had happened between Yash and me. We made mistakes. I held on to a grudge and risked something very special. And although we'd talked through it and were mending the fractures in our once-solid foundation, the concept of renewal hit harder in this moment. Like a ceremonial cleansing. A weight off my shoulders, chasing away darkness by allowing my light to grow. It didn't just affect me.

\* \* \*

Mandir had been chock-full of vibrancy, and I thought nothing could outdo it. Until Yash and I broke off from the family and arrived at Al Seef for the main event.

My breath caught as we, decked out in our finest, emerged from the taxi and stepped onto the streets where everyone, everywhere breathed Diwali.

Girls twirled around for pictures in glimmering outfits, and guys smoothed over their best clothes. Booths sold food and sweets and juices. There was even an area set up where women painted palms with mehndi in front of expectant lines. Music flared up around us.

Palm trees lining Dubai Creek were wrapped in both white and colored lights. Lights everywhere! Twinkles against the darkness breathing life into the night.

A ceremony was taking place in the middle of crowds too thick to get into. I tried to see on tiptoes. Yash took my wrist and led me to a bench and pulled me up to stand beside him, pointing at the lighting ceremony. The throngs had gathered around a giant diya shape created from tea lights. Workers lit up the last flames. The crowds cheered and I hastily took pictures.

"I have to get closer!" I yelled to Yash over the noise.

"OK! But we can't get separated!"

I nodded. If we did, we had a plan to WhatsApp a meeting location. Yash didn't leave that to chance. He held my hand and helped me down as I clutched my skirt high enough that I wouldn't trip. He didn't release my hand and I relished his soft, warm touch as he led me through the crowd like a torpedo, offering a "please excuse us" along the way until we stopped at the base of the lighting ceremony.

Hundreds of dancing flames were meticulously arranged before us. We both gasped at the beauty and wonder.

Nothing said Diwali better than this. Nothing symbolized our inner strength and light as well as . . . well . . . actual light!

Extinguish the darkness by setting it ablaze. The day of new beginnings was at hand. And I couldn't be happier than to experience this with Yash.

Yash seemed to huddle around me to give me time for as many photographs as I needed, moving here and there to capture the most with the least amount of shadow. But alas, perfecting this shot in a crowd was pointless.

Getting out of the throng of onlookers flashing away with their own cameras and ruining everyone else's shot was nice. We came. We saw. We enjoyed. And we left.

The string light–wrapped palm trees made for great shots, though, their reflection glimmering on the surface of the creek water like a million stars.

We weaved in and out of crowds to try to see as much as possible. I pulled back on Yash's hand when he walked a little too fast for me. He looked back at me with a questioning look.

"What's up?" he asked.

"A little slower?" A welcoming breeze picked up and I fanned myself.

"Do you need to sit down?"

I shook my head, hiked my skirt to my ankle, and showed him my sandals. "Think I'd be wearing anything uncomfortable?"

"Honestly thought you'd be in sneakers."

Ah, darn it. I should've worn sneakers.

A new round of music boomed through the air. The crowds went wild as a procession cut through the streets behind us.

"What *is* that?" Yash asked, swerving his head to check it out. "Let's go see!"

He pulled me behind him, and I followed in step. Yash walked slower this time and kept me close, holding our joined hands out of view. Wasn't going to lie that I didn't love being close to him, that I didn't love the touch or how he always made sure that I was protected and accounted for.

I didn't think either of us was prepared for what we saw when Yash pried through the crowds. We stumbled to the edge of the sidewalk, our jaws dropping at the marching band playing upbeat Bollywood-style music led by dhol drummers in traditional outfits, from head garment to mojri. They were followed by dancers.

Here, I thought my lehenga was heavy and hot. These women were all dressed up in glitzy, flowing skirts and glimmering tops, covered in chunky costume jewelry. The men were in shimmering kurtas, and away they danced, inciting ear-piercing cheers.

Everyone, and I mean *everyone*, whipped out their cameras and phones and tablets. But we were front and center, thanks to Yash, capturing prime shots.

Yash was grinning and banging his head like this was some rock concert, looking to me with the biggest grin ever.

I, naturally, turned the camera to Yash. The device just gravitated toward him, and he was part of the best shots. Thank goodness he didn't go insta-rigid, as he was too engrossed in the music and show to notice me taking pictures of him.

When the procession passed, we headed back toward the creek to find the best place to get situated for the fireworks, sitting on a bench farther down. We were close enough to the water but far enough from the masses. With the dark sky speckled with stars, the illuminated buildings in the background, and the brilliant reflection off the water, these were sure to be some of the greatest of all pictures.

Even though the bench was big enough for four people, we found ourselves in the middle. Now I was the one going rigid. My hands were turning clammy, and ugh! I wanted to tell him I *like* liked him, but what if he didn't feel the same way?

"Are you OK?" he asked.

I snapped back to reality. "Yeah. Why?"

"You're tense. Something up?" He glanced at his hands as he wiped them across his pants.

My lips parted. I'd always been able to say anything to him. We didn't have many secrets between us. But this was different.

I sighed. *Woman up.* I ended up running a finger through my hair, forgetting the mogra. "Oops!"

Yash went to help as soon as he saw me struggling to pin it back in and make sure it lay correctly.

"Hey, you have the flowers you like in your hair," he stated, as if he was just now seeing them. "There."

"Thanks," I said, entangled beneath his hands.

Before Yash moved away, he leaned over and smelled the blooms. I froze, holding my breath. His cheek had almost brushed mine. He was so close that I could kiss his jaw, if I wanted to be so bold. He seemed to still, before clearing his throat and sitting upright, away from me.

I guessed he still liked how they smelled, too?

He blurted, "Do you want ice cream or something to drink?"

"Yes."

"What do you want?" He cocked his chin toward some vendors and an ice cream shop down the way.

"Surprise me!"

He laughed nervously. "OK. You stay here and keep our spot. I won't be too far or gone for too long."

Yash hurried off and left me to protect the bench. I grunted. Why did I want to tell him anything? If this was a crush, it would go away quickly enough. Crushes usually did. They came fast and furious and wilted away just as quickly. And if Yash never found out, then we'd never have the awkwardness like this again.

Yeah. That sounded like a plan.

But then I remembered today was Diwali, and in two days, we would celebrate sibling bonds. Which meant treating him like a brother. I couldn't go through with those traditions knowing I no longer saw him as a brother. But we celebrated as a family, and everyone would notice if I refused to participate. And they'd want to know why. I couldn't even pretend it was because I was still mad at Yash. And worst of all? I could imagine the pain of rejection on his face.

If we sat down for brother-sister traditions and I straight up refused to do gift exchanges, he would be absolutely crushed.

I groaned and dropped my face into my palms. I didn't have a choice except to explain to him. I was sweating as I mulled over what to say. It seemed like he'd been gone only ten seconds instead of ten minutes when he returned with a sugarcane drink for us to share and two ice-cream cups with flavors I couldn't have guessed.

"Thanks!" I took a cup.

He explained, "So, this is Nouq. It's an Emirati brand. You have baklava flavor because I know you love that stuff."

I tasted the creamy dessert. "Mm! They really did that!"

"It's made with camel milk."

I paused as he took a spoonful of my ice cream, shoved it into his mouth, and grinned.

"See?" he said. "You wouldn't have eaten it otherwise. Just like the chocolates all over again."

"No. I like it, and I would've tried it now that I've had camel's milk. But why did you take a chunk out of my ice cream!"

"I wanted to try it! I got hibiscus," he added, digging into his own cup.

I stabbed my spoon into his ice cream.

"Hey!"

I shoveled the bite into my mouth, ignoring the brain freeze. "Mm! So good!"

We quieted and enjoyed the ice cream before sharing the lightly spiced sugarcane drink.

Yash slouched back and took a sip. He looked out at the lights and asked, "Was there something you were going to tell me?"

I played with my dupatta, the ends of which gathered on my lap.

He bent over and fiddled with the straw and waited.

I clenched my eyes. God, was I really about to confess my feelings for my best friend?

"Something's up," he said quietly. "Did I do something—"

I blurted, "I like you!"

He froze, avoiding my eyes.

I quivered as the words exploded out of me. My face heated to a million degrees. "Oh my god. We just got back to being friends though. I don't want to mess that up or for it to be weird between us. I want you as my best friend first and foremost and forever, OK? I won't jeopardize that again . . . but like . . . Bhai Beej is coming up and I can't do sibling traditions with you. But I didn't want you to not know the reason and feel hurt or rejected or whatever because of me not explaining. Not again."

I clamped one hand over the other to stop them from shaking, but that didn't help. "I don't expect you to like me like that, and honestly, it'll probably just pass, and we can laugh about it one day. Anyway . . . I didn't want you to feel bad when I don't do the brother-sister stuff."

I clenched my eyes and grunted. "That's all."

I bunched up the dupatta in my hands. Why wasn't he saying anything? Was he weirded out? Was he mad that I'd jeopardize us?

My stomach convulsed.

I kept talking, because I didn't know what else to do. "I didn't express myself after the falling out. I was mad for so long that I can't even remember what we used to be like, and I caused a lot of hurt. It's OK if you don't feel the same way. I just . . . couldn't let you think it was anything bad. Well, hopefully it isn't too bad? I don't want to lose you as a friend again."

I bit my lip and forced myself to look at him. He was staring at the cup in his hand.

He snickered then. "You were definitely a jerk for a while."

"Hey!" I said on instinct. I started to get misty-eyed the second I saw him watching me, his soft expression anything but angry.

"Nikki, why are you crying?" He wrapped his arms around me, and I nearly bawled into his shoulder.

"I'm so mortified," I muttered. "And now I'm getting makeup and snot on your nice kurta."

"Yeah, you're pretty gross," he whispered against my hair.

For a moment, we didn't say anything but just hugged. In the back of my mind, I vaguely recalled how PDA wasn't allowed here, but was this PDA?

I weaved my arms around his waist and hugged him tighter. "I'm a mess."

"For liking me? Nah. You can't help it. I'm pretty likable."

I laughed against him. He always knew how to make me feel better, how to ease whatever intense emotion was hitting me.

He pulled away, and I wiped my face, but he wouldn't look me in the eye. I knew it. I knew there was going to be weirdness between us. But all things considered, it could be so much worse.

Yash turned my hands over in his so that he was looking at the palms. "Girls with dark mehndi shouldn't be crying."

I stared at him. I wanted to ask what he meant by that. Well, the saying was: The darker the mehndi turned out, the more that person was loved. But did he mean being loved by him? By family? Or was he just reminding me of how happy I was to have my mehndi come out so well?

He parted his lips when he finally looked at me, like maybe he would say something profound. Instead, in perfect Yash fashion, he said, "You look like a pufferfish."

"Shut up."

The corner of his mouth hiked up. "You're not going to lose me," he promised.

My lips trembled.

"Oh my god, don't cry again!" He smooshed my face against his chest as I breathed through my tears.

"I mished shuz," I croaked against Yash.

"I missed you, too, you big crybaby."

"Wah!"

"Hey, look!"

I pulled away, wiping my face, and a gigantic weight lifted off my shoulders. Although I was trying my best not to feel hurt if he didn't like me back in this way, I at least took comfort in knowing one thing: We were going to be OK.

We turned toward the water. The telltale shrieking of fireworks had started. Crowds cheered and oohed and ahhed and huddled closer to the creek.

"Come on." He stood, pulling me up and toward the water.

Photography could always calm and focus me. I would deal with this whole mess later. But for now, I concentrated on the fireworks, capturing crowds and joy as the night sky lit up and sizzled with bursts of every color imaginable.

Whatever awkward tension there was melted away as Yash laughed, looking like he was ten again at Lake Travis for Fourth of July fireworks. I twisted just a little to get him in some of the shots as the faraway buildings lit up to say: HAPPY DIWALI!

Yash was effortless and natural when he didn't realize he was being photographed. Right now? He had no clue. His eyes glinted with pure joy as different colors lit up small surfaces of his face, his chin tilted up at the night sky.

What was he thinking? Or was he just enjoying the moment like everyone else?

Catching him at his relaxed best—and with all the right angles, best lighting, and soft shadows—was rare.

In this moment, having Yash in the corner of the picture completed a perfect shot. Perfect squared? Was that a thing? Well, it was now.

Behind him were sparkling bursts of bright blue, green, pink, red, purple, yellow, and white. The fireworks swelled into a fantastical crescendo, their exploding lights and shapes obliterating the darkness of the sky. Glitter lit up the night as celebrations boomed around us in cacophonies of cheers, laughter, and the distant crackle of fireworks. The water mirrored the sky, creating an endless loop of shimmer against darkness, a full circle of radiance.

The play of light and shadow softened the contours of the otherwise sharp lines of Yash's features—his jaw, his face, his shoulders—and brushed glowing lines of light against the silhouette of his frame.

Breathtaking. It was the most magical moment teeming with artistic bursts.

Thank goodness for the noise drowning out the clicks of the camera. Otherwise, he'd realize what I was doing and go stiff.

Yash was so incredibly photogenic.

*Stay just like that.*

Yash was lost in the show above him, his hands relaxed and dangling at his side and not balled up as if having his picture taken destroyed a piece of his soul.

I glanced at the screen to study the shots before taking another. I couldn't lose this moment, but I also had to make sure I was getting decent shots and adjusting anything that wasn't working.

"This is awesome!" Yash called back, glancing at me just as I captured my last photo of him. "What are you doing over there? Don't get separated."

I nodded and pressed my arm against his. The knuckles of our pinkies touched, and a flutter swam through me.

Yash was watching the last of the show, and I wondered what was going through his thoughts. But then his finger twitched and caressed my pinky, and I didn't move away. Instead, I sank into his touch and tried to tamp down my smile.

A second later, he hooked a finger with mine. We were sort of holding hands, but this time, it had a whole new meaning. Not kids or just friends, and definitely not like siblings. Maybe this felt new to him, too, the way it did for me.

I pressed closer against his arm, tilting my head toward his shoulder while he tilted his head toward me. His chest was going in and out, like maybe he was breathing a little harder.

Was he feeling this, too? Did he have flutters in his stomach? Was his skin warm and tingly? I really hoped so. And I really hoped that we could always feel this way with each other.

All around us, the last of the magical fireworks glimmered in what was quite possibly the most romantic moment of my entire life.

# CHAPTER TWENTY-FOUR

L ast night had been perfect. The taxi ride back had been quiet but pleasantly content. We'd returned to our rooms, where our families were waiting with boxes of sweets. We stole glances at one another while we ate and told our parents about the amazing experiences of Diwali in Dubai.

The following day was Gujarati New Year, which meant we were due back at mandir at some point for worship followed by a big ole family dinner, per tradition. Usually, we'd have this at home, alternating between our house and Yash's house and sometimes with other family or friends, depending on who was in town and available.

Here, we had a reservation at a nice restaurant, according to Ankit Mama. It only made sense that our parents had hit it off with Mummie's cousins and would end up doing dinner together. Instead of going all the way back to Mama's house in Abu Dhabi, we went out for dinner. This was apparently the tradition for Ankit Mama anyway. Between all the dads and uncles, there was sure to be a big, drawn-out back-and-forth about the bill, because Indian dads always fought to pay for everyone's meals.

I woke up refreshed and still a bit sleepy until I remembered how I'd confessed my feelings to Yash. *Cringe.* But also how he had sort of held my hand. *Squeal!*

Our families met in the lobby for breakfast. Yash and I kept trading looks, and I was trying my hardest not to smile. Our parents were oblivious as they planned out the day, while Lilly quietly watched us.

Whenever we'd make eye contact, she'd look from me to Yash and back to me. Then smirk. Oh my lord.

But I had more pressing things to worry over, because after breakfast, Yash and I would be taking a taxi to . . . *skydiving*.

Nervous energy was a thing, and we both had it all through breakfast, not that we could eat, and straight into the drive toward the biggest leap of our lives (pun intended). We tapped our feet in the taxi, tugged the hems of our shirts, and babbled on about how things would be fun and fine.

I even kept checking my phone to busy myself, noting how Jalebi_Writer had never responded. He probably thought I was definitely a weirdo now, and creeping into that "too-familiar space." Oh, well.

"Are you sure want to do this?" I asked Yash. "Because clearly you're freaking out."

"I'm good!" he said.

Well, if he insisted that he was fine, then I wouldn't back out.

We checked in, signed more paperwork, weighed in, watched a video, went over detailed instructions, practiced, and got onto a plane.

Oh my lord, I couldn't believe I was about to be strapped to someone who jumped out of planes for a living. My entire body was shaking as we stood at the door of the plane, waiting for the green light. There was one extra jumper: a camera guy to capture everything.

I clutched onto the straps at my shoulders and tried not to heave. But no matter how visceral, my anxiety wasn't anything in comparison to how pale Yash suddenly turned. Ashen.

"You look like a ghost!" I yelled to him over the sound of the small plane. "Are you OK?"

He shook his head.

I took his hand and managed a smile. We'd made it this far, and this was something Yash had really wanted to do. He'd regret this if he backed out now. "You got this!"

"No, I don't. I don't know what I was thinking!"

"We're here! *I'm* here! We're doing this together, OK?"

Yash shook his head again, his eyes wide behind the goggles.

I tapped the GoPro attached firmly to his strapped-in chest. "Are you the GOAT or what? First person at our school to sky-dive!"

"Forget them! This is scary!"

Yeah, didn't I know it. My teeth were chattering and my stomach was doing flips. I squeezed his hand and hugged him. "If you can put up with me, you can do anything!"

Then, for some weird reason beyond me, I gave him a clandestine peck on his cheek.

He froze and I awkwardly smiled, hopeful the kiss had made him feel better instead of weird. His look of surprise melted away, replaced by determination. With lips pressed, he nodded once and gave the guys behind us a thumbs-up.

*All right.*

*Here we go.*

*We're really doing this, huh?*

Yash and his tandem guy went first, hooting on the way out and dropping into a cloudless sky. Um, was the ground really *that* far off?

Oh crap. We were doing this! OH MY GOD!

The camera guy gave me a thumbs-up, and here we went!

We. *Jumped.*

Like, freaking superheroes. Yes, this totally counted as being a superhero.

The speed was . . . *intense.* Free-falling had my insides churning and yet pushed up against my spine. One minute. One minute of falling through the air felt like forever. The pressure kept my arms wide open, my body straight, and my hair whipping back in its ponytail. Good thing the tandem guy strapped to my back had on a helmet and a face shield!

The warm wind pulled the skin on my arms and face back and felt like a hundred tiny ice picks drifting over my flesh. I couldn't even smile at the cameraman. My face wasn't cooperating, and I was probably going to look super horrified in all the pictures.

Once I let go of the staggering fear clawing into my bones, I began to appreciate the awesomeness that was skydiving. How freeing and magnificent this all was. And when I managed to unclench my eyes, my breath sputtered as I took in the bliss.

First off, the world looked round on the curvature of the land and sea.

Second, there was so much blue water ahead and peaks of

buildings and city below, and just desert behind us in a sheet of beige.

Third, Palm Jumeirah really looked like a big palm tree from the sky.

When they gave us signals, we tried to face the camera guy and throw peace signs, heart shapes, thumbs-ups, hook 'em horns, or whatever else we could think of.

Then the parachutes opened. The sudden jerk snatched the breath from my lungs. After free-falling, this gliding felt more like we'd completely stopped and were hovering high above the world. Was this what it felt like to fly? Magnificent!

The terror that had filled me seconds ago melted into utter bliss and peace. I pushed out a breath.

The serenity I harnessed in this moment and during Diwali was surreal.

The world was too big, too glorious to be stuck on negative things.

I just felt so alive! Like I could conquer anything!

We landed with a little fall gently hitting the ground and were quickly unbuckled from all the straps by ground staff.

I bent over, trying to fight off a headache and not hurl.

Yash rushed over to me, embracing me in a hug and swinging me in a circle before dropping me. He bent over and held up one finger.

"Don't barf!" I told him.

He laughed through his heaves. "That. Was. Amazing!"

He hiccupped and flung an arm around my shoulders. "Did you like it? Are you OK?"

"It was incredible!" I thrust my arms out. "I feel like I can take on the whole freaking world! Like, come at me, bro!"

Yash's cheeks were flushed and his eyes watery as the sun hit him. He wiped his brow like he'd been sweating. His hair was so windblown that it was standing straight up.

I shoved my fingers through his hair. "You need a haircut."

His hands landed on my hips, and I stilled. This seemed like one of those implausibly romantic scenes in the movies, ripe for a passionate, adrenaline-infused kiss. Wait. Did I want to kiss him? Yeah . . . I really did.

I swallowed hard. "Up there, I felt like I was literally on top of the world, *invincible*."

"Invincible, huh?" he asked, his gaze dropping to my mouth for the briefest of seconds.

I bit my lip and tilted toward him. Yash leaned down. But then we remembered where we were and stepped back. I heaved out a breath, my skin flaring.

Yash cleared his throat and rubbed the side of his neck. "They're calling for us. We better follow them inside and get out of the drop zone."

"Oh right. Of course."

We followed procedure and checked out. This time, when we took a taxi back, we didn't sit at opposite ends in a weird, quiet space. We sat closer to each other, and Yash took my hand in his. We kept our stare straight ahead. I tried to tamp down a smile and control the belly flips.

This was definitely a non-friend handhold.

Skydiving had been epic. It had me feeling like a total badass, like I could do anything. The aftermath? Eh. Not so much.

Mummie stood over me as I lay helpless in bed, the lights off, my body surging from the aftereffects. I hadn't vomited, but man this headache was going to shatter my skull.

"You took all the ibuprofen I gave you?" she asked, checking my forehead as if I might have a fever.

"Yes," I muttered.

"And you ate some food with it?" She glared at the plate of cheese, grapes, and crackers at my bedside table.

"I can't."

"You need to have something in your stomach."

Because that was the cure-all for Indian moms: Food. Feed everyone for any reason and then overfeed them for good measure. Got a headache? Eat. Period cramps obliterating your insides? Eat. Feeling bloated? Eat. Feeling weak? Eat. Have an exam? Eat. Fell off your bike? Eat. Suffering from heartache? Eat extra.

There was a knock on the door. So loud.

Lilly let Yash and his parents in. Hetal Auntie immediately sat beside me and checked my forehead.

"Did she eat?" she asked Mummie.

My mother clucked her tongue.

"Oh, beta, you have to eat," Auntie insisted.

I mumbled nonsense into the pillow.

"Should we stay until she's better?" she asked Mummie.

"You guys can go. I'll stay with her," Yash offered. Dude didn't like having to go mandir so often, either.

"Lilly?" he asked. "You wanna stay with us?"

"No," she said. "They have food. And it's really good."

Our parents fussed over me some more, hemming and hawing until I forced myself to sit up and nibble on a cracker. "I'm OK. See, I'm eating. You guys go if you want. Don't waste a whole afternoon because of me. Nothing will happen. We're not that far. Yash can WhatsApp you if something happens."

They eventually conceded and Papa told him, "Message us in group chat every half hour and immediately if she gets worse, hah?"

Yash nodded. "Of course, Uncle."

After they got ready, not nearly as quietly as I wanted them to, they hustled out the door.

Finally, silence.

Yash sat at the desk and pulled out his tablet.

"You don't have to stay."

"It's fine," he insisted. "I didn't want to go. I have a headache, too."

"What? And how does no one know? Why is your mom not babying you?"

He swiveled in the chair to face me. "Because I'm not a crybaby like you," he teased. "Actually, mine's not too bad. Are you OK?"

I lay back down and draped an arm over my eyes. "This is the mother of all headaches."

"They said this could happen, but should go away after a little while. Just take a nap."

"Are you drawing?" I asked instead.

"Yeah."

"That's cool."

He let out a breath and got up. The mattress depressed beside me, and I turned to find him sitting against the headboard, his legs extended, feet crossed at the ankles.

He showed me the tablet. A drawing of The Atlantis hotel with shimmering pale blue water in front of it, but this time he'd used a watercolor style. He was getting so versatile.

He tapped the screen with his stylus and showed me a girl with a ponytail at the souk drinking from a coconut.

"Is that . . ." I started to ask before realizing how egotistical it sounded to assume he was drawing me.

"Yeah, it's you," he said.

I beamed.

He added nervously, "I have to tell you something."

"Hmm?" I turned onto my side to face him, eager to know what had him worked up. But the headache wasn't having it. The pain was shutting my brain down.

In the silence, in the near dark with the glow of his tablet, Yash drew as he started talking, but I fell asleep without registering a single word.

* * *

When I woke up, my headache had diminished, and Yash was still working. Although now, he had his legs crossed and was hunched over the tablet resting on his lap.

I didn't see what he was working on, but it looked like homework. Ugh. There was going to be so much to catch up on, but whatever. I couldn't believe he was staying on top of his while on vacation.

"Hey, Snoring Beauty, do you feel better?"

I weakly pushed him. It did nothing. "Yes. Thanks for staying with me."

"You should try to eat something, though."

"You sound like our moms."

"Well, they're all hammering into me on the group chat about getting you to eat. So, please eat something. Your dad said we can order food, or he'll dip out to bring you something."

"Oh my god, no. I can't take any more Indian food. So much, so close together. Can I just get a salad?"

He chortled. "Too spicy for you?"

"Spicy, heavy, saucy, fried, the kind of carbs that hurt my stomach. I just want salad. And crackers."

Yash poked me in the side, and I nearly screamed out a laugh. "You could use a salad."

"Don't fat-shame me."

He pinched my side and a pleasant flutter crashed against my insides. "I meant you *should* eat something aside from chips and sweets. And we had so many sweets last night. That gets you sick, remember?"

I rammed my finger into his armpit. "You're not my mom."

He jumped, grabbing my wrist, and tugged me into his chest.

That flutter? All-out raging. Maniacal thrashing. And in no uncertain terms, declaring, *You are, indeed, crushing hard on Yash. In case you forgot.*

He warned, "I will tickle the hell out of you, Nikki."

I ducked my head into his chest to hide whatever telling look I had on my face. "You can't. I don't feel good, and you have to be nice," I mumbled. "Can you order me a salad?"

He reached over to the bedside phone, ordered, and hung up, returning to the position we'd been in. Both of us were slouched against the headboard on many pillows. I was lying halfway down, and our legs were extended in front of us.

"You're lucky," he whispered in my ear; and dear lord, my breath hitched.

"Yash . . ."

"Yeah?" he asked, tilting his head so that we were staring into each other's eyes.

I panicked and pulled the covers to my face. "Did you actually have fun skydiving?"

"Yeah, I did. I know. Don't remind me. I freaked out beforehand," he groaned, draping an arm across his eyes.

"I was freaking out, too."

"Really?" he lowered his arm to look at me. "You seemed way cooler than I was."

"I was scared, but I didn't want you to regret not jumping when we'd made it that far. Are you glad you jumped?"

"Yeah. Thanks for that."

"Why were you so insistent on skydiving in the first place?"

He looked at the ceiling. "Uh. You know how you were accusing me of skydiving to impress some girl?"

My heart splintered. "Yeah . . ."

"Well, you were right."

I frowned. I was about to barf all these crackers back up.

He pinched his lips together. "I was trying to impress you."

I let out a sigh of relief. "Why did you think that would impress me?" Wait. Was he trying to impress me because he was crushing on me? I wondered how long he'd felt this way about me, but I didn't have the nerve to ask.

"Not the part about me jumping out of a plane, but the fact that we got to do something so amazing together."

He was trying not to smile, and here I was grinning like a fool. "You coerced me into a moment of a lifetime."

"Are you mad?" he asked.

I pulled the covers down from my face and shifted, propped up on my elbow so that I was on my side facing him, his chin at eye level. "I'm glad. Can I ask you a question?"

"Maybe."

I clenched my fists to keep from shaking, but I had to know. "Do you like me?"

"I've always liked you."

"No. Not as in friends. I mean, the way I like you."

He swallowed and my gaze fell to his throat. "I've always *like* liked you, Nikki."

Then he drew an arm back over his eyes and tamped down a smile. Yash was, for the first time ever, wholly embarrassed.

My entire body was trembling, but here went nothing and everything.

I leaned over, dipping beneath his arm, and kissed him. It was just a peck on his chin, partially on his jaw. But it was probably just as defining a moment as a kiss on the lips, bringing all the stomach flips with it.

Yash slid his arm off his eyes. I ducked down, tucking my face against his neck. His hand fell to my hip.

Yash nudged my forehead with his chin, and I looked up at him. He was watching me with a soft expression that could destroy a girl. His gaze dropped to my mouth. My breath hitched as he leaned down toward me.

Oh my god. Oh my god. Was this happening? My first kiss? With *Yash*?

Our lips met. Softly, delicately.

All the feels hit my gut like we were on one of Dubai's many fastest/biggest/highest-in-the-world roller coasters. Forget Diwali fireworks. Sparks were going off in this tiny space between us.

He pulled back and I gasped. Why had he stopped?

His mouth came crashing down against mine. Guess he didn't want it to end, either.

I'd never felt so warm, so volatile, but in the best, euphoric way.

We parted, breathing heavily. My cheeks flushed as I buried my face against his arm, smiling and maybe laughing. His body convulsed beneath mine like maybe he was laughing, too.

I leaned back. "Wait. You liked me all that time?"

He nodded.

"Why didn't you ever say anything?"

He shrugged. "Worried it would ruin our friendship. Sound familiar?"

"Why didn't you tell me when I told you?"

"I dunno. I'm shy?"

I pinched his side and he flopped, chuckling. "Since when?"

"Since this!"

Our phones pinged and Yash reached over to the bedside table to check his messages. "Parents will be on their way back soon. You better eat something before they ask what I was doing all this time."

Eeek! For the love of all that was good, my dad could *not* find out that we'd been locking lips!

I jumped out of bed, asking, "Where's my salad?"

"Should be here any minute. We gotta get ready for dinner soon. You OK to eat dinner with us?"

"Yeah. Maybe another salad or soup with everyone?" I went through my clothes to find my outfit for our big family New Year dinner.

"Why are you grinning so hard?" he asked, sporting a grin of his own.

"Yash . . . you kissed me."

He hopped off the bed. "So, what you're saying is that if I ever want to make you smile, I just have to kiss you?"

"Oh my god." I tried to control the flutters sweeping up and down my body and asked, "Oh. What was it that you were telling me when I fell asleep?"

"You didn't hear anything I said?"

"No. Sorry. My headache got me and then I was out. Or were you trying to tell me how much you adore me?"

He smirked. "Adore, huh?"

"What else?"

His brows furrowed, pensive. "Um, we gotta fill out a follow-up for skydiving so that they know we're alive and OK."

"Sure," I said. The way Yash had sounded had me thinking it was super important, but eh, guess a company making sure that they hadn't killed us was sorta vital.

# CHAPTER TWENTY-FIVE

y headache had completely vanished by the next day. But now it was also the last day of Diwali, and I was *not* looking forward to it. Not because I didn't want our time in Dubai to end or for the festive season to wilt away, but because it was . . .

"Everyone almost ready for Bhai Beej? We were thinking about going to the park for this," Papa said.

"What did you get Hetalben, again?" Mummie asked him.

"Surprise," Papa said with a wag of his finger.

Mummie pulled his hand down. "Surprise for her, not me!"

"We're sharing sweets?" he asked instead.

"Yes. I bought them for everyone." She nodded at a red and gold box on the desk. Even though sisters fed one to their brothers, or in our case, people close enough to be siblings, Mummie must've gotten something for us girls, too.

Mummie would place a cashew-laden kaju katli to Pranav Uncle's mouth and he would give her a gift in return.

Hetal Auntie would place a chocolate barfi to Papa's mouth, and he would give her a gift.

Lilly and I would do the same with Yash, his flavor of sweets being the very popular bright orange jalebi soaked in sugary rose water with a hint of cardamon and topped off with saffron.

Meanwhile, I loved stuffed kala jamun and Lilly would trip for some rose-scented gulab jamun. Our parents didn't usually eat much in the way of sweets, but here we were, with a big ole box full of them.

Our parents had their own siblings but couldn't always go visit for Bhai Beej since they were spread out across the States. Since we were essentially one giant family, we just celebrated together. The parents seemed to love the fact that single-child Yash had "sisters" next door and that we brotherless girls had him in return.

It was a lot like Raksha Bhandan, except on that day sisters gave brothers sweets and tied threads around their wrist, and brothers gave sisters money and a promise of protection. Lilly and I exchanged threads, too, and did our own version because we decided that we didn't need brothers to protect us. On the other hand, getting a lifetime's worth of protection and money in a trade-off for decadent mithai seemed like a pretty sweet deal. Pun absolutely intended!

"Today is very important," Papa reminded us.

I cringed. I couldn't do a tradition with Yash that had us treating each other like brother and sister when we clearly weren't. We saw one another as something entirely different, and going through with Bhai (which literally meant "brother") Beej was about to get weird AF.

I wondered, if Yash had liked me all this time, whether this was why he took his duties with Lilly seriously but with me had always found ways to get around the more traditional steps. Why he refused to let me put a sweet to his mouth and always snatched the Raksha Bhandan thread before I could tie it on him. He refused to ever wear mine and instead had insisted that he liked to keep them intact in a journal instead. It was all symbolic anyway. Aside from meals during these times, we didn't get much more into it than that.

"I don't want to do this with Yash anymore," I confessed, rubbing my arm and evading eye contact like it was a monster.

"Why not? Don't tell me that you haven't taken Diwali seriously and put things behind you. Have you only been pretending to get along with him?" Mummie scolded.

"No."

"Not doing this might offend Yash."

"We're on the same page. He won't be offended."

"Then explain why," she pressed. "So that we're *all* on the same page."

"Um . . . because . . ."

Papa lifted his hand in a gesture for me to continue, and Mummie tilted her head and cocked her brows as if saying I'd better hurry up because she didn't have all day.

My skin flared hot. If confessing my feelings to Yash had been mortifying, then this took the cake. I'd been so worried about losing Yash as a friend, but what about our parents? Would mine no longer see him as their son, but like any other boy they wanted me to retain boundaries with, creating a rift with his parents? Would they no longer trust us together? Would we stop hanging out as a giant family with our random meals?

How could I say this without telling them the truth but also offer enough of an excuse to get away with it and—

"Because they like each other," Lilly interjected, rolling her eyes and sighing dramatically. "They *like* like each other and it's so weird to treat a boy like your brother when you're crushing on him. God. How does no one else see what's happening? I saw this miles away, like from Austin miles away."

She took off her glasses and held them out in an offering. "Maybe y'all need glasses?"

Heat obliterated my face. It was on fire.

"Oh . . ." Papa breathed, his jaw hanging open.

"Hmm . . ." Mummie hummed, pressing her lips together and looking me up and down like she wanted to say, "Get it, girl!"

*No! Mother of mine, do not be like that.* She was probably planning out our entire future, thinking how wonderful it would be for her best friends to become her in-laws.

"Please don't tell his parents or say anything to Yash," I grumbled.

"Aha!" Lilly said, pointing at me. "You confess! I called it."

Mummie blew out a breath and looked to Papa. "How are we going to handle this? They'll want to know the reason. They deserve to know."

"Please don't tell them!" I exclaimed, clutching onto Mummie's arm and trembling. Yash and I hadn't even figured out what we were doing and where we were heading with our relationship, and maybe he didn't want his parents to know. It seemed like something he should tell them when he was ready.

She clucked her tongue and hugged me. "Are you scared that you like him?"

"Um, yes. Duh. But, also, this is mortifying. Why do parents have to know about everything? Crushes are supposed to be private, but also this might be cosmic karma for how mean I was, and I totally accept it."

Papa chuckled and rubbed my back. "Oh, beta. Any boy is nuts not to like you. Doesn't mean I want you two—"

"Oh my god, no," I interrupted. "Don't finish that sentence. This is why you shouldn't know if I like him. Don't be weird around him, OK? Don't give him evil eyes *or* smirks. Don't go either way. Everything has to be the same."

He ignored me and said, "How about this? We just celebrate together. No official sweet offering and present giving for pictures? We do our thing with his parents. You and Lilly do your thing with Yash."

I nodded.

"I'll still participate," Lilly said, hugging me. "He's still like a brother to me. And I want a gift from him because he gives the best ones."

So here I was, between my parents and against my sister, all willing to slyly conceal this from Yash's parents. But Yash himself? I'd have to tell him that my parents knew. My feelings for him, which should've been private, were snowballing, gathering more and more people.

\* \* \*

We'd packed our things and got ready to check out. The hotel let us leave our bags in their holding room until we returned, since our flight wasn't scheduled until much later.

In the meantime, we'd picked up lunch to head out to the park, and by lunch, I meant we'd gathered loads of food from vendors and cafés and hauled everything out to a nice, shady area. We first exchanged gifts and sweets, and true to their word, my parents took Yash's parents aside and did their exchange away from us. They didn't seem to mind once Papa started cracking jokes. We were far enough away to have some privacy when talking but close enough that our parents could watch us.

Lilly fed Yash a jalebi first and he plucked a flower from beside him and handed it to her.

She was delighted and didn't care one iota when I said, "Lame. That's not a gift."

"My presence is a gift," Yash replied.

I plucked some grass and threw it at him. He laughed and swiped shredded grass blades from his hair. Then we sort of sat there and eyed the other.

I cleared my throat, tossing a jalebi at him, which he caught in the air and bit into. "You can feed yourself," I said.

"That's fine. I didn't get you anything anyway." Even though he pointedly looked at my camera.

I stuck my tongue out at him, and that was kinda the end of that.

And the Most Anticlimactic Award goes to . . . *Nikki*!

I turned to my camera and took family shots to capture the day before going through the ones from Diwali.

"Anything good?" Yash asked, glancing over his plate of food.

I landed on the firework scenes—*the* perfect picture with *the* prefect subject—and smiled. "Yeah, something really good."

"Lemme see?"

"You're not ready to behold this level of beauty."

We checked into the airport and made it past customs with some extra time on our hands to peruse the mighty, glimmering shops. We avoided the super pricey stores and went straight for the treats.

"Here's your gift," Yash said.

"What?" I asked, taking the familiar Al Nassma bronze box.

"You liked camel milk chocolate, right?"

I smiled, imagining how I was going to savor these little squares of rich, smooth, gourmet camel milk chocolate with creamy nougat, pistachio, and espresso centers. But then my smile vanished.

"Not for Bhai Beej," he added quickly, scratching the back of his head.

"Obvs," I said with a nervous chuckle.

"But you're not going to be able to find these anywhere else."

"Thank you. So, as a heads-up. My parents know I like you."

He tapped my fingers, still clutching the box, and added, "Well, my parents know that I like you."

"How long do you think before they ignore our pleas and tell each other?"

"I give it to the end of takeoff."

"Can't trust them with anything."

Lilly appeared at my side with a grin.

"Oh! How long have you been standing there?" I asked, stepping away from Yash.

Lilly put a hand on my back and pushed me toward him. "Go on. God, only took y'all forever. Seriously, *am* I the only one who saw this coming from miles away? Sure you don't need my glasses?"

Yash cleared his throat as I mouthed, "Sorry."

"Plane's boarding!" Auntie yelled from across the seating area. "Go to the bathroom! Then we can divide leftover thepla."

"Oh, my god," he muttered.

In a matter of minutes, we'd boarded the plane and shuffled ever so slowly toward our seats. The novelty of air travel had lost all meaning, now that I was dead tired and not looking forward to catching up on mounds of homework. As we suspected, our parents had arranged for Yash and I to sit together again. But this time, neither one of us wanted it any other way.

We shuffled toward the back and settled in while our families sat farther up. I slipped into the window seat and Yash took the aisle seat with an empty seat in between us, now piled with three seats' worth of "airline swag." Namely toiletries and blankets.

"Is that really your seat?" I asked.

"Yep. My dad said the trick is to book seats with an empty one in the middle because who wants a seat in between two people?"

"Smart. Hopefully no one booked it."

"At least I can change seats with them, but looks like a half-empty flight."

"Hey. Don't forget your Garfield and Nermal picture."

He laughed. "Who forgot?"

Yash situated the two stuffed animals in the seat between us, buckled them up, and took pictures before stashing them in his backpack. Then he moved all the swag to the aisle seat and slid into the middle seat beside me.

# CHAPTER TWENTY-SIX

The plane went into dark mode after everyone had had their meals. Also, we did *not* accept thepla from our moms but ate delicious airline food plus endless snacks from the snack cart.

Outside, the skies were pitch-black. I pulled down the visor to cover the window. Just looking out there made me cold. I tapped the screen off on the back of the seat in front of me, yawning and fighting droopy eyelids.

"Not watching anything?" Yash asked.

"I was thinking about catching up on my shows or some movies, but I'm so tired. Just want to close my eyes to the dark." In fact, most everyone had chosen the dark route around us, their screens off.

I jerked my chin at his screen. "You?"

"Nah, gonna get some work done, maybe."

"Eh." I shrugged. I could ignore homework for another day.

I shivered in the sudden chill. I crossed my arms, glad for the hoodie, kicked off my shoes, and tucked my feet underneath me.

"You cold?" Yash asked, pulling out two blankets from their plastic packaging.

He unfolded one and draped it over me to cover my feet against the wall and partially over my arm closer to him. Then he unfolded the second one to cover himself.

I pressed my lips together and clamped down on a smile as I leaned against his shoulder. He lifted up the armrest between us and I scooted closer with a sigh. This was as comfortable as one could get on a plane.

The flight attendants seemed to vanish into their area behind us, some taking their breaks and naps while others prepared whatever they needed to prepare, and Yash took in a long breath, his chest expanding so the movement lifted me off him for a second.

He swallowed hard. I could hear the slight sound as he adjusted the second blanket to fully cover my left side against him so that we shared it. And then he . . . left his hand on my knee. The simple touch pressing lightly against the thick fabric of my sweats sent flutters through me. My heart palpitated and my skin turned warm in an instant. Could he hear the pulse raging behind my ears?

The last of the lights went off, leaving only the strip of walkway lights illuminating the aisles to the restrooms and the starry speckles on the overhead bins and ceiling mimicking the sky.

Yash kissed my forehead, muttering, "Good night," and I'd never felt more complete than in that moment.

* * *

I kept coming to with heavy eyelids, my brain fighting to stay awake while simultaneously dragging me back to sleep. In those seconds of the in-between, through the haze created behind my lashes, my brain tried hard to register the flickers of images.

Yash was drawing on his tablet, something that looked familiar.

I fell back asleep and groggily tried to open my eyes sometime later. Yash's screen was halfway turned toward me while he colored his art. Those panels. Those strokes. Those characters and that world. They all whooshed into my head and startled me fully awake, though I stayed absolutely still.

Without him knowing that I could see what he was working on, there was no need for him to try to hide it. And now I knew why he hid his work from me all this time. Sure, it was his personal business, and I didn't need to know. On the other hand, why was he drawing scenes so incredibly similar to *The Fall*?

My eyes widened as he attached text to what was undoubtedly the episode readers had been waiting for. No way could this be fan art.

I steeled myself. Was the teen breakthrough WebToon artist that I'd been DMing with all summer actually *Yash*? The guy who knew about the fight? The guy I'd accidentally messaged about my crush?

I stirred only for Yash to immediately turn off his tablet.

"What are you doing?" I asked, my voice hoarse.

"Just working on stuff."

"Homework?" I sat up and moved away from him.

"Due dates," he circumvented.

Oh my god. I was an *idiot*.

I swallowed. Was he evading the truth or dancing around lies? Heat coursed through me, paired with nausea. "Wait. Are you . . . Jalebi_Writer?"

He froze, his stare darting from me to the tablet.

I shoved off the blanket we'd been sharing, pulled my feet down, and leaned against the window as far from him as I could. "Oh my god," I muttered. "All this time I wasn't talking to you, but I *was* DMing you?"

"Nikki, let me explain."

"Explain what?" I shot back. "How you lied to me all summer?"

"I didn't lie," he protested, turning toward me.

"You just never told me it was you?"

"It was the only way you'd talk to me."

"So it was OK that you tricked me into talking to you? All this time, I was telling you everything about the fight and then about me liking you?"

"It wasn't my intention to trick you, and I tried to tell you."

"When?" I snapped.

"In Dubai."

"Instead of during the months we'd been chatting?"

"So you can be pissed at me all over again?"

"Yes," I hissed. "Didn't you think I'd be more pissed the longer it went on? Or were you just never going to tell me it was you?"

I threw my hands up. Argh! I was so mad at him for this, but I was even angrier that I couldn't simply be happy with him breaking through with his art in such a huge way. "This is how you had money for the camera, then."

"Yeah," he said quietly.

Tears welled up in my eyes, my anger bleeding into mortification. But as upset as I was, all I really wanted to say was . . . YOU ARE AN AMAZING ARTIST AND I AM SO PROUD OF YOU.

I wanted to congratulate him on his success, but the words wouldn't come out. They got tangled in my throat, battling my inclination to be angry when I just needed to grow the hell up. But still! Wasn't it wrong for him to keep his identity from me?

I clenched my eyes. Ugh! Why couldn't I just feel the right thing, the responsible, grown-up thing?

He whispered, "I'm sorry for not telling you. I really didn't know how. I avoided your early DMs, but then felt bad because you were such a fan. I just meant to say thanks and have that be the end of that, not end up chatting. Nikki, please say something."

I sucked in a breath and said, "I need to go to the bathroom."

"Oh, uh, OK."

He slid out and I hurried to the back. I actually did have to pee, but then I stared at my reflection in the mirror. I wanted to cry, to let it out, and then move on. It wasn't the worst thing a person could do, and he hadn't violated—no, wait. He *had* violated my trust. But dang it! I hated being mad at him!

After spending what seemed like hours in the small stall, I emerged and found him standing by our seats.

I flipped around and went to get snacks and drinks and to stretch my legs and clear my head. Just like the flight into Dubai, the attendants were cool with letting me take whatever I needed from the cart setup.

Yash gave me room, but I had to eventually return to my seat. Before he could sit beside me, I said, "Could you not sit there? I need some space."

He sighed but quietly sat in his assigned aisle seat, leaving me to process the situation.

We didn't speak for the rest of the flight, but Yash, after some time, returned to working on his tablet. Maybe he had deadlines to meet. Maybe he was working on the one episode we'd all been waiting for with bated breath.

He glanced at me every now and then, and every time I looked away, pretending I wasn't trying to see what he was working on.

"Do you, um, want to see?" he asked.

He actually, finally, wanted to share his work with me?

I shook my head, but my heart screamed, *YES!*

"Oh, OK," he replied, defeated, and returned to his art.

I nibbled on my nail. Oh, to be the first person to see his work, to be privy to the episode. More than that, I just wanted to see his work unfurl. How did he do it all? Where did he get the idea from? When had he started this style? How did his work with WebToon start in the first place? Ugh. I wanted to know everything and be happy for him and with him.

# CHAPTER TWENTY-SEVEN

There wasn't much time to talk to Yash when we returned. We'd been thrown back into our lives. Work and house stuff for the parents, homework galore and school for us kids. Plus, I'd scrambled to edit and send off the perfect shot for the internship after going back and forth on the top three pictures. Just seeing Yash made my chest hurt. I was still upset with him, but also, I just *really* missed him.

Before our falling-out last spring, Yash and I had driven to school together. After the fight, when my car privileges had been taken away, I either rode the bus or Tamara would go out of her way to give me a lift.

I went with Tamara the first few days back to catch up. She had all the details on homework and classes and of course the latest drama. She was more interested in my trip, though, specifically Yash. I told her everything, minus the WebToon and kissing. I'd never heard her squeal with delight before!

"I thought you didn't like him?" I said.

"Of course I like Yash! Who doesn't? But I had to support you. Well, to some extent. Girl, you petty as hell. It took this long to make up?"

"I know, I know."

Tamara turned onto a side street to avoid morning traffic without missing a beat. "Are y'all dating or what?"

My skin flared hot. "No."

She side-eyed me. "For someone who pretty much fell in love in a romantic city, you sure seem angry. Are you sure you forgave him?"

I bit my thumbnail and looked out the window. Ugh, Austin was so ugly compared to Dubai. "Something else came up."

"What?"

"I can't say."

She sighed. "That bad?"

"I don't know."

"What do you mean you don't know?"

I tried to frame this in a way that removed the whole Web-Toon thing, because that was Yash's personal, and apparently secret, business. It wasn't my place to tell anyone about it. "So, you know how Yash draws?"

"Yeah."

"I came across . . . his artsy social stuff that he has under a pen name. And I messaged him to tell him how cool his work was. Long story short, we'd been lowkey DMing all summer and he never told me it was him."

"Shut. Up." She swerved into a parking spot that was, for once, not a hike to the first school building.

I lunged forward when she hit the brakes.

"Sorry." She pulled the parking brake and turned toward me. "Go on."

"That's all. I found out it was him."

"So you're mad at him all over again?"

"Kind of. I don't really know! It was a violation of trust. But I don't want to be upset with him."

"Did you ever ask him if he was Yash?"

"Well, no. I would've never thought to ask!"

"Did you ever give him a chance to tell you?"

"Duh. He had all summer while we were DMing."

She twisted her mouth in thought. "What kind of chats were y'all having?"

"Just superficial things. I liked his work and he'd thank me, tell me it was nice to hear from me, etcetera. I guess, no different than any other artist I've messaged, if they respond at all."

"What did Yash have to say about this?"

I groaned. "Well, first he claimed he tried to tell me. Even though we weren't speaking all summer, he could've told me in DMs."

"Maybe he wanted to tell you to your face? Or, maybe he thought you didn't have a right to know since it was his personal art stuff. Obviously, he had a pen name to separate himself from it."

"Well, he had all Dubai when we were getting close."

"Maybe he didn't want to ruin the vacation?"

I watched some students walk across the parking lot to school.

Tamara asked, "Did he say why he didn't tell you?"

"He . . . didn't know how, and he didn't want me to get mad."

"Hmm. I'd be afraid of pissing you off, too. You did go off on him and stopped talking for so long that no one thought you'd be friends again. Guess you have to ask yourself if he's worth losing over this. It doesn't seem like he was trying to be shady. Honestly? He doesn't deserve to go through another falling-out with you."

I swallowed hard and stared at my backpack in my lap. It made sense now, how Jalebi_Writer had ignored my many comments and messages at first. Maybe he didn't want to open up because of this very situation. Yash had said that he just wanted to thank me because I was such a fan. And, as I thought about it, I was the one who usually messaged him. Maybe he felt obligated to reply?

"I didn't know he was drawing again," I said quietly. "I'm glad he is. It makes him happy."

The truth was, nothing was worth losing Yash over. And I'd much rather be celebrating his artistic success than fighting again. I just wanted some time to process, to articulate my thoughts, but also, there were some other things I had to take care of.

\* \* \*

After dinner that night, I told my parents, "I know what I did was wrong."

They paused, setting down their drinks to look at me while Lilly pretended to be attached to her tablet.

"The whole fake IDs and club thing. And of course, being mad at Yash. That was all wrong, expert-level deflection. I'm sorry."

"We know you are, and we appreciate the apology."

"Can we discuss the photography internship?" I asked, biting my lip, bracing for them to laugh me right out of the room.

"Oh, you still think you can go if you get accepted?" Papa asked.

"I'm hoping? Being grounded *all* summer gave me lots of time to think. I paid the price, didn't I?" I pointed out nervously.

"Did you get in?" Papa asked.

"I submitted the final photograph. Supposed to hear back in a couple of weeks."

"Did you get the shot you needed?"

I beamed and showed them on my phone which shot I'd submitted. They gasped the second they saw.

Mummie gave Lilly a misty-eyed look and said to me, "Oh my, beta. That is the most beautiful picture I've ever seen! I truly adore this."

"So worth the camera," Papa added with a touch of awe.

Eek. I should probably come clean about the camera, but maybe I could hold off until after I'd paid Yash back for it.

"The internship will be a great opportunity for you," Papa said, lifting my hopes perilously high. "It'll teach you skills but also some life experience while temporarily on your own, not to mention how hard it can be to earn a dollar. We've been discussing it." He glanced at Mummie.

She nodded at him and said, "You're a good girl who made a few bad decisions. You learned from them, hah?"

"Yes," I replied eagerly.

"And it would be unfair to damage your future if we were simply . . . what's the word?" she asked Papa.

"Petty," Lilly chimed in.

Mummie smiled. "Yes. Pettiness is ugly and destructive."

"So, if I get accepted, I can go?" I asked.

My parents nodded. Papa said, "We told you last year, when you wanted to apply, that you could attend if you were accepted. We don't go back on our word."

"Thank you!" I ambush-hugged my parents, nearly knocking them off their chairs, but they just laughed and patted my head.

"Let me see the picture," Lilly said, taking my phone. Her eyes lit up and a big grin spread across her face. "This is your entry?"

"Yeah." I smiled, my heart warming.

She glanced at the picture again, the one I'd taken of her beaming with the fullest joy at the concert. There had been several really good photos, but this one of my little sister took the cake.

"What do you think?" I asked.

She shoved away from the table and rushed me with a hug. "I think you're super talented," she muttered into my shoulder. "And I'm going to miss you when you're away at the internship."

* * *

I paced my room that evening, wondering how to approach Yash. First things first. I understood how we got into this situation. In his shoes, I probably would've done the same thing. Most importantly, I knew he wasn't trying to deceive me and that he just didn't know how to tell me, but also his art world was his. If he wanted to be totally private about it, then who was I to force him out?

I opened my phone and saw a text from him. Not Jalebi_Writer. Jalebi_Writer hadn't messaged me since I accidentally told him about my crush on Yash.

Followed by an emoji with sad, pleading eyes and a bouquet emoji. I found myself smiling, but also sadness welled up inside of me. He shouldn't have to keep apologizing.

And that was it. Well, it wasn't asking much of me to read the episode I'd been anticipating, maybe even the episode he'd been working on during the flight when he offered me the chance to get first look.

I grabbed my tablet and flopped onto my bed, opening the WebToon app to *The Fall*.

Instead of the black and gloomy opening panel, there was only the title on an unassuming, plain white backdrop.

There was a large text box that made up an entire panel.

Hey, everyone! Sorry for the unexpected delay in getting the next episode to you! As you'll see, it's still delayed, but let me explain why. See, this whole series came about because I was going through some things. My best friend of a million years and I had a falling out, and to cope with the loss, I turned to drawing again. Like, a lot. I didn't think I'd show anyone these drawings, but here ya go. It's the truth. Also, shout-out to my editor and WebToon for allowing me to post this very personal non-episode.

I scrolled down to find sketches of our neighborhood and drawings of our high school football field with half-drawn players and track runners in soft colors of blue and green like a watercolor painting. There were occasional sad faces here and there and partial images of Jalebi_Writer staring out his window at night, but never showing his entire identity.

My heart was breaking all over again. These drawings sucked me into the moments when he suffered the most, especially the rough sketch of him sitting in the corner with his knees pulled up to his chest, his arms wrapped around them, and his head down like he was sad. Beside him was a plate of food with text that read, "*Not eating*," with a looped arrow pointing at the untouched sandwich.

My eyes welled up as I ran a finger over the panel, touching his head as if that would make him feel better.

Then I came up with *The Fall* and worked on it nonstop. So, yeah, while something incredibly agonizing was happening to me, something unbelievably wonderful came from it. And WebToon loved it! And it kinda exploded into something surreal thanks to you guys.

Subsequent panels showed his back hunched over a tablet on his desk and a partially eaten sandwich beside him. He'd found so much joy in art.

I had to take a break recently because my family and I went to Dubai to celebrate Diwali. We went with my former best friend and her family. We spent a lot of time together. We ate, bickered, did touristy things, ate some more, and reconciled. We found friendship. And more.

There were sketches of Dubai in various styles. Of me shopping in a souk while drinking from a coconut. Of us on cutesy, confused camels and me looking purely terrified with him laughing. Of us sliding down dunes where he had a squiggly line that relayed nothing short of "OMFG" for a mouth while I was grinning with squished eyes. Of us skydiving making heart shapes with our hands. Of us . . . holding pinkies beneath colorful fireworks.

Well, the thing is, she's a huge fan of this WebToon and messaged me a while back. We'd been chatting all summer and she didn't know this was me. I didn't want to tell her because this was MY thing, and she didn't have the right to be let in on my personal life when she wouldn't even look at me in real life. So I thanked her politely for being a reader and tried to avoid real convo. But then we got to chatting and it was like talking to her like old times, and I couldn't help it. I really missed her, and this was the only way she'd talk to me. I was going to tell her the truth in Dubai. But then she accidentally messaged me that she liked me (the real me). So I couldn't tell her then!

There was a black-and-white panel, the only color a blush at his cheeks while he read the message, although he didn't include our real names.

Then she told me in person, and I told her I liked her, too.

Followed by a panel of us leaning against each other under a blanket on a plane with the lights of the overhead bins looking like smiling stars.

But that wasn't the entire truth.

My heart sank.

She discovered the guy she'd been chatting with online for months was . . . ME.

There was a panel of me looking upset and glaring out the airplane window with my chin on my fist, my elbow on the armrest.

I know you're reading this. And I should've told you from the beginning, even though I tried to tell you at some point. But how, when we were in a rocky place? You asked if we could be friends again. Well, the truth is . . .

My heart skipped a beat as the screen stayed on this in-between panel text. I couldn't swipe up to read what his verdict was. And at the same time, everything came crashing back into me. This was not my true light shining, and I couldn't damage his light, either.

I closed the app, marched downstairs, out the door, across the backyard, and through the gate between our yards, to find Yash sitting on his deck with his tablet in his lap.

He looked up to find me trudging toward him. Yash stood, shoving his hands into his pockets. His face flushed, and he kept glancing at the grass between us when I was trying my hardest to maintain eye contact.

"Did you read it?" he asked, his voice shaky.

"Yeah," I replied, my own voice quivering.

He dragged his gaze up to meet mine. "Did you . . . see the ending?"

"No."

He frowned.

"I mean, I read until the 'truth' part because I had to come over and say this first. Whether or not you decided that you don't want to be friends. I know I have a lot to work on, and I said I would never hurt you again."

"Nikki . . ."

"I'm sorry." I wiped a tear as it rolled down my cheek.

Yash took a few steps to close the gap between us and swiped his thumbs across my face. "Hey, why are you crying?"

I stared at his throat. "Those drawings. So much talent and so much pain. I just wanted to tell you how amazing they are, but instead I was mad about the chatting."

"You were right to be mad. I'd be mad, too," he said quietly.

"But I get it. I didn't have the right to know that you were this big WebToon star, and you wanted to keep that private. And things sorta evolved. We didn't mean to keep talking to each other. We didn't mean to hurt one another. But I don't want to lose you again. Those months were hard—and yeah, I know, it was my own fault and that time was way harder for you—but I'm not letting that happen again. So, whatever your truth was at the end of the episode, just know that I can't lose you. But I understand whatever you decide."

I finally looked up at him. A smile cracked across his face

before he ambushed me with a hug, knocking the breath from my lungs and crushing me. I gasped but hugged him back.

"You're so dramatic," he muttered into my hair before kissing my head. "And you should read it, because I can't tell you what it says when you're standing in front of me."

"You still like me?" I squeaked.

"Yes, Nikki."

"More than camel milk chocolate?"

He laughed. "Yes. More than jalebi even."

Yash led me to the porch and handed me his tablet, already opened to the episode, and scrolled down to the section I'd left off at.

**Well, the truth is . . .**

Followed by a panel zoomed in to the skydiving drawing showing just his hands forming a heart against his chest.

**. . . I think I'm in love with you, *and I would draw a million sketches to be with you.***

My breath caught as I looked up from the end of the episode, only glancing at the ninety-nine thousand plus likes and top comments filled with heart emojis.

"Are you serious?" I blurted, my heart spasming with so much joy flooding my veins.

Yash started, "What do you—"

I swung my arms around his neck and said, "I love you, too."

"Bro," he jested, but man, how I'd missed his teasing.

"You better not say you're not in love with me and this was all just an episode for likes."

He wrapped his arms around my waist and planted a kiss on my shoulder. "I'd never joke about loving you."

He kissed my neck and added, "But I *am* sorta terrified of your dad now."

I laughed. "He just went from beloved Uncle to Hawkeye."

"Are we OK?" he asked softly.

I breathed him in, held him tight, and said, "We'll *always* be OK."

# Acknowledgments

I hope you enjoyed this trip through the UAE, inspired by my own family trip. I can still remember the glamour and sugarcane drinks. Thank you to my parents and brother who made this once-in-a-lifetime family trip bigger than life! And the joining of my brother's then fiancé and her family (now wife and in-laws) as we traveled in preparation for their big, fat, Indian wedding (which is literally a whole other book). This was an amazing time with amazing people.

*Sleepless in Dubai* took me back to those days of feverishly (as in, I had an actual fever!) running around Dubai and acting like kids with my brother as we went to amusement parks and rode every single ride we could fit into, doing all the touristy things with my parents, my dad who brought daily fruit, and my mom who gave me strings of white jasmines for my hair every morning. I had a blast writing this book and hope that it made you smile, laugh, and feel like you were on an adventure right alongside Nikki and Yash.

As with all things book related, I wouldn't be here without the support and guidance of my *incredible* agent, Katelyn. You truly are the best! Thank you for all your enthusiasm, encouragement, and the many (probably too many) times you lent a listening ear.

Many thanks to my editors Jessica, Erum, and Anne, and the entire Abrams team for helping me bring this book into the world.

I will forever rain upon my husband a million thank-you's for supporting this writerly lifestyle in which I sit as a hermit behind a desk for days on end in a vast assortment of sweatpants while nibbling on cheese. He doesn't seem to think it's weird at all.

I'm grateful for my family, who appears to be tickled at the idea that the biggest introvert in their lives can in fact produce so many words. Special shout-out to Papa utilizing the power of WhatsApp to spread the news of my writing adventures through the uncle-network, and to Mummie, who will forever be feeding me thepla (even when we're not traveling). Despite my theatrical objections, I wouldn't want it any other way. To my brother, who has always been there for me and makes me feel like I'm doing this adulting thing right, you truly are the pillar to so many lives. And Prapti, baby girl. You can't read yet, but may you travel a thousand worlds and live a thousand lives through the written word.

Thank you to all the wonderful readers! I've delighted in your messages, comments, posts, podcasts, videos, and meeting some in person. I've enjoyed connecting with so many of you over the years and look forward to more. Books truly are magical in the way they bring us together.

Meet ya in the next story!